For my sister, Maria, who's been saving
lives in A&E for over thirty years.
Super Nurse – Super Woman.

THE NEW BOY

PAULA RAWSTHORNE

SCHOLASTIC

Scholastic Children's Books
An imprint of Scholastic Ltd
Euston House, 24 Eversholt Street, London, NW1 1DB, UK
Registered office: Westfield Road, Southam, Warwickshire, CV47 0RA
SCHOLASTIC and associated logos are trademarks and/or
registered trademarks of Scholastic Inc.

First published in the UK by Scholastic Ltd, 2019

ISBN 978 1407 18026 7

A CIP catalogue record for this book
is available from the British Library.

Printed by CPI Group (UK) Ltd, Croydon, CR0 4YY
Papers used by Scholastic Children's Books are made
from wood grown in sustainable forests.

3 5 7 9 10 8 6 4 2

www.scholastic.co.uk

PROLOGUE

As we get nearer to the edge it's as if there's no one else on earth except me and him. Even the birds seem to have abandoned the sky. I hear the moaning wind as it whips my face, feel the grey clouds pressing down, see the whole of the city laid out in front of me.

There's another high-rise opposite Lennon Towers, walls of windows facing this way, there must be hundreds of people inside, getting on with their lives, oblivious to what's happening to me. *Someone* must be watching. Surely someone must be out on their balcony . . . must be looking up . . . all the way up, beyond the twentieth floor – gasping as they spot us on the roof. Are they calling the police right now? Is their voice rising as they tell the operator that there are people on the roof of Lennon Towers: teenagers. They shouldn't be up there. They could get themselves killed.

How clearly can they see us? Can they see his face? Can

they see how he holds me, never wanting to let go? Can they hear how he says my name?

"Zoe." His voice is full of tenderness as his grip tightens around my crushed hand. "We're going to do this."

"But, Ethan—?" I look over my shoulder at him.

He holds a finger up to his lips. "Hush. This is how it's meant to be."

He hauls me forward, closer to the edge. I jerk back, trying to get a foothold on the rough concrete, but my bare feet skid along painfully as he drags me towards him. I cry out in pain and terror.

He gathers me to him; holds me close, strokes windswept hair out of my eyes. "Don't be afraid, Zoe. This way we'll be together for ever."

My body shakes uncontrollably as I take his face in my hands and look deep into his eyes. Dead eyes. When I speak, I try to make him hear passion in my voice, knowing my life depends on it.

"There's no need to do this. We can still be together. I love you. I love you!"

"Then prove it."

I scream as he lifts me up and carries me over the metal barrier that stands between us and the narrow ridge. He carefully places me down, the tips of my toes touching the very edge of the roof. He calmly tells me not to struggle as he seizes my hand again. I can't stop my legs shaking. I try to look straight ahead but my eyes are drawn downwards. My stomach lurches at the sight of the drop; miniature cars and trees hundreds of feet below. Everything suddenly feels unreal. This can't be happening. This can't be how my life ends.

No one is coming. No one can reach me . . . save me. In a second he'll step off this roof, taking me with him.

He stands next to me, tall, solid, looking out over the city like he's king of the world. He turns his head, a rictus smile on his face, the wind carrying his words to me.

"Everyone will know that our love was real. They'll write about us. Tell stories about us, be jealous that they've never loved so deeply."

Sobs burst out of me, tears blind me.

I hear his voice in my ear. "Don't be afraid, my love. It's time. . ."

CHAPTER 1

Three Months Earlier

The dress code for Hinton Dale states that only smart clothing is acceptable, which seems a bit hypocritical, seeing as the college is so scruffy. Even so, I suppose that ripped jeans, a battered biker jacket and red DMs are pushing it; but I'm seventeen in a few weeks and no one should be telling me what I can and can't wear.

I put the collar up on my jacket as the cold air prickles my exposed neck. I'm still getting used to my hair. I haven't had it this short since I was a little kid, but I love messing around with the colour and trying out new styles. I've gone from shoulder-length peroxide blonde to a cropped lilac bob. I'm not sure what Mum thinks about it, but she didn't complain when I left the house for college this morning. Mind you, she was a bit preoccupied. I looked over her shoulder at breakfast and caught her staring at a photo on Petra's Instagram posted a few days ago – Dad in a ridiculous white suit and Petra in a low-cut, skin-tight wedding dress – *Happiest day of my life, marrying my soul mate in #Vegas*, the caption declared.

My heart ached as I watched Mum's face crumple. I kissed the top of her head and told her not to torture herself, and she quickly turned the phone over, embarrassed. "I'm not, love. Don't you worry about me," she said, fixing her lips into a smile.

It's the first time that I've walked the route to college. There's a maze of streets to get through before I reach Fellfoot Park, where I've arranged to meet Jodie, Sonja and Ethan in the playground.

I'm so glad that we all decided to go to the same college. When the exam results came out over summer I was worried that Ethan wouldn't be enrolling. He was gutted about some of his grades and his mum and dad were pushing for him to do an apprenticeship. But when he heard that I was definitely going to Hinton Dale, he signed up. It wouldn't be the same without him. We've been best mates since primary school. We bonded in after-school club over Lego and toast. It's a miracle that we stayed friends all the way through high school. Ethan was friendly with other people, but we always stuck together. He was the one who got me through the trauma of Dad leaving. His family's flat in Lennon Towers became a bit of a sanctuary for me. I don't know what I would have done without him.

I take a left turn and walk down the mossy alleyway that

leads to Fellfoot Park. Rows of well-kept gardens back on to it but, as I pass a tatty-looking plot of land, a bullet-faced dog rockets towards me, snapping and snarling through a flimsy wooden gate. I jump back with a yelp and hurry away as the dog's piercing bark follows me down the alleyway and into the park.

My pulse starts to calm as I spot Jodie and Sonja sitting on the roundabout, waiting for me. I can't help smiling. Jodie has gone all "college preppy" in a gloss-black short skirt with thick tights and a delicate pink top. Her nut-brown hair cascades over the fluffy collar of her jacket and her pretty face is dominated by big-framed glasses. Sonja looks ultra-smart. People often assume that she's unapproachable because of her ice-queen beauty, but we know her better than that. Her long white-blonde hair is tied in an intricate plait that sits straight down her back. She looks like she's going into a business meeting, with her dark, tailored trouser suit and leather briefcase. I swear that girl will be CEO of some multinational before she's thirty.

"Looking good, girls!" I call to them as they jump up to hug me.

"I like your hair, Zoe." Sonja nods approvingly. "The colour makes your hazel eyes *pop*."

Jodie holds me at arms-length. "Zoe, you know that I adore your face – you're like a Viking warrior princess."

"Come off it!" I snort, creasing up with laughter. "I think you need to be a bit taller than five foot three to qualify as a Viking warrior princess."

"But it's your big eyes, wide face, strong jawline; you're gorgeous but this haircut isn't quite right. We need to soften it." She sweeps my fringe off my forehead like an artist perfecting a painting. "Hey presto!" She takes a mirror from her jacket and shows me her work. She's right, as usual. That looks a lot better.

"Thank you, oh, great style guru." I bow. "And am I right in assuming those glasses are just for show?"

"Of course. I want to make the right impression on our first day. I'm hoping they scream intelligent *and* cool," Jodie says, sliding them to the end of her nose and narrowing her eyes.

I love the girls, even though, from the outside, we probably seem too different to be friends. Me and Ethan met Sonja and Jodie when we were teamed up on a geography field trip in Year Eight. Sonja and her family had recently arrived from Poland and Jodie was also new to St Nic's. The so-called "archaeological dig" we were meant to be doing ended up with us four having a massive mud-slinging fight in a field. We all got detention the next day but it was such a laugh that it was worth it.

"Where's Ethan?" I ask, as we all sit down on the roundabout.

"He'll be here in a minute," Sonja answers, pushing her foot against the ground, making the creaking roundabout slowly rotate.

"So, what are we looking forward to at Hinton Dale?" I ask, as Fellfoot Park spins gently in front of our eyes.

"Some decent teachers," Sonja says briskly. "Business studies at St Nic's was so lame. Mr Roberts just used to play us episodes of *The Apprentice* and get on with his marking."

"I want their fashion textiles course to be as good as it looked on the open day," Jodie says. "Plus, if it's not too much to ask, I'd like there to be a few hot boys at college who'll throw themselves at my feet and worship me."

"Amen to that!" Sonja declares.

"I can't be bothered with boys," I sigh. "I've decided that for the next two years at Hinton Dale I'm going to have fun without them."

Jodie puts her lecturing face on. "Zoe, don't let one bad holiday romance make you give up on the entire male population."

I give her a little shove and she screeches, grabbing hold of the rusting rails. "Don't worry, Jodie," I say, rolling my eyes, "Matt Gillingham hasn't turned me into Miss Havisham. He was just someone I snogged on holiday – who turned out to be a pathetic, lying loser."

Sonja jumps off the roundabout and pulls it to a halt. She holds her phone in front of my face. "Look at him," she says, scowling. "You can tell he loves himself just from his profile picture."

I put my fingers in my mouth, pretending to gag when I see Matt Gillingham's image on her screen. He's bare-chested, deeply tanned, lying on the beach with a smirk plastered on his face.

Jodie shakes her head. "Zoe, I'm trying to respect your

stance on the whole social media thing, but if you'd only return to the twenty-first century and join the rest of humanity on Facebook, Instagram, *anything*, then in a couple of clicks you'd have been able to find out that he already had a girlfriend at home and saved yourself some heartache in Spain."

I let out an exasperated sigh. "It's not a *stance*, Jodie. I came off all the social media stuff because I have no *incredible life* or *profound thoughts* to share with the rest of the world," I say. "And I don't want to be holding my breath to see how many likes I get every time I put up a photo."

"But you're missing out on so much, Zoe. You don't know what's going on in the world," Sonja says pityingly.

"That's not true, you and Jodie keep me updated with all the gossip," I say with a grin. "Anyway, it's all such a time suck. I'd rather be reading *Jane Eyre* or watching *Moulin Rouge* than checking my notifications."

"But what good have they done you? You're always reading old books and watching those strange romantic films, but you *still* end up snogging a loser on holiday." Jodie shrugs.

I laugh. "Just because I happen to appreciate great literature and classic movies doesn't mean that I'm looking for some kind of romantic hero to come and sweep me off my feet."

"Whatever, but I'm hitting the dating apps if I haven't found anyone decent by the time I'm eighteen," Jodie replies cheerfully.

Ethan's voice calls out to us from across the park. "Hey, guys. Sorry I'm a bit late, I had to take Reece and Jimmy to school."

I grin as his gangly frame ambles towards us. It's been three weeks since I've seen him; when I got back from Spain he'd already gone camping with his family. I watch his mass of soft brown curls bounce as he walks. His jeans sit precariously on his bony hips. He always looks cutely dishevelled, like he's just got out of bed, but I know he works harder than any of us; most of his spare time is spent babysitting his little brothers and sister.

He stops in front of me and it hits me just how much I've missed him, especially after this long, weird summer. Everything seems right with the world when Ethan is around.

He gives me his sweet lopsided smile. "How are you doing, Zoe?"

"Great!" I reply, springing off the roundabout to hug him, my head hardly reaching his chest.

"Heard anything from that fool you met in Spain?" he asks.

"No, I haven't," I groan. "And would you lot stop making a big deal of it? It was nothing. He's a no one. I'm sorry I ever told you about it. Can we all just move on now?"

"Yeah, sure," Ethan says, pretending to zip his lips.

"I will never speak his name again," Sonja says earnestly.

"Agreed. Matt Gillingham is now officially, He Who Must Not Be Named," Jodie teases.

"Hey, your hair looks great, Zo. And you got those piercings you were talking about," Ethan says, gently running his finger over the small hoops that curve around my ear.

"Oh, yes, I hadn't noticed them," Sonja says, inspecting my ear approvingly. "You're so observant, Ethan."

His cheeks pink up. "Just call me Sherlock."

Sonja reaches her hands out to him. "Shall we?" she says, as we all link arms and head off.

*

We leave the park and dash across the busy main road and through the gates of the college. A frayed banner is displayed above the entrance, proclaiming: *Welcome to Hinton Dale College, Where Learning and Excellence Meet.* The soft September sun breaks through the cloud, bathing the college, and its acres of grounds, in a yellow haze. I can see the churned-up football pitches and overgrown cricket squares, the tennis courts with plants sprouting out of the tarmac and an athletics stadium with its weather-beaten stand.

On the open day, it's the outside of the building that sells it to potential students and their parents: it looks like a stately home in need of some TLC. Of course, once you get inside the oak-panelled hallway, there's a strong musty smell that can't be disguised by the air fresheners dotted around. But Hinton Dale still has a charm that sets it apart from the new-build college on the other side of town. When I went to look around there it felt like walking through an airport lounge – impersonal and characterless.

Anyway, I don't need anywhere flash. If I'm willing to put the effort in, I reckon I can get decent enough results at Hinton Dale. Jen, my sister, came here and now she's in her third year at uni studying biology. She's having the best time, so she hardly ever comes home. I wish she'd visit more.

I know how much Mum misses her and, despite the age gap between us, she's always fun to have around.

As we walk into the hallway, a pinched-faced boy in a grey suit approaches us. He's wearing a silky yellow *Here-to-help* sash like he's an overdressed greeter in a supermarket. "Hey, guys, first day?"

We nod in unison.

"Cool. I'm Ned, upper sixth. I'll take you to your common room."

We follow him along the dark corridors, the floorboards creaking with every step. Ned talks at the speed of light, never once turning to look at us.

"You should've already received an email with your personalized timetables and tutor groups. The college is a bit of a rabbit warren, but you'll soon find your way around. The dining hall is on this floor, to the left – my advice is to avoid anything that isn't pre-packed, unless you like hairs with your chips."

We all shoot each other looks of disgust as Ned marches on, leading us up the sweeping oak staircase. A kaleidoscope of coloured light shines through a large stained-glass window at the top of the landing, creating a church-like atmosphere. Ned takes a right and stops outside an enormous wooden door. A gold plaque screwed on to it reads, *Lower Common Room*.

He swings the door and a wall of noise hits us.

"As you can hear, a few students have already arrived," he shouts above the multitude of voices. "I'll leave you to it, but just grab anyone with a yellow sash if you've got any questions. Mr Dunn, the head of the college, will be along soon to give you his classic welcome speech." He grimaces. "Enjoy!"

He ushers us in and disappears. The room reminds me of a draughty Tudor hall, with black and white beams, a vaulted ceiling and mullioned windows which are streaming with condensation inside. Massive dusty tapestries hang from the walls, depicting hunting scenes, banquets and battles. It's like stepping back in time.

There must be about two hundred students in here, all checking each other out. I recognize quite a few of them from St Nic's, our old school. We wave at each other as people stand around chatting on the threadbare rugs that cover the uneven floor.

People are crammed on sagging sofas, balancing on orange plastic chairs, perched on the window sills staring at their phones, and even sitting inside the cavernous inglenook fireplace with its vast stone surround. The tables full of computers at the far end of the room are the only things that look like they belong in this century.

I spot Harry Sherwood out of the corner of my eye and let out an involuntary groan. Ethan's face tenses as he notices him too. I tap Ethan's arm to divert his attention and go cross-eyed to make his mouth twitch into a smile.

I was hoping that when we finished St Nic's we'd never see Harry Sherwood again; he's toxic. He likes to get laughs by taking the piss out of people. Ethan has never been very sporty and PE became a nightmare for him with Sherwood humiliating him every time he ran for the football or tried to bowl in cricket. Ethan would pretend to shrug it off, but I know how much he dreaded those lessons.

Sherwood looks over and says something to his girlfriend, Justine Collins. They both glance at me and laugh. They're probably slagging off my hair, but I just turn my back on them. I don't care what they think – about me *or* my hair.

There's surprise as a recording of church bells suddenly rings out from two speakers high up on the walls. Slowly, silence descends as people realize that a wizened-looking man has entered the room. He's wearing a black schoolmaster cape over a heavy tweed suit and he tries not to make eye contact with anyone as he positions himself in front of the fireplace.

"Have we come to Hogwarts by mistake?" Ethan whispers in my ear, making me stifle a chuckle.

Unfortunately for us, the head, Mr Dunn, is no Dumbledore, and his monotone voice makes his uninspiring welcome speech seem endless as people start to yawn, cough and sneakily check their phones.

He's in the middle of a list of health and safety rules when Sonja simultaneously elbows me and Jodie in the ribs. She's grinning from ear to ear. "Guys," she mutters. "Eyes left!"

We look at the crowd of students. "What are we meant to be looking at?" I whisper.

"Only the most beautiful boy I've ever seen in my life," she declares. "There – standing by the window, blue sweater, black hair, drop dead gorgeous."

I follow her stare and see him. Despite myself, my eyes widen. He's standing so straight and tall, listening to Mr Dunn attentively. I'd say he's about six foot, trim, fit . . . like a footballer. Cheekbones to die for, full bow-shaped lips, jet-black hair, his skin a sun-kissed golden brown. I glance at Jodie, who drops her jaw like a cartoon character.

Just then, as though he knows he's being watched, he turns. He stares for a moment, then he smiles. Probably the most perfect smile I have ever seen. I look down at the ground, embarrassed, but Jodie gives him a little wave, speaking through closed teeth like a ventriloquist. "He's smiling at me."

Sonja joins her hands together in prayer. "Thank you, God," she laughs.

Ethan shakes his head at us in exaggerated disapproval. "You're such hypocrites. You bang on about 'the objectification of women' and then. . ."

"Don't be jealous, babe, we'll always love you best," Jodie cackles.

Mr Dunn coughs loudly, glaring at us. "And one last thing. Please remember that you're at college now. We expect a level of maturity and dedication to your studies befitting of young adults. I won't delay you any longer. Classes start in ten minutes. Do use this time to mingle and get to know each other." He smiles tightly and sweeps out of the hall, his cape wafting behind him.

The room erupts into noise again.

"Come on," Jodie says, and before I can protest she grabs my hand and starts pulling me through the crowd towards the boy.

"What are you doing?" I say.

"Mingling," she winks.

Sonja is right behind us, dragging a reluctant Ethan.

"Come on, Ethan. I need you. He might be scared off if it's just girls," Sonja says, as she barges onwards.

When we reach him, the boy has his head bowed, zipping up his rucksack.

"Hi!" Jodie says brightly. "We're new. Obviously!"

The boy raises his head and smiles. "Hi." He puts out his hand to her. "I'm Jack Cartwright." His voice is smooth and mellow. There isn't a trace of an accent; he could be from anywhere.

"I like a bit of formality," Jodie jokes, as she takes his hand and he shakes it. "I'm Jodie."

"Nice glasses, Jodie."

She tries to contain her delight and play it cool. "What, these things? They're just something I picked up off this new website."

"Any on there that you think would suit me?" he asks.

"*Anything* on there would suit you," she says in full flirtatious mode. "I'll send you the link, if you like?"

"Thanks, that'd be great."

Jodie cracks me up. She certainly knows how to get a boy's number quickly. I discreetly look him up and down now we're closer. He's definitely Jodie's type: perfectly gorgeous and a fashionista's dream. He wouldn't look out of place on a Paris catwalk.

Determined not to be pushed out, Sonja leans across Jodie, saying, "Hi, I'm Sonja Bartkowski."

"*Miło mi ci pozna, Sonja,*" he replies, shaking her hand. We stare at him in amazement.

"Oh, you know Polish?" Sonja looks thrilled.

"Only the odd phrase. I'm trying to learn a few sentences from every language, just so I can impress girls," he says, straight-faced.

Ethan laughs but Sonja looks uncertain.

"I'm joking!" The boy grins and I can practically hear the sigh of relief from Sonja. "But I really am trying to learn languages. I just think it's nice to be able to communicate with people. Why should I expect everyone to learn English?"

"Well, I think that's wonderful." Sonja's wide-eyed with admiration. "I've been friends with this lot for years and they haven't bothered to learn any Polish."

She's still holding Jack's hand. I give her a little nudge, and she lets go, her cheeks flushing.

I turn to walk away, not wanting to interrupt Jodie and Sonja's battle for the new boy's attention, but Jack holds out his hand to me.

"Hi," he says warmly. His hand closes over mine in a firm grip. I get a waft of his aftershave – he smells divine and his *eyes* ... his eyes are amazing. They're so dark, like inky bottomless pools.

"I'm Zoe Littlewood," I say, trying not to stare. "And this is Ethan."

"Oh, yeah, Ethan Mansfield. I think we'll all have psychology classes together. I saw your names on the list."

"Good memory." Ethan looks impressed. "I struggle to remember what I had for breakfast."

I tug on Ethan's denim jacket. "We've got to go. They're going to ring the bell in a minute and I don't want to get caught in the crush."

Ethan looks at me, surprised, but lets me drag him away. I've got no intention of joining Jodie and Sonja in their fawning over the new boy. I don't care how handsome and charming he is, wasting time on boys is not on my timetable at Hinton Dale College.

CHAPTER 2

We're sitting in the stands of the dilapidated athletics stadium, catching some afternoon sun before we make our way home. We're meant to be having a debrief about our first day, but Sonja and Jodie are glued to their phones.

"What's so interesting?" I ask.

"Just finding out about the *delicious* Jack Cartwright. You should see his Instagram. He's a legend!" Jodie says. She scrolls through feverishly.

"No, thanks." I open a bag of crisps and hold them out. Only Ethan registers and takes one.

"We were with him in psychology this afternoon. He was making notes on the new MacBook!" Ethan says, sounding impressed.

"Oh, come on, Zoe. Just look at Jack's profile picture. It's *so* cute," Jodie says, showing me her phone.

I glance at the screen displaying Jack's Instagram page.

His photo is a close-up of a fluffy ginger cat nuzzling his cheek as he gives a million-watt smile. Yes, it's cute. *Too* cute.

"Talk about trying too hard," I mutter.

"He's got nearly five thousand followers and he's only following two hundred and twenty," Ethan says, looking over her shoulder. "How's he done that?"

Jodie gasps. "There's a photo of him with The Haunted!" She reads out the caption. "*You never know who you're going to bump into backstage @theo2london #TheHaunted*. Have you seen how many comments and shares it's got?"

"He's into his fitness," Sonja says, showing us images of a super-toned Jack on a rowing machine, the cross trainer, lifting weights. In each of the photos there's an older woman training with him. She's attractively flushed, with a lovely smile, while Jack doesn't look like he's broken a sweat. I read the captions. *Day thirty-five of marathon training with Super-Mum. Raising funds for #DementiaCare. Please support us.*

"Oh my god, he's running a marathon with his *mum*! I can't even get my mum to run me to the shops," Jodie says.

"He's raising funds for a dementia charity," Sonja says admiringly. "I could tell as soon as I met him that he was a caring person. You just get those kind of vibes off him."

My eyes can't help flitting to his Facebook page that Sonja is now, eagerly, scrolling down. In between shared posts about global warming, alerts about missing teenagers, funny Gifs and YouTube videos, are photos of him and his friends, all good-looking boys and girls. There are pictures of him having BBQs in a sunshine-filled field, looking handsomely dishevelled at a music festival, and James Bond-suave in a tuxedo at a leavers' ball.

"What school has he come from?" I ask, being drawn in despite myself. It's hard to imagine someone so perfect coming from anywhere.

Sonja and Jodie race to find the answer.

"Lenton Academy, Somerset," Sonja says, reading. "Looks like he moved here in July. Family: Annie and Rob Cartwright. No mention of brothers or sisters."

"Forget that," Jodie proclaims. "I've found the most important information. Relationship status: *single*! Jack Cartwright is available." Jodie and Sonja high-five each other.

"Hold on. Why are you assuming he's interested in a relationship?" I say teasingly.

Jodie scowls at me. "Zoe, don't put a downer on things. He was the only hot boy in that common room! He's new in town. He'll need some friends, so I'll just be . . . friendly."

"I take personal offence that you consider Jack Cartwright to be the *only* hot boy in that room," Ethan jokes.

"Well, it goes without saying that *you're* the hottest and Jack is way behind in second place," Jodie grins.

"But you've got to admit that running a marathon is pretty impressive," Sonja says.

"I could run a marathon if I wanted to," Ethan says unconvincingly.

"Yeah, I suppose you're the right build – nice and skinny," Jodie says sincerely.

"I prefer to call it lean," he laughs, patting his non-existent belly. "Obviously, I'd need to do a bit of fine-tuning to build up my stamina."

"Go on, then. Go down to the track and do a few laps, and then we'll treat you like the Adonis that you are." Jodie hauls him off the bench.

"Fine!" Ethan searches through his rucksack and pulls out his battered trainers. "I'll show you what a real athlete looks like. Now, who's going to run with me?"

"I'd love to, babe, but I can't run in these," Jodie says, pointing to her platform shoes.

Ethan looks to me and Sonja.

"I'm hardly dressed for exercise," Sonja says, sweeping her hands down her trouser suit.

"No can do, Ethan. It's been so long since I ran that I'd keel over and need an ambulance," I say apologetically.

"Suit yourselves," he replies, putting on his trainers and walking purposefully down the steps to the crumbling track. He wheels his arms in the air, shakes out his legs and then starts to jog. Adorable as Ethan looks, he's no athlete. His running is too loose-limbed and he's wasting energy.

We start to clap and whoop as he completes a circuit.

"One more lap, Ethan," I shout to him. "Doing great!"

He gives a thumbs-up, trying to conserve his breath as he continues.

Suddenly, music blares from the stadium entrance and I see a group of St Nic's students stroll in. My heart sinks as I spot Harry Sherwood among the crowd. I look back at Ethan, still doggedly running; he hasn't noticed them yet.

Harry Sherwood stands in front of the group and starts flapping his arms and legs as if it's how Ethan runs. He calls out, his voice echoing around the stadium, "Usain Bolt had better watch out because Ethan Mansfield is on the track!"

There's laughter from the crowd. Ethan looks over, mortified and stumbles to a halt.

I get to my feet, anger surging through me. I'm not going to let Sherwood continue his bullying in our new college. I head down the steps, determined to confront him, but stop as I see Jack Cartwright walk straight past Sherwood and the mocking crowd, and approach Ethan. He says something to Ethan and they both laugh, and then he gestures to the track and, to my amazement, they both start running. Jack lets Ethan set the pace and they jog steadily, side by side.

The laughter from the group has stopped. Instead they stand, silent, looking in curiosity as the handsome boy casually chats to Ethan as if they do this every day. Ethan's posture becomes more upright, his chest isn't heaving with the strain, his head is held high as they jog past the crowd, ignoring them. As Ethan and Jack continue around the track, Harry Sherwood's group starts to look restless and minutes later they drift away.

"Oh my god!" I hear Sonja exclaim. "What a beautiful thing to do. He doesn't even know Ethan and he's helped him out like that."

Sonja's right. It's such a kind and even brave thing for the new boy to do, so I feel mean for secretly thinking it was also a bit strange.

CHAPTER 3

"Zoe and Sonja, go either side of Jack," Jodie directs. "Ethan, make sure we're all centred this time."

Sonja stands on tiptoes to be seen over Jack's shoulder. I stand next to him, trying not to look fed up while Jodie crouches, winking up at the screen. The camera clicks and I'm relieved to be able to relax.

Jodie takes her phone from Ethan and inspects the shot critically. "It's not bad, but maybe you should take another one."

"No!" Ethan and I protest in unison. This is the fifth photo she's taken and I swear if she takes any more I'm going to have to hide her phone.

"OK, then, I'll just have to use this one. I'll tag everyone . . . except you, Zoe, of course." Jodie rolls her eyes at me.

"Why aren't you tagging Zoe?" Jack asks curiously.

"Zoe's not on Instagram. She's given up social media. She's got a *thing* about it," Jodie answers.

Jack looks at me intently. I wait for the inevitable questions, but he doesn't interrogate me. Instead he gives a little nod, almost like he's impressed. He spots Aaron Lewis and the football crowd coming into the common room.

"Excuse me a minute," he says to us and heads towards them, calling out, "Hey, Aaron, how's that team of yours doing?"

The crowd of boys greet him warmly. "We need you, man," Aaron says, slapping him on the back. "You were phenomenal last match."

I watch him chatting and laughing with them like they're old friends. We've only been at Hinton Dale a couple of weeks but already there's no shortage of people who want to hang out with Jack. I've seen how he gets on with people; discussing music, politics, clothes, climate change, YouTubers, clips of talking animals – whatever it is, whoever they are, he can always find something in common with them. The strangest thing of all, is that it always seems genuine – never like he's trying too hard. I wish I had his social skills.

It's great having him in our psychology class. We've only had a few lessons but already me and Ethan are struggling, partly because Mrs Taylor's method of teaching just seems to be overloading us with hand-outs. It's Jack who knows what to ask to make her actually explain the theories; although I'm pretty sure he only does it to help the rest of us out, because he's even corrected her a couple of times. Like, the other day, she was rattling through the ethical guidelines for psychological research when she read out, "*The BPS guidelines state that participants in research studies should always give informed consent.*"

That was when Jack very politely said, "Yes, miss, but aren't there exceptions to that? For instance, in naturalistic observation studies, in a public location, where people would expect to be observed by others, informed consent isn't a necessity."

Mrs Taylor fumbled with her notes, mumbling that he was quite right. Now she looks panicked every time Jack puts his hand up.

Sonja said he's the same in maths and physics. I've heard people saying he's some kind of genius. Mr Dunn must be grateful that Jack enrolled; he's going to single-handedly drag Hinton Dales up the results tables.

Jack wanders back over, but he's immediately intercepted by Pete West who appears in front of us, flicking his fringe out of his eyes. I know that he isn't here to speak to us. Even though he went to St Nic's, I've never had a conversation with him. He's way too cool to bother with me and my little gang.

"Hey, Jack, I was thinking of setting up a WhatsApp group for Underground Revolution. A few of the lads want to hook up online. We could sort out times . . . teams. What do you reckon?" he drawls, nonchalantly.

"Sure, sounds good to me," Jack replies equally casually.

Pete fist-bumps him and wanders off, tapping into his phone.

"What's Underground Revolution?" I ask Jack.

"It's a game."

"What, a video game?" Ethan's face is a question mark. "But that's Pete West. He's not a gamer. He's just spent the summer partying in Ibiza!"

"Well, it looks like Underground Revolution has changed his mind." Jack shrugs. "I put him on to it. It's new, so word hasn't spread yet, but it's going to be huge and I mean *huge*! We should play each other online, Ethan."

Disappointment flickers across Ethan's face. "I can't," Ethan says. "I haven't got an Xbox at the moment. I did have, but my little brother Reece poured his juice down the back of it and . . . you know . . . I haven't got around to replacing it."

I sense Ethan's unease. He doesn't want to tell Jack that he can't afford a replacement. He's too busy babysitting at home to get a Saturday job and his parents already work around the clock to try to keep up with the bills.

"We'll sort something out," Jack says.

I wait expectantly for Jack to finish his sentence. The obvious thing to do would be to invite Ethan around to his house to play, but the invitation never comes. There's an awkward silence so I jump in to fill it.

"M&Ms, anyone?" I say, holding out the packet of sweets. Ethan and Jodie dig in, but Jack politely declines. From the shape he's in, I can't imagine that anything unhealthy has ever passed his lips.

Sonja catches our attention by growling loudly at her phone.

"What's wrong?" I ask.

"I've been refreshing this page to get hold of tickets

for The Cave Dwellers' gig," she cries. "And now it's saying they've sold out. How could they have sold out so quickly? It's ridiculous!"

"Oh, Sonja!" Jodie groans. "This is their first tour in two years. I can't believe we're not going."

"It's not my fault," Sonja protests.

"Hang on," Jack says, typing into his phone and frowning in concentration. "Yeah, I thought so. Look – I've found a site with tickets left at face value." He grins. "You'd better hurry up and buy them. I'll send you the link."

Jodie and Sonja look like they'll explode with joy as they open the link. "Oh my god, this website is amazing. It's *literally* going to change my life," Jodie says melodramatically.

"What about you two?" Jack says to me and Ethan. "Don't you want tickets?"

"The Cave Dwellers aren't my thing," Ethan replies.

"And I can't afford it right now," I say lightly, although the truth is I'm completely gutted not to be going. Me, Jodie and Sonja were into them way before they got big. I'd love to see them live, but I'm skint and I'd never ask Mum to help; paying for the holiday in Spain used up all her savings and I know how tight money is since Dad left.

A big shout goes up from the other end of the room where a crowd is surrounding one of the tables. Curiosity drags us over and we find Harry Sherwood sitting at the table, his sleeve rolled up, grinning triumphantly. Arm wrestling, like the Neanderthal he is. Justine Collins is playfully massaging his shoulders like he's a boxer in his corner.

"OK, winner stays on," Amanda Parry announces loudly. "Would the next challenger please come forward?"

No one offers. Sherwood scans the crowd, his eyes resting on Ethan. "I challenge Ethan Mansfield," he says with a smirk.

I see Ethan's face twitch. Sherwood's such a bastard.

"Come on, Ethan. It's only a bit of fun. There's nothing else to do in this crappy common room," Sherwood says brightly. "Unless you're afraid, that is?"

Ethan hesitates.

"Don't bother," I whisper to him. "He's pathetic."

He shakes his head, his chin jutting out determinedly. "It's OK," he says quietly.

The crowd claps supportively as Ethan takes his place opposite Sherwood and rests his elbow on the table, clasping their palms together. The skin on his hand immediately starts to blanch as Sherwood squeezes hard.

Amanda leans over the table and inspects their interlocked hands and positioning of their elbows. "OK, then, on the count of three," she says excitedly. "One . . . two . . . *three*!"

Ethan's face creases with strain as Sherwood's hand tightens around his. Sherwood takes a moment to grin at the spectators as he starts to push Ethan's hand towards the table. I grit my teeth, willing Ethan on as he pushes Sherwood back a fraction, his arm quivering, but Sherwood is just playing with him.

The next second he slams Ethan's arm into the table.

There's a muted clap around the room as Ethan gets up, trying to disguise his pain with a weak smile.

"Hard luck, Ethan," Sherwood says insincerely. Ethan grimaces and slides to the back of the crowd.

"Who's next, then?" Amanda surveys the crowd saying theatrically, "Is anyone brave enough to challenge our Common Room Champ?"

There's a silence, and then, "I'll have a go," Jack says politely, causing whoops of excitement from the girls in the crowd.

"Go, Jack!" Jodie shouts as he takes his place at the table.

"At last I get some proper competition," Sherwood says, but his smirk has disappeared. He looks just the tiniest bit worried.

People hold up their phones to film the encounter. Jack doesn't even bother to roll up his sleeve. He keeps a poker face as he clasps Sherwood's palm in his, but Sherwood keeps shifting his hand, adjusting the grip and shuffling in his seat.

"Settle down, Harry," Amanda orders. She scrutinizes their hold and straightens Harry's elbow. "No cheating, and may the best man win!"

Sherwood braces himself, the veins in his forearm already raised in anticipation, but Jack remains calm and composed. I lean in, holding my breath.

"One . . . two . . . *three*!"

Immediately there's a thud and a howl as Sherwood's hand slams down on the table.

The crowd erupts into applause. Harry is cradling his arm

and looking at Jack with a mixture of fury and astonishment. I exhale in relief.

Jack is standing up already, not a hair out of place. He extends his hand to Sherwood. "Hard luck, Harry."

Sherwood doesn't take it. He is still cradling his arm. "You've broken it!" he whimpers angrily.

"It's not broken," Jack says, matter of fact. "It might be sprained. You can go and see the nurse if you want a second opinion."

Amanda climbs up on the table in delight. "Any more challengers for our new champ?"

People shake their heads, laughing. "I need my arm, thanks very much," Aaron Lewis calls out.

"Then I declare Jack Cartwright our Common Room Champion!" she hollers, throwing her arms out to loud cheers.

People are congratulating Jack as he makes his way to us. Sonja has already posted the clip – *Common Room Champ #TeamJack*

Ethan grins from ear to ear. "Thanks, Jack, that's made my day! I just wish I could have beaten him, but there's no chance with these things." He flexes his long, thin arms suddenly looking dejected as the grin falls from his face.

"There's no reason to be intimated by idiots like Harry Sherwood," Jack says. "But if you want to get fitter, I could help you get into shape, maybe build up more muscle?"

I shoot a look at Ethan, expecting him to find it hilarious that Jack would even think he'd want to "pump iron" but, instead, Ethan's face lights up.

"Would you?" Ethan asks.

"Sure," says Jack warmly. "But to see results you'd need to be committed and put the work in."

"Of course. I'll put in a hundred and ten per cent!" Ethan says, with a cheesy smile.

I'm taken aback. This isn't like Ethan. He's always seemed happy being the cute, gangly boy I know and love. As I listen to them chatting enthusiastically about training timetables and goal-setting, I know that I ought to be impressed, but something, deep in my stomach, tightens with an inexplicable anxiety.

CHAPTER 4

I look out of my bedroom window. Everyone is home and cars line both sides of our street. Dad is going to struggle to find a parking space. He always texts me when he arrives to say he's waiting outside. He doesn't ever come to the front door. Mum still can't bring herself to actually talk to him.

I keep one eye out for him as I call Jen. I haven't spoken to her for a while, but knowing what a great time she's having makes me even more determined to work hard for my exams so I can go to uni. I've got this stupid idea in my head that doing a psychology degree will help me understand men like Dad – men who seem to be happy and then throw it all away to chase young women. I'm hoping that there's a deeper psychological reason for his behaviour rather than the obvious one. I suppose I want to find an excuse for him. It's too hard to think of my dad as being that selfish and shallow.

I sigh as soon as I hear the voicemail message kick in.

"Hi, this is Jennifer. Sorry I can't take your call, but leave a message and I'll get back to you."

I try to sound upbeat. "Hi, Jen, it's Zo. I know that you'll be in the library studying – *not*. Anyway, Dad's just about to pick me up for the monthly 'I'm a good father really' meet-up. Just wondered if you had a message for him, but obviously you can always call him yourself. OK, well . . . ring me some time. Love you. Bye."

I rest my forehead on the windowpane. Jen was lucky; she'd just left for university when it all blew up with Mum and Dad, so she didn't have to deal with any of it. It was me who got the full blast.

One morning everything was normal: Mum hassling me out of the door for school, Dad saying he'd be back late. Then, that afternoon, I returned home and discovered Mum, destroyed. She'd found his phone and the text messages between him and Petra. And that was it; everything was shattered. There would be no more "normal" again.

Mum tried to keep it together, even when our house had to be sold and we moved here. I know, every day, what a struggle it is for her. She never wants me to see her upset but her fake cheerfulness is no disguise. I'm so proud of her. Over this last year she's been getting her confidence back – loving her job as a dental receptionist, going out with her friends more – but Dad marrying Petra the other week hit her hard. I think Mum had convinced herself that it wouldn't last.

As I watch the street lamp outside our house flickering on and off, my phone buzzes. It's Dad.

Parked outside no 32.

I grab my coat and call out to Mum. "He's here!"

She appears in the hallway, cradling a glass of white wine. I notice that she's had her roots done and is wearing a lovely turquoise blouse that reflects the colour of her eyes. But she still looks thin and her face is gaunt. All the stress of the divorce made the weight fall off her. I keep thinking that, when I can hug her without feeling just skin and bone, then I'll know that she's really coming through it.

"You're looking lovely, Mum," I say. "Are you going out somewhere?"

"Just for a quick drink with the girls." She looks a bit sheepish, fiddling with the stem of her glass. "Actually, Zoe, they've been trying to persuade me to sign up to one of those dating websites. Obviously, one of the *nice* ones." She flushes. "What do you think?"

I'm startled for a moment, but then I see her anxious expression and I force an enthusiastic smile on to my face. This will be good for Mum – why should Dad get to move on and not her?

"I think you should go for it, Mum. There'll be s*ome* good blokes out there."

She smiles, relieved. I know that she wants my approval, even if she doesn't really need it. "OK, then. I might just do it," she says. "Now, you have a nice time with your dad."

I step out into the chilly night air – winter has definitely arrived. Dad waves at me from inside a polished deep red

Jaguar. As I open the door and climb in, the smell of the leather interior hits me.

He stares at me, disapproval in his eyes. I realize that this is the first time he's seen my new lilac hair. "Hello, darling." He leans across and kisses me on the cheek. His face is tanned but there are dark circles under his eyes. He starts the engine and casts me another sideways look.

"Is there something the matter, Dad?" I say lightly.

"No . . . nothing." He pauses and then says, "It's just . . . do you have to keep messing with your hair? And have you had *more* ear piercings?" He looks exasperated.

"Get over it, Dad," I say. I'm not going to let him wind me up. "It's not like I've gone and got a tattoo . . . yet." I enjoy the look of alarm that jumps on his face.

I lean back in my comfortable seat.

"Nice wheels." I prickle with resentment, thinking of Mum's clapped-out car on the driveway.

"Not mine, sadly. It's a company car," Dad says. "They gave me an upgrade. I'm covering a much bigger region, so it means more travelling."

"Are you having to stay places overnight, then?" I ask. I try not to make it loaded, but that's how he managed to have an affair in the first place. So many nights away that Mum never even questioned where he was.

He tries to hold in a sigh. "No, I've been managing to get home every day so far." He glances at me. "Petra doesn't like me being away."

I instinctively cross my arms at the mention of her

name, but who can blame her for wanting to know where Dad is?

"This place OK?" he asks, turning left into a retail park full of superstores and chain restaurants.

"Yeah, fine," I answer, secretly disappointed. We haven't seen each other in weeks, I thought that he might choose somewhere special to eat. Make a bit of an effort.

We walk into the empty pizzeria and the young greeter pounces on us.

"Good evening. Where would you like to sit?" she says enthusiastically.

We survey the room of vacant tables.

"In a booth by the window would be great," Dad smiles at her.

As we sit down and look at the menu, Dad's phone rings. He looks at the screen and says apologetically, "I've just got to get this." He turns his back to me and mutters into the phone, "Hi, darling. Everything OK?"

My stomach turns. Petra. Can't we even have five minutes alone?

"Yep, just got here. All good." He flashes me a nervous smile. "Yes, I will. OK, see you real soon." He hangs up. "Petra says hello."

I glare at him across the table. Luckily for Dad, the young waitress comes over and breaks the tension.

"Can I take your order?" she says eagerly.

"Yes, please." I study the menu. "Can I have a Coke, and I'll have calamari to start, then a calzone pizza for my main.

I'll order pudding after, if that's OK?" I smile and hand her back the menu.

"And for you, sir?"

Dad keeps his eyes on the menu as he says, "I'll have an orange juice and a tuna salad . . . hold the dressing."

I look at him mockingly, knowing that he's paranoid about his weight now he's with Petra. "On a diet are you, Dad?"

"No, no. Just keeping healthy," he replies, looking embarrassed.

"Any starter?" the waitress asks hopefully.

"No, thanks, and you might as well bring the calamari and main courses at the same time." He hands the menu back.

I shake my head. He's so transparent. He wants our dinner together over as soon as possible so that he can get back to *her*.

Dad always says that Petra is keen to get to know me and Jen. He's invited me to stay with them a few times, but there's no way I even want to be in the same room as that woman. Sometimes I wonder what would have happened if Mum had never seen those texts. Would Dad have left us anyway? Would the affair have ended and life gone back to normal? Or would he have just done it again, knowing he'd got away with it once?

"Are you going to take off your jacket?" I ask. He looks like we're having a business meeting.

"Sure," he says, sliding it off, revealing a brightly-patterned, slim-fitting shirt which is too tight for him. I could *almost* feel sorry for him. Dad has become a walking cliché. The middle-aged man with the young wife, desperately trying to keep in shape at the gym, dressing in clothes far too young for him. Going out to clubs to try to keep up with her. Trying to hide his receding hairline in photos by wearing beanie hats. Terrified of letting his guard drop, in case she sees he's just a flash salesman with the gift of the gab, who used to like staying in on a Saturday night and watching the history channel.

"Oh, before I forget, I got you and Jen presents from Vegas," he says brightly, pulling out two boxes from his bag. Headphones with pictures of 'Vegas Elvis' on them. "They're cool, aren't they? We got them from the Elvis museum." He looks pleased with himself.

I thank him and put them down on the ground. I'm not going to ask him about his wedding and honeymoon, if that's what he's expecting.

"You'd like Vegas. I'll take you and Jen there one day," he says.

I instinctively grit my teeth. I don't want a free holiday if it involves Petra coming.

"So, you want me to give Jen her present?" I ask him, as the waitress brings over our food and drinks.

"Yeah, would you? I don't think I'll be seeing her for a while yet," he replies casually, knowing that he hasn't seen her for seven months. "Anyway, how was your holiday? France, wasn't it?"

"Spain," I reply, trying to keep the coldness out of my

voice. Clearly, nothing about our lives interests him. "Yeah, it was fine, thanks."

"And college?" He's shovelling in his salad as I take a bite of my calamari and chew slowly.

"Yeah . . . I've only been there three weeks but, so far, it's all good."

"Well, what subjects did you decide to study?" He takes a sip of orange juice.

"Psychology, English literature and history."

He leans over and takes some of my calamari. I knew he wouldn't be able to stick to his diet.

"Oh, history!" he says, like it's an old friend. "What periods are you doing?"

I can't stop a creeping smile. Dad is a frustrated historian who became a sales rep because he never got a chance to go to college. He always loved it when we watched history documentaries together.

"Well, we've already started on the Tudors and we're going to cover the Stuarts as well."

His eyes brighten. "You lucky girl! They're my favourites. Of course, Elizabeth I was the greatest monarch among them. Did you know. . ." He stops mid-sentence, silenced by the ringing of his phone. He looks at the screen and flushes. "One minute," he says, turning away. He listens for a minute, then puts his hand over the phone, whispering to me, "Petra's saying that she's finished at work and could drive over and join us."

I stare at him. "Is she joking? No! This is our time

together. I hardly get to see you as it is." My voice rises despite myself. I bite back tears.

He looks panicked and puts his finger to his lips, scared that she's heard me. "Sorry, Petra, there's no point. We've nearly finished anyway. Another time, hey."

He hangs up and forces a smile. He pushes away his salad. I stare at my pizza. I don't feel like eating.

"I was going to order banoffee pie for pudding. Do you want one?" I ask challengingly. I know what the answer will be, but I want to make him say it.

He flushes again beneath his tan. "Actually, Zoe, could we skip pudding tonight and next time we'll go to this fantastic place that *only* does puddings? You can have as many as you like, I promise."

I nod. And that's that. Our night out together, over in less than an hour.

On the drive home Dad tries to continue the conversation about Elizabeth I, but I'm not interested any more. Eventually he puts on the radio to ease the awkward silence. He pulls up outside the house and kisses me on the cheek. I turn away.

"Remember to give Jen her present," he says as I'm climbing out. "See you soon, love."

I close the car door without saying a word. I don't look back as he pips the horn and drives away.

The house is in darkness. I walk quietly through to the kitchen and turn on the light. There's a note on the worktop.

Gone for that drink with the girls from work. Don't put the bolt on the door. Mum xx

Good, I'm glad she's having fun. She deserves it. I lie on my bed and check my phone. No message from Jen. I'll text her tomorrow, tell her about the gift from Dad, not that she'll be interested. A message from Ethan appears.

Hope it's going OK with your dad.

A lump rises in my throat. That's typical of Ethan – checking that I'm all right. He knows that meeting up with Dad usually leaves me feeling let down. It's eight o'clock. Ethan will probably be at home, babysitting, while his mum and dad do the late shift at the hospital. They're so lovely and caring – the perfect people to be health-care assistants.

I call him and my spirits lift at the sound of his voice.

"Hi, Zo. You still with your dad?" I can hear his little sister, Amy, chattering in the background.

"No." I pick at my bedspread. "He couldn't get out of there fast enough. Petra kept phoning. She wanted to join us!"

"Oh, that's a bit crap. I'm sorry."

"Yeah." I try to sound like I'm not bothered. "What are you up to?"

"I'm babysitting, of course. What else does a sixteen-year old man about town do of a Saturday night? I'm knackered, though. Getting Reece and Jimmy to bed was like herding cats, and now Amy is refusing to go to sleep unless I read her a story."

Amy shouts excitedly down the phone. "Zoe . . . Zoe, tell Ethan to read me *Beauty and the Beast*."

"Ethan, read Amy *Beauty and the Beast*. In fact, put me on speakerphone, so I can hear it too. It's been years since anyone read me a bedtime story." An image flashes into my head; I must have been about five. I'm cuddling up to Dad on the sofa as he reads me *The Gruffalo*. He used to make me feel so safe and loved. But he's not *that* Dad any more.

Ethan gives a mock sigh of resignation. "OK, fine." There's a rustling as Amy settles on to his lap. "If you're all sitting comfortably, then I'll begin."

Ethan's great at reading. He reads the simple story with such drama that I hear Amy gasp and giggle as he tells the tale. At the climax, when it seems like Beast has been killed, I find myself holding my breath and, when he transforms back into the handsome prince, stupid tears well in my eyes. As the story ends, Amy claps and I join in.

"Again, again!" Amy demands.

"No, we made a deal. It's sleep time. Hang on, Zo." I hear the distant noise of a door shutting, and then, after a few minutes, Ethan picks up the phone again.

"Still there?" he asks.

"That was lovely, Ethan," I say, and I mean it. "Can I phone you every night for a bedtime story?"

There's a moment's pause that feels oddly loaded. I find myself saying quickly, "Have you done the psychology that's due on Monday?"

"No," he groans. "I can't get excited about research methods. Why can't we do an essay on that Milgram experiment we read about? I mean, *that* was just crazy."

I nod eagerly to myself. That experiment was unbelievable. "I know, right? I still can't believe that sixty-five per cent of them gave what they thought was a *lethal* electric shock to innocent people, just because they were told to by a man in a technician's coat?"

"I wouldn't have done it," Ethan says emphatically. "No way."

"But that's the terrifying thing – you might have done. Those participants were just ordinary people, and I bet they would have said the same before they were actually in that situation."

"Well, that's what happens when people blindly follow orders, so maybe we should ignore Mrs Taylor's order to do the research methods essay. She'll respect us for it, won't she?" he says, making me laugh. "Listen, why don't you come over to mine tomorrow and we can work on the stupid essay together?"

"Great! That'll make it less painful," I say. "I'll bring toffee popcorn and crisps to keep us going."

"No popcorn and crisps for me, thanks. I'm sticking to Jack's fitness plan," Ethan says determinedly.

I have to bite my tongue. Ethan has really thrown himself into training with Jack. I hope Jack's not pushing him too hard. I can't imagine my friend as a muscle-bound hunk. And I wouldn't want him to be that way. He's just . . . Ethan. My Ethan, and he's adorable as he is.

"I hope he knows what he's doing," I say.

He laughs. "This is *Jack* we're talking about. He's worked out a personalized diet and exercise regime for me to build stamina and muscle mass. People have seen us working together and been asking him whether he'll do the same for them, so he's starting fitness training after college on Mondays and Wednesdays. Why don't you come along?"

I wince at the thought of it. Still, I try and sound diplomatic for Ethan; he's so excited about this. "I read his post on the message board inviting everyone, but I'm not sure it's for me."

"Oh, come on. You might enjoy it – a *load* of the girls have signed up."

"I bet they have," I say, knowing how the girls at college flock around Jack. "And have you seen his post asking what people want for the common room?" Jack seems to have taken on the role of student rep and everyone seems happy enough with it.

"Yeah, there are some hilarious suggestions. I particularly like the votes for a Jacuzzi and spa-treatment area, but I thought I'd keep it real, so I put down air hockey. What about you?"

"I went for a home cinema system," I laugh.

"Dream on."

"To be honest, I think we're all dreaming. I don't know how we're going to persuade Mr Dunn to give us *anything*," I reply, wondering whether Jack might end up regretting raising people's hopes.

"If anyone can persuade Mr Dunn then Jack can," Ethan says his voice brimming with admiration.

CHAPTER 5

The doorbell rings as I'm finishing breakfast. Mum is upstairs, so I shovel another spoonful of cornflakes into my mouth and head to the front door, wondering who could be ringing so early.

Jack stands on the doorstep, looking immaculate, and Ethan is beside him with beads of sweat running down his sweet face. Every morning Jack has started calling for Ethan so that they can "stride" to college together.

"Hi, Zoe," says Jack. "Wondered if you wanted to walk in with us?"

Mum comes downstairs and grabs her coat from the end of the banister. She waves at Ethan but stops abruptly when she sees Jack. "Hello," she says, smiling broadly. "I'm Emma, Zoe's mum."

Jack holds out his hand. "Good morning, Mrs Littlewood. I'm Jack Cartwright, a friend of Zoe's."

Mum takes his hand. "Nice to meet you. Sorry to rush

off but I don't want to be late for work." She fishes out her car keys from her handbag.

"You may want to take a detour if you're driving to the surgery. There's been a crash on the ring-road. Perhaps use Parsons Lane instead," Jack says.

Mum gives him a puzzled look and he grins. "I noticed your badge . . . Longton Surgery," he explains, pointing to her jacket.

"Well, aren't you an observant young man? Right, Parsons Lane it is." Mum waves at us cheerfully and heads out.

"Look at you, charming the parents, sickening," Ethan teases. "Come on, let's get going before I seize up." He presses a button on the slick black watch around his wrist. "No way! I've done five thousand two hundred steps already," he declares in happy disbelief.

"That's because you're walking eight flights of stairs. I told you ditching the lift at Lennon Towers would be good for you," Jack says.

"I didn't know you had a fitness monitor," I say, eyeing it up.

"Yeah, Jack gave me it. It's a Go-Getter. It's pretty amazing. It already knows more about my body than I do!" he laughs. "It logs all your data, does continual health checks, offers loads of mad apps, it even tells me when to go to sleep and what to eat," Ethan says incredulously.

"Would you like one, Zoe?" Jack says, looking at me with his inkwell eyes. "I've got a spare. I wouldn't want any money for it."

I hesitate. It's nice of him to offer but I'm not sure I want a watch telling me when to sleep and what to eat.

"Go on, Zoe. I didn't think it was my kind of thing either, but after a few days you'll wonder how you ever lived without it," Ethan enthuses.

"Thanks, I'll think about it," I say politely.

Jack gives a little respectful nod and heads out of the door, striding up the street as me and Ethan lag behind. I hear a buzz from Ethan's wrist and Dwayne Johnson's voice rings out. "Come on, Ethan! Move your butt. Remember, if you do twenty thousand steps by 20.00 hours today, you'll get ten pounds off your next purchase from Lean Machine sports and casual wear."

I elbow Ethan. "That's creepy!

"Admit it, Zo, you think it's fun really. It's like having 'The Rock' as your own personal trainer. You can choose which celebrity voice you want to motivate you. Just imagine, you could have Leonardo DiCaprio whispering to you, as Romeo, 'Go forth, sweet Zoe, and quicken thy step as thee quickens my heart.'" Ethan bows at me, fluttering his thick dark lashes.

"Don't give up your day job, Ethan," I say drily.

Jodie and Sonja are waiting for us at the entrance to the alleyway. Jodie strolls up to Jack, takes a deep breath and says, "*Dzie dobry*, Jack."

"Jodie, have you been learning Polish?" Jack sounds impressed.

"Sure. I'm doing it for my pal here," Jodie replies, squeezing Sonja.

Sonja shrugs her off playfully. "She's doing it to impress you, so that *you* think she's a good friend to me, which actually proves what a *bad* friend she is."

"But does it matter why Jodie's doing it, as long as she learning your language?" Jack says lightly.

"*Dziękuję*, Jack," Jodie says, slinging her arm around Sonja's shoulders. "As I keep telling her, Sonja is very lucky to have such a thoughtful friend as me."

We head into the alley and my stomach knots as it always does when I walk down here. I hate this walk; since the first day of college that vicious dog is always there. I'd love to avoid it, but to take the alternative route would mean a massive detour and I'm usually running late.

"Guys, be careful when we pass this house coming up," I warn. "There's a mad dog running wild in the back garden."

"Yeah, yeah," says Jodie. "We can handle some little pug."

And just then, the dog comes out of nowhere, slamming its face against the rotting gate, snarling and slobbering. I gasp and draw back, and Ethan catches my arm. Sonja and Jodie shriek, but Jack doesn't seem to flinch.

"Get back, Jack," Ethan calls out, as the dog hurls itself at the fence again. Its overgrown nails scratch at the wood and, to my horror, it starts leaping up, frantically trying to get over the fence. I spot a man smoking a cigarette in the kitchen window, just watching.

"Hey! Hey!" I shout above the dog's barking. "Get out here and get your dog under control!"

The gnarled-faced man in a grey vest opens the kitchen

window and leans out, shouting at us, "Stop upsetting my dog."

The dog becomes even wilder on hearing the man's voice. It circles around the filthy kennel on the patio and then runs again at the gate, bounding up and looking like it's going to clear it. Before any of us has time to react, Jack has whipped his rucksack off his shoulder and swung it at the dog with such force that it's sent flying backwards into the garden.

My mouth is slack as I watch the disorientated animal stagger to its feet. The man barrels out of the house, swearing at us and holding the dog by the collar.

"Bullseye, are you OK, boy?" He turns to Jack, his eyes bulging in fury. "I'm calling the police. You don't do that to my animal."

"Go ahead," Jack says coolly, putting his rucksack back over his shoulder. "It was self-defence and there are four witnesses to back me up. Though we can see what the police say, if you like."

"Piss off!" the man roars.

I'm trembling with anger and fright, but Jack's calm helps me find my voice. "What if your dog got loose when a little kid was walking past?" I say furiously. "He could kill them. You've got to make it safe."

The man takes another drag of his cigarette before answering. "Listen, darling, it's very simple. If you're worried about my dog chewing your face off, I suggest you don't walk down this alley."

"Hey!" Ethan snaps, stepping forward. "You don't talk to

her like that. You keep your dog under control or – or I'll sort it out for you!"

The man laughs scornfully. "I'd like to see you try." He lets go of the dog's collar and Bullseye flies at the gate again, growling and baring his teeth.

We turn and sprint down the alleyway with barks and curses following us. We don't stop running until we're in the college grounds.

"Oh my god, Jack. You were amazing," Jodie pants, dropping on to a moss-covered bench. "The way you stopped that dog. If he'd got over that gate he could have torn us apart."

"Yeah. Thanks, Jack, you were great," I say, a little in awe of him.

"What have you got in that rucksack ... bricks?" Sonja says, plonking herself down next to Jodie.

"Just text books," he says matter of factly, as he sweeps his dark hair out of his eyes.

"I *knew* texts books would come in handy one day," Jodie says, sending us girls into a fit of tension-releasing laughter.

I'm laughing so hard that I can hardly breathe and when I see tears rolling down Sonja and Jodie's faces it just makes me laugh even more. I glance at Jack through blurry eyes – he's looking at me, smiling.

Ethan's gaze flits between me and Jack as he says tetchily, "I don't know why you're all laughing like this is some sort of joke. We need to call the police about that dog."

"The police won't be any help," Jack says. "Look it up.

The owner isn't legally required to tether his dog on private property."

"But he could escape and attack someone," Ethan says, outraged.

"Yes, but it hasn't happened yet," Jack says.

"So, you actually have to get hurt before the police will do anything?" I murmur.

"Basically, yes," says Jack. He shrugs. "But at least we're all OK."

"We can't just leave it. Zoe walks past that dog twice a day," Ethan says. "We need to do something."

"Sure, but what?" Sonja says defeatedly.

Ethan stares right through us. "I'll think of something," he says so softly that only I hear him.

CHAPTER 6

The common room is packed with students waiting for our weekly assembly. It's far too noisy to concentrate so I go and grab one of the computers at the far end of the room. My next psychology assessment is due this afternoon and I want to work on it some more. I was given a bad grade for my research methods essay and Ethan's was even worse. I have to get this right but I'm getting distracted by Jason Caston who's in the seat next to me, his head's down, his eyes transfixed on his phone as his thumbs shift around the screen.

"Yes!" he suddenly exclaims, punching the air.

I see his screen fill with flashing signs and floating balloons. He's playing some kind of game.

"Did you win?" I say trying to be friendly.

"Yeah – Five . . . thousand . . . pounds!" he grins triumphantly.

"What? Really?"

He looks at me like I'm stupid. "*No,* it's not real money,

but it will be one day," he says confidently. "It's a casino app. I love stuff like this. Jack Cartwright put me onto it . . . it's free. You should try it; it's addictive though."

"Oh, right," I say turning back to my work. The last thing I need is to get hooked on some gambling app.

The church bells ring out from the speakers and Mr Dunn walks into the room. As everyone grabs somewhere to sit, it strikes me just how many people have congregated around Jack. People seem drawn to him, even people who usually stay in their own cliques – the footballers, the indie kids, the straight-A students, the geeks, the gamers, the too-cool for school crowd – he seems to attract them all. More and more of them are turning up for his after-school fitness training. I've noticed some have even started wearing the same brand of sports gear and trainers as him. I'm still resisting going along, despite Ethan trying to persuade me. I'm sticking to my own form of exercise, which consists of dancing around my bedroom to The Killers.

Assembly only lasts ten minutes, but Mr Dunn's dull delivery makes it feel like an hour. He wishes us "a happy day of learning" and turns to leave, but Jack stands up. "Mr Dunn, you mentioned we could discuss the common room."

Mr Dunn looks irritable. "Certainly, certainly. Make an appointment."

"Actually, sir, it's a matter that affects *all* students so it's more appropriate to discuss it here in assembly." He smiles disarmingly.

"Leave it, will you, Cartwright?" Harry Sherwood shouts

to Jack. "We all just want to get out of here."

Someone tells Sherwood to keep quiet. Others call-out in support of Jack. Harry isn't used to being put in his place and I watch his face as he quietly seethes. It's been obvious that he can't stand Jack getting all the attention, and I bet he's still feeling humiliated from being beaten by him at arm wrestling and it being posted on Instagram for everyone to see.

"It sounds like people agree with you, Jack." Mr Dunn clasps his hands together, his tone patronizing. "So, what's on your mind?"

"Well, I'm sure you'll agree, sir, that our common room is poorly resourced, particularly compared to the ones at other sixth-form college in the area."

Mr Dunn doesn't look impressed. "I would take exception to that. It's quite adequate for your needs. This room is just a space to congregate."

"But it isn't sir," Jack says gently. "This is our space to relax and socialize between lessons, as well as a place to study. As a sixth-form cohort, it's vital we have a room that we can value and take ownership of. A welcoming space will help bring people together." Jack sounds so self-assured, so natural. There is a murmur of assent in the room.

"So, what are you proposing, Jack? A bouncy castle, a fairground ride?" Mr Dunn looks at him over his glasses.

Jack gives a polite laugh. "No, sir, but the student body have been discussing our needs and have come up with a number of things that will greatly improve our environment and make us proud to be Hinton Dale students."

Mr Dunn stares him. "Let's hear them, then."

"Firstly, we need comfortable seating. Decent sofas and armchairs."

"Hmm," Mr Dunn responds. "Perhaps."

"We'll need vending machines, a pool table, table tennis and air hockey. There's also been a high demand for an Xbox."

"Absolutely not." Mr Dunn bristles. "This is a college not a youth club."

"I understand, sir. I think on consideration we could let that one go."

Someone snorts with laughter. Jack had better watch it. He's winding up Mr Dunn.

"There's nothing I'd like more than to improve the common room facilities, but unfortunately, all this would take money we haven't got," Mr Dunn says firmly.

"I'm not sure that's factually correct, sir," Jack replies calmly. "I've been having a look at the college financial statements from the last academic year." Everyone falls silent. "And they show that Hinton Dale is in profit. Wouldn't it be appropriate to use at least some of that money for the good of your students?"

There are whoops of approval around the hall.

Mr Dunn is fiddling with his glasses agitatedly. "Everybody needs to quieten down and show some decorum. Jack, I don't appreciate being ambushed like this and, unless you've got an accountancy degree, you're hardly in a position to understand the intricacies of this college's finances."

"It's not difficult, Mr Dunn. It's all broken down in

black and white. The document is accessible online to the public. I'm sure that when I bring the financial statement to the attention of parents, they'd agree that monies should be invested in the college for the benefit of their children."

Mr Dunn is rubbing his glasses so hard I swear they're going to smash. "Finances are a matter for the governors and stakeholders. I'll put your request on the agenda for our next meeting. And yes, perhaps we can look at some new seating. However – " he draws himself up, running his hand over his thinning hair – "I can guarantee that they won't release money for everything you've outlined. That would require separate fundraising," he says peevishly.

Jack turns to face us all, wearing that all-encompassing smile of his. "Fundraising. We can do that, can't we?"

"I'm not doing any sponsored bloody run," Jodie calls out.

"And no bake sales!" Amanda Parry shouts.

"I'd be up for it, but only if it involves a club and bangin' music," Pete West declares, to cheers.

"Fine." Jack nods. "A club and bangin' music it is!"

Excitement fizzes in the room. People start heated debates about venues. Ethan, Jodie and Sonja are checking out clubs on their phones. Mr Dunn tries to order us to our classes, but his voice is lost in the noise. He gives up and walks out of the room like he's leaving Jack in charge.

I stand apart from it all, watching Jack moving among the crowd of excited students.

Who is this boy? Because he seems to be changing everything.

CHAPTER 7

I take the lift to the eighth floor of Lennon Towers, standing rigid in the centre and holding my breath to stop the stench of whatever's smeared on the walls from sailing up my nose. I probably should have used the stairs, like Ethan does, but these heels weren't designed for mountaineering.

I hear his family before I even reach their door down the dimly-lit corridor, laughter and squeals coming from number 814. I grin to myself as I ring the bell. Jimmy opens the door in his tartan pyjamas and bedhead hair.

"Hi, Zoe, we're watching *Paddington*. Do you want to watch it with us?" he asks sleepily, wrapping his chubby hand around my fingers and leading me inside.

"I love *Paddington*, Jimmy, but it's going to have to be another time. Me and Ethan are going out," I say. I poke my head into the steamed-up kitchen to say hi to his parents.

"Hello, Zoe, love," Simon says, opening the oven to a

great blast of heat. "Do you want some fish fingers and chips?"

"No, thanks." I smile at Ethan's dad. "Me and Ethan are going on the sixth-form *big night out*," I say with jazz hands.

"Don't I know it?" Simon laughs. "He's been in that bathroom for nearly an hour. Reece had to get washed in the kitchen sink."

I raise my eyebrows. What's Ethan doing in there? It's not like him to take his time getting ready. Usually he has a quick shower and grabs whatever clothes he finds on his bedroom floor.

"Is Lily at St Monica's?" I ask.

"Yep, she's on the ward until ten and then I'm doing the eleven to seven shift. We're like ships in the night," he sighs. "Anyway, how's your mum?"

"Fine. You know how much she loves her job at that dental surgery? She gets to chat to people all day as she calms their nerves in the waiting room."

"I'm so pleased she's doing well. Will you send her our love?" Simon says as he dishes out the fish fingers and oven chips on to plates. "Are you meeting Jack at the club?"

"Yeah, we're meeting everyone there." I steal a chip off a plate. "Have you met Jack, then?" I'm curious to know what Ethan's dad makes of him.

"Yeah, a few times. The kids love him. He gave them his old iPad. I told him not to, but he insisted. He's so patient, isn't he? He sat with the three of them and taught them how to play all these computer games. I got on with the housework. Even snuck in a cup of tea."

"That's nice of him." I find myself frowning. Is there no one Jack Cartwright can't charm?

"He seems like a great lad." Simon puts the ketchup on the table. "Me and Lily couldn't be happier that Ethan's friends with a boy like Jack; someone who's confident and comfortable in his own skin." Simon sticks his head into the hallway and calls out, "Come and get it!"

There's a stampede as the three of them rush into the kitchen. Amy is still in her uniform, her wild frizzy hair escaping from a ponytail. Her freckled face lights up as she sees me.

"Zoe, you look like a princess!" she exclaims.

I can't help chuckling at her excited face. My hair is short and lilac, my eyes are lined with heavy black kohl and my wide mouth is coated in plum lipstick. I'm wearing a shimmering silver sleeveless top, faux leather trousers with chunky high heels, and a mass of earrings and bangles reaching halfway up my arms – I hardly look like a princess going to a ball. Still, it's nice to hear.

"Thank you, Amy," I say, giving her a kiss.

"Yeah, you look all right, Zoe," Reece says, glancing at me. He lifts his plate off the table and starts to carry it, unsteadily, out of the kitchen.

"Where do you think you're going, Reece?" Simon asks, his arms folded.

"*Please*, Dad, can I eat it watching *Paddington*? It's a *really* good bit." Reece's pleading face is too cute.

"OK, but don't tell your mum," Simon winks.

I help Jimmy carry his plate as we parade into the sunflower-yellow living room with its poppy patterned curtains. I love this room, even though the sofas are too big for it and storage boxes line the walls and there are always clothes drying on radiators and toys scattered on the floor like an obstacle course. I love this room because I always knew that I could find laughter and fun here when I was feeling low after Dad left.

I settle the kids in front of the TV and go and knock on Ethan's bedroom door.

"Come in," he says.

As I open the door to his tiny bedroom I'm hit by a choking cloud of aftershave. I crawl over his bed and open the window as far as it will go with its safety lock. "Ethan, go easy on that, will you?" I splutter.

"Too much?" He looks puzzled.

I nod my head, coughing. It's only when the smell starts to thin out that I recognize it; Ethan's bought the same aftershave as Jack! My eyes stop stinging and I'm able to look at him properly. I'm struck by the difference in his appearance. He's gelled his soft curly hair into an impressive quiff and his usually pale skin is glowing. When he looks at me it's as if I'm only just noticing the electric blue of his hooded eyes. He's wearing a paisley shirt tucked into smart black jeans with a chunky belt, which makes his torso into a V-shape. I hadn't realized how much he'd filled out and toned up. My eyes flit to his bed where more clothes are laid out. There's no sign of his usual baggy T-shirts and slouching jeans.

"New clothes?" I ask.

"Yeah," he says bashfully. "Don't laugh, but Jack helped me pick them online. He's good at stuff like that. I got this as well." He holds up a hoodie covered in a retro Union Jack design.

I don't want to be unfair to Jack, but I can't help feeling annoyed. I don't like the thought of Jack changing how Ethan looks and even how he smells. And how's Ethan meant to pay for all this? It's OK for Jack; money doesn't seem to be a problem for him. He has all the latest gadgets, and every day he comes into college in a new brand of top or jacket, and I've never met anyone with so many pairs of trainers.

"Well, you look great," I say, and it's true. I catch a glimpse of myself in his wardrobe mirror and suddenly feel self-conscious. My top was Jen's; she bequeathed it to me last time she was home, and the trousers and shoes are my latest finds from the charity shops on the high street. I sigh without even realizing and, as always, Ethan seems to know what I'm thinking.

"You look gorgeous, Zoe," he says quietly. "You'd look gorgeous in anything."

"Thank you," I reply shyly. There is an odd, long pause.

This is ridiculous. I've been in Ethan's bedroom hundreds of times, chilling on the bed together, studying, sharing music and funny YouTube clips. But this feels different. His room feels even smaller as we stand opposite each other . . . so close. His eyes search my face like he's soaking in every detail. One of his curls falls forward onto his forehead. Instinctively I brush it back into place with my fingertips, and I see him swallow hard. He hesitates and then, very gently, takes my hand. He raises it to his lips and kisses it, his soft, warm lips on my skin.

"Ethan?" I whisper in surprise.

One of the kids yells in the living room and I pull my hand away. As I do, my bangles slide off and cascade on to the carpet. We both immediately bend down to pick them up and clash heads. I yelp and rub my forehead as Ethan winces, apologizing over and over.

I'm too unsure and confused to know how to react so I give him a shove and start laughing. He joins in. We sit on the floor, rubbing our heads, laughing unconvincingly and *not* mentioning what just happened.

CHAPTER 8

The air in the Blue Angel club is humid and the walls seem to be throbbing as the beat of the bass rebounds off them. Lights flash around the dark room, momentarily illuminating people dancing, shouting into each other's ears and throwing their hands around, trying to make themselves understood. Ethan and I are standing in silence sipping bottles of overpriced fizzy drink. There's no alcohol on sale; the club know that we're from Hinton Dale and they don't want any underage drinking.

I sneak a look at Ethan out of the corner of my eye. He was full of nervous chatter in the taxi on the way here, but now he looks deep in thought. I wonder if he's feeling embarrassed about what happened. Or I wonder if he wants it to happen again. Do *I* want that? The atmosphere between us in his bedroom felt like something had shifted, like I was seeing him, for the first time, as something more than a friend.

I shake myself. No, I shouldn't go there. We need to forget it – he's too precious to me to complicate things. Ethan has always been my best friend. I don't want anything getting in the way of what we've got.

I spot Harry Sherwood and Justine Collins in a corner booth. Harry's arm is firmly around her as he pours something from a covered bottle into their glasses of Coke. Jodie and Sonja are in the throng of girls around Jack, trying to drag him on to the dance floor. He's head and shoulders above them. The light from the rotating glitter ball reflects on his handsome features, making him look impossibly glamorous.

Aaron Lewis approaches him, like they're best mates – Jack has been playing in Aaron's football team and seems to be single-handedly saving them from relegation. From around his neck, Aaron pulls out a beaded silver chain with military-style dog-tags attached. Jack responds by fist-bumping him and getting out his own necklace from beneath his dark pink shirt. People seem curious and ask to see them, as Aaron takes a photo of them both, proudly displaying their dog-tags.

"Do you want to dance?" Ethan yells in my ear, as one of my favourite tracks starts to boom through the speakers.

"Yeah," I reply. We squeeze on to the dance floor. Even this feels weird though. When we used to dance at the school discos we'd be whirling each other around and dancing like there was no one looking, but now we're swaying stiffly, avoiding each other's gaze.

"Hi, Ethan! Hi, Zoe!" Jack appears next to us with an entourage of admirers. I smile tightly but Ethan greets him warmly. "They're making me dance," Jack says, so deadpan that I have to suppress a laugh.

Amanda Parry grabs Jack's hands and wraps them around her waist. He politely disentangles himself and takes a step back.

"Dance, Jack. Dance!" Amanda demands, like he's a performing bear.

He nods resignedly. "Fine . . . I'll dance."

He stops, his head lowered. One or two of the girls shoot each other unsure looks; is there about to be something Jack can't do? And then, with unnerving suddenness, he starts to move, and it's as if his body is in complete unison with the rhythm of the music. His dance becomes hypnotic as his whole body undulates, his head rolls, his arms and feet flick and snap to the beat, his eyes blank, like he's lost in a trance.

Others join him, laughing and joking at first, and then gradually falling into step alongside him. I stand back and watch as the whole floor of students move with Jack, smiles glowing on their faces. I turn to comment to Ethan, but realize that he's been swept up in it too. I seem to be the only one not caught in Jack's rhythm.

As the track segues into another, I move to the bar, watching Justine Collins howl with laughter as she struggles to get out of the corner booth. She's so unsteady on her feet that she can hardly stand up as she waves her sparkly clutch-bag in the air to the beat of the music. She and Sherwood must have been drinking long before they got here.

I'm taking another sip of my drink when I feel a hand on my arm.

"Ethan." I swing around with a smile, but it's Jack I'm facing.

"Hi," he says cheerfully. I stare at him for just a second too long. He doesn't appear to be out of breath at all after dancing like *that*. He must be so fit. "Are you having a good time?"

"Sure." I gulp down my drink. I don't know what to say to him. I can see why everyone thinks he's amazing . . . I mean, he *is* amazing. But there's just something about Jack that makes me hold back.

"Do you want to dance, Zoe?" he says. I hesitate and he holds out his hand. "With me?"

"Oh, I – no . . . no, thanks," I say hurriedly. "I'm taking a breather."

"No worries. Another time." He gives me an easy grin and heads back to the dance floor, to whoops and cheers. I turn to the bar, only to find Jodie and Sonja are beside me.

"Did we just see Jack asking you to dance?" Sonja says, clasping my hands.

I shrug and nod, embarrassed.

"And you turned him down?" Jodie looks stunned.

I nod again, bracing myself for their reaction.

"What is wrong with you?" Jodie sounds outraged. "There are a hundred girls in here who'd throw each other under a bus just to get close to Jack Cartwright and *you* turn him down!"

"Get over it. I only said no to a dance. It's no big deal," I say defiantly.

"No big deal," Sonja repeats, shaking her head in disbelief. "There's no hope for you, Zoe Littlewood."

"Do you want a drink?" I ask them, trying to change the subject.

"No, thanks, babe. We'll catch you later, but if Jack asks you again, just point him in our direction." Jodie blows me a kiss and they disappear into the crowd.

I see Ethan heading my way and I wave in relief. At last, a bit of sanity.

"Where did Jack learn to dance like that?" he says. "That was insane . . . but in a good way."

"He certainly got everyone moving," I shout above the noise.

"Yeah, everyone except you, Zoe." Ethan is grinning. "You, er, didn't fancy dancing with Jack, then?"

"No! So, what?" I say defensively.

"No reason," he says cheerfully.

"I'm going to the loo," I say into his ear. I need some space. I don't want Ethan to be reading too much into the fact that I rejected a chance to dance with Jack.

I stop and chat to a few people as I pick my way through the club and into the chilly air of the corridor. The women's toilets are at the far end but as I pass the cloakroom I hear Harry Sherwood's voice. He sounds angry. I hesitate. I want to keep walking, but I know I should check that whoever he's shouting at is OK.

I steel myself and go in. Harry is yelling at someone – Jack, who stands there watching him calmly. Beyond them I spot Justine, slumped against the back wall, her mascara-smudged eyes flickering, her face pale and clammy. On the floor next to her is her clutch bag. It's wide open with lipstick, foundation and door keys scattered around it.

"What's going on?" I ask.

"I'll tell you what's going on," Harry growls. "I've just stopped this piece of scum from robbing Justine."

I look at Jack, confused. "What do you mean?" I ask.

"Look. He's got her bank card, money and phone," Harry says.

To my astonishment, I see that he's right – Jack is holding her stuff. My eyes flicker to his face. He looks relaxed, amused.

"Of course, I've got them – she gave them to me," he says. "And Harry knows it."

"I know what I saw," Harry says, jabbing his finger into Jack's face. He doesn't even blink. "When I came in, he was taking stuff from her bag." He shakes his head. "Taking advantage when she's barely conscious."

I'm thrown into confusion. Jack couldn't . . . he wouldn't. Would he?

I walk over to Justine and take her hand. "Justine, are you all right?" I try to make contact with her glassy eyes. "Justine, what's happened?"

She puts her finger to her lips, slurring, "Shush." She waves me away like I'm a fly.

"*She* won't know what happened. She's too out of it,"

Harry says savagely. "But I do. I saw it for myself."

Jack makes eye contact with me. "I was walking past the cloakroom and saw Justine slumped against the wall. She looked . . . yeah, out of it, so I came to help her. I told her I'd get her friends and book a taxi. She opened up her bag and gave me her phone, money and card. Said I should call her mum. That's when Harry stormed in and started accusing me." He gives Harry a measured look. "He knew what was really going on. He just wants to use this against me. But he's a liar."

"You don't call me a liar!" Harry says, clenching and unclenching his fists. "You make me sick. You come into our college from nowhere, conning everyone that you're something special. Lapping up all the attention, when all the time you're just a low-life who'll rob vulnerable girls." Without warning, he takes a wavering swing at Jack, who swerves neatly out of the way.

I shout at Harry to stop. He ignores me as he takes another swing and then another, aiming for Jack's face but he can't land his punches as Jack ducks and dives, but doesn't retaliate. Harry grunts and his face contorts as he drives a right hook towards the side of Jack's head. Jack grabs his fist in mid-flight and pushes him back so Harry falls to the sticky ground.

I stand between them with my arms outstretched, looking down at Harry. "Stop it! Don't you think you should be checking if Justine is OK?"

Harry scrambles to his feet, panting and swearing as I try and gather my thoughts

"Harry, Justine needs to go home and you should call the police and let them sort this out."

"What's the point?" Harry seethes as he dusts himself down. "Justine isn't going to be able to remember anything and *he'll* just tell them his little story, then it'll be my word against his. But don't worry, he's not getting away with this."

Harry's on the verge of erupting again. I have to keep them apart.

"You need to go," I say urgently to Jack.

He steps towards me, his head cocked to one side like he's baffled. "You don't believe him, do you, Zoe? You know that I wouldn't steal anything. I was trying to help her."

My mouth opens. I don't know what to say. How can I tell him that I believe him when I didn't see what happened? How well do I know him, anyway?

"Just go, Jack," I say, avoiding his gaze.

He nods, then leaves the cloakroom without another word.

I tend to Justine as she lolls her head on me. "Justine," I say gently, "this is really important, so try to concentrate. Did you give Jack your phone and money to get you a taxi?"

She momentarily opens her eyes wide, like she's been startled and mumbles, "Go home," before her head flops back on my shoulder.

Harry Sherwood crouches in front of her, his face like granite. "It's OK, babe," he says, "I saw what happened and I'm going to make sure that everyone knows what he's really like. People need to be warned about scum like him."

*

We had to help Justine into a taxi. She was so drunk that she threw her arms around me and gave me a kiss as I placed a plastic bag on her lap in case she threw up. I made sure a couple of her friends went home with her.

When I get back inside, I'm surprised to see that Jack is still here, acting as though nothing has happened. He moves through the crowd, chatting, dancing, smiling, as if he hasn't a care in the world. But word is spreading like a virus; Harry is making sure of that. I watch Harry flit from group to group, talking with his hands, still pumped up. Each time nodding in Jack's direction. People turn to stare at Jack in disbelief, before throwing themselves into intense discussions.

Ethan joins me, looking anxious. He's obviously heard. "It's not true, is it?" he asks.

"I came in after it happened," I say. "Jack *did* have Justine's things in his hand. She was really drunk. He said she'd given them to him to call a taxi, but Harry's swearing he saw Jack stealing them."

Ethan shakes his head. "Sherwood's lying."

"It's his word against Jack's. I wouldn't count on Justine being able to remember much."

"This is Harry Sherwood we're talking about. People won't believe him over Jack."

"Maybe, but you know how people are and Jack can't prove he's innocent."

"But you believe him, don't you?" Ethan asks. "Why would someone as loaded as Jack need to steal stuff anyway?"

"I don't know?" I say hesitantly, doubts swirling round my mind. "People do all kinds of strange things. Sometimes there's no logic to it."

Ethan looks at me frowningly. "Oh, come on, Zoe. This is our friend we're talking about."

"Sure, but he's *everyone's* friend, Ethan. That's the problem," I say, and it comes out too harshly. "We don't really know him. I can't say one hundred per cent that I believe him."

We look across at Jack. Amanda Parry is talking to him, throwing her head back with laughter. A girl Sherwood has just spoken to walks over to Amanda and whispers in her ear. Instantly the smile falls from Amanda's face.

Suddenly the music stops and the club lights go up, hurting my eyes after hours in near darkness. Everyone clears out quickly and I reluctantly follow Ethan as he heads towards Jack.

"Jack," Ethan calls out. "Look – I've got to ask, Sherwood's lying, isn't he?"

Jack focuses his dark gaze on Ethan. "You're my friend, aren't you, Ethan?"

"Yes."

"So, you *know* Harry Sherwood is lying."

Ethan pauses before saying, "Of course he's lying."

Jack lands his hands on Ethan's shoulders. "Thank you."

My heart sinks a little. I know that Ethan is right; that

Harry Sherwood is vile and not to be trusted. But can we really believe Jack so blindly?

We make our way into the frosty night. It's chaos outside the club, with people desperately trying to grab taxis. Cars are pulling out all over the place. Drivers are reversing without warning. An argument erupts between two groups fighting over the same taxi. Harry Sherwood is among them, trying to get his mates in the car first. Things are getting heated and I spot Jack walking into the crowd, trying to calm the situation. The next moment there's some kind of scuffle and suddenly I see Jack falling backwards on to the road like a felled tree. I watch in horrified slow motion as his head slams against the tarmac with a sickening thud.

It takes a few seconds for people to realize what's happened and then an eerie silence descends. Ethan and I push our way through the crowd that's forming around Jack. His eyes are closed. He's not moving.

I kneel down to him, tapping his cheek gently. "Jack! Jack! Are you OK?" He doesn't respond. I try not to panic. He's out cold but there's no blood. He mustn't have cracked his head open.

Ethan places his fingers on Jack's neck. He looks at me, his eyes wide with panic. "I can't find a pulse." His voice quivers.

I fumble for my phone and hit 999. The operator tells me she's sending an ambulance, but it'll be ten minutes – ten minutes! It's too long, he needs help now. I swallow my panic and try to focus as she gives me instructions. "Don't move him but check his breathing again."

I pass my phone to Sonja, who's as white as a ghost. "Sonja, keep listening to the operator." I bend right down and put my face to Jack's. I can't feel any breath coming from him. My hands tremble as I place them on his chest, praying for any movement, but I don't feel anything . . . anything at all.

"I don't think he's breathing," I whisper. Panic escalates around me. People are shouting at me to give him CPR, but I'm struggling to remember what to do. "Chest compressions!" a voice calls out.

Yes . . . yes! I straddle him, interlock my hands and hover them over the centre of his chest, ready to pump down . . . quick, firm compressions to start the heart beating again. I take a deep breath and begin. "One . . . two . . . three . . . four. . ." I freeze mid-compression as Jack's eyes open. There's a communal gasp as he levers his torso off the ground.

I'm still straddling him. We're face to face as he sits up. I try not to show my alarm as I see that his left eyelid is drooping. I move off him and place my hand on his shoulder.

"Jack, you should stay lying down. Don't try and move," I say gently. "The ambulance will be here in just a minute."

He seems confused, disorientated. He tries to get up but other students surround him, coaxing him to lie still.

"No . . . ambulance," he says.

"You've had a bad fall, Jack. You need to get checked out in hospital." I speak slowly. I slip my hand into his pocket and draw out his phone. It's still working, thank goodness; I can call his parents.

He looks around at everyone, even though I beg him not to move his head.

"I'm f . . . f . . . fine." He struggles to his feet as people support him.

"Don't let him try and walk," I say as I peer at his phone. I scroll down his contacts. He seems to have the numbers of most of the sixth form. I press on "Mum", gritting my teeth as I wait for her to pick up, but an automated voicemail kicks in.

"Hello, Mrs Cartwright, my name's Zoe Littlewood. I'm using Jack's phone. Please don't panic, but Jack's had a fall outside. The Blue Angel club. An ambulance will be here any minute. He'll probably be taken to St Monica's, but I'll ring you back when I know for sure."

We're still trying to get Jack to sit down when a white four-wheel drive roars up the road, braking in front of us. A middle-aged woman and younger man jump out. I recognize her from Jack's Instagram pictures. They push through the crowd.

"We're Jack's parents," the woman says, as she loops Jack's arm over her shoulder, signalling to her husband to do the same. "We were on our way to pick him up, but I've just heard the voicemail. It's best if we get him to hospital without delay."

I follow them. "Mrs Cartwright, the ambulance will be here soon. We were told not to move him. He hit his head." I gesture to his drooping eye.

Jack's dad waves me out of the way. "We understand, but we can't waste time waiting for an ambulance. He could have a brain bleed . . . every second counts." His voice rings with authority and we drop back.

"St Monica's has the closest A&E," Ethan says, walking beside them as they head to the car. "Do you want me to come with you? I could show you the quickest route."

"No, it's OK, we know the way," Jack's mum says, looking deathly pale. "Cancel the ambulance, tell them we're taking him." The crowd looks on as Jack's parents manoeuvre him into the back seat and buckle him in. He starts to ramble incoherently again, the stammer worse than before.

His mum climbs in next to him, cradling his head on her shoulder. "Don't try and speak, Jack," I hear her say as she strokes his hair. "You're going to be all right, darling."

The car tyres squeal as Jack's dad reverses, swings out on to the main road and storms into the distance.

CHAPTER 9

It's been six days now without news of Jack. We've all been trying to find out how he is, but his mobile is off and he hasn't replied to messages on his social media. Ethan, Jodie and Sonja are so worried about him that, when the college refused to give us his address, they decided to walk around the new estate where he lives, looking for a white four-wheel drive to try and identify his house. It seems strange to me that no one has ever been invited to Jack's house when he's so sociable and has become such good mates with people.

Although news of the cloakroom incident hasn't reached Mr Dunn yet, he found out about Jack's accident and promptly banned any other sixth-form club nights. The police woman, who turned up after Jack's parents had taken him away, spoke to witnesses but, in all the confusion, no one could say exactly what caused the fall. The incident was recorded as accidental and no further action is going to be taken, but both me and Ethan suspect it could have been Sherwood who pushed him, although we've got no proof.

As rain batters the windows in the common room, we're standing in the vast fireplace. The whole year seems to be talking about Jack and the accident . . . Jack and what happened in the cloakroom, but the mood is low; everyone's upset. They seem almost lost.

People have been hassling Justine, asking if Jack was *really* stealing her stuff at the club. I actually feel sorry for her. She's obviously stressed and embarrassed about it all. She keeps repeating that she can't remember anything, but Harry is always by her side, reassuring her that he saw what happened. Usually Ethan would keep his head down around Sherwood, but all week I've seen him getting more wound up as Sherwood repeats his accusation about Jack. So, when we hear Sherwood spouting off again about what a low life Jack has turned out to be, I see the muscles twitch in Ethan's cheek and, before I know it, he's squared up to Sherwood.

"You're lying!" Ethan seethes. "So, keep your mouth shut."

Sherwood looks amused. "Well, Ethan, what's this? Have you suddenly grown a pair? You look angry. Do you want to hit me? Come on, then, why don't you give it a go?"

"Don't, Ethan," I say urgently. I take his arm to guide him away, but he shakes me off, not backing down.

"Ethan!" Jack's unmistakably self-assured voice calls out from the behind us. The whole common room stops and turns to see him standing in the doorway. There's a silence and then a low, gossipy murmur. Most people can't stop themselves smiling at him.

Ethan's pumped-up expression relaxes into a relieved grin. Jack comes over, ignoring Sherwood, and gives Ethan a manly hug. I study him carefully. He looks completely normal.

"It's good to see you, Jack," Ethan says.

"Sorry I haven't been in touch. I didn't want you guys to worry," Jack says apologetically. "But they didn't want me to speak to anyone while I was having tests."

"What did they say about your head injury?" I ask.

"There's no harm done. I know I must have seemed a mess," he says.

"It was a bit scary . . . your eyelid was drooping. You were stammering a bit," I say.

"Yeah, apparently those symptoms are common with concussion, or so the doctor told me. They gave me a CAT scan and everything looks fine. I was kept in a couple of nights for observation. They were brilliant at St Monica's. Mum bought the staff the biggest box of chocolates I've ever seen."

"Good," is all I can manage. I can't stop staring. He's looking as healthy and perfect as ever.

"I owe you a massive thank you, Zoe." His eyes meet mine. "I've heard that you stepped in and gave me CPR," he says, placing his hands over his chest.

I'm flustered with embarrassment. "Yeah, but you didn't need it. I don't think you ever stopped breathing. It was just our panic. I'd hardly touched you when you opened your eyes."

"Well, whatever. I'll never forget that you were the one who helped me. I don't know how I'll ever be able to repay you." The pupils of his eyes are enormous. I flush under his gaze. I don't know how to react to him.

Harry Sherwood interrupts, standing in front of Jack with his arms folded. "Great to see you back on your feet." He oozes with sarcasm. "Thing is, I don't think people are too keen to have you here, not when you're the kind of person who robs semi-conscious girls."

Jack ignores him and strides over to the computer tables, everyone's eyes on him. He remains standing as he types on the keyboard. Then he calls out loudly to everyone in the common room. "Excuse me!"

It doesn't take anything more to bring the watching room to silence.

"I've just uploaded something on my Facebook page which may be of interest to you all." With this, he steps back as everyone starts feverishly getting up his page on their phones.

Gasps fill the room as the video plays, showing the starkly lit cloakroom of the Blue Angel.

The footage seems to be taken from the doorway. It shows Justine Collins slumped against the back wall, her sparkly clutch bag on her lap. She's groaning and muttering to herself. The shot moves inside the cloakroom and closes in on her. Justine's long raven hair is plastered to her clammy face, her smudged eyes flicker.

"Justine, are you OK?" It's Jack's voice, but he can't be seen.

Justine mumbles something incomprehensible.

We see Jack's hands brushing Justine's hair off her face and gently straightening her lolling head.

"Listen, Justine, it's Jack. You look like you've had too much to drink. I think you need to go home."

"Home," Justine repeats wistfully.

"I'll book you a taxi then I'll go and find your friends to look after you, OK?"

With this Justine starts to fumble with the catch on the clutch bag in front of her. She gets it open then tips it upside down, shaking the contents onto the carpet.

"What are you doing, Justine?" Jack's voice says.

She peers at the objects on the carpet like she's struggling to identify them. Then she slowly picks up her phone, bank card and a twenty pound note and thrusts them into Jack's hand. "Phone Mum . . . get taxi," she slurs.

"Yes, I will, but I don't need your money."

Jack's hand reaches for the clutch bag, but Justine is swatting him away saying, "No! Phone Mum . . . get taxi."

Suddenly Harry Sherwood's voice rings out. "Hey, get away from her. What the hell are you doing?"

He comes into shot, waving his arms around, chest out, spoiling for a fight.

Jack must stand up to face him as Harry's twisted face fills the frame.

"I was helping Justine. She's had too much to drink.

Maybe you can take over now," Jack says calmly.

"Helping her? You were robbing her!" he snarls. "You've got her stuff in your hand . . . you were going through her bag."

"No, I wasn't."

Sherwood starts to sway in front of Jack, shouting. "You've blown it now, golden boy. I'll tell everyone you were robbing Justine. How could you do that, especially when she's like this . . . when she needed your help." There's a sneer on his face.

"But you must have seen that I was trying to give it back?"

Sherwood shrugs and smirks. "It doesn't matter what I saw. It's your word against mine, pal."

Then my voice can be heard, asking, "What's going on?" and the rest of the video plays out just as I remember it, only now I know the truth.

My cheeks burn with shame.

Ethan looks up from his phone and gives me a look that says, *I told you so*.

The atmosphere in the common room feels like a baying crowd at a public hanging, as everyone reacts to the video. A hailstorm of outrage falls on Harry Sherwood, and all his swagger and arrogance drains from him. He turns to Justine, but she looks ready to explode with fury.

"Get lost, you lying bastard!" she shouts at him. "I never want to see you again."

Sherwood throws curses at everyone and slams the door behind him. As soon as he's left, people start to swarm around

Jack – the girls hugging him, boys slapping him on the back, everyone eager to tell him that they never believed Sherwood for one second.

I'm staring into space. On the one hand, I'm relieved, hugely relieved. On the other, I'm confused. How did Jack get that footage of what happened in the cloakroom and who would have been filming it?

CHAPTER 10

In psychology later, I sit as far away from Jack as possible. I'm trying to avoid having to speak to him. I'm embarrassed that I didn't just believe him. Why couldn't I have been like Ethan and given him my support, instead of doubting him and sitting on the fence?

There's a groan as Mrs Taylor announces that we'll begin the lesson with a very simple maths question to wake us all up.

"Hannah, what's seven times seven?" she asks.

"Forty-eight, miss," Hannah replies immediately, making me double-check my mental arithmetic.

"Now, Aaron, seven times seven?"

"Forty-eight!" he says, like it's a no brainer.

"Ben, same question?"

"Forty-eight, Mrs Taylor," he says.

She asks four other students, who all answer forty-eight

without hesitation. I don't know what's going on. Am I hearing the same question as them?

"Eliza, seven times seven?"

Eliza looks uncertain as she says hesitantly, "I make it forty-nine."

Mrs Taylor doesn't comment as she moves on to Jack. "Jack, seven times seven?"

"Forty-eight," he says with absolute certainty.

I look around the classroom curiously. People are nodding in agreement.

"Amanda, seven times seven?"

"Forty-eight," she mutters.

"Ethan, seven times seven?"

Ethan pulls a comic face of confusion. He glances at Jack, who gives him an encouraging smile.

"Forty-eight?"

"Zoe, seven times seven?"

I look to Jack. The encouraging smile returns to his face.

"Forty-nine," I say, confused. "I'm pretty sure that seven times seven has always been forty-nine."

Mrs Taylor gives us all a little clap. "Well done, everybody. You've just taken part in a version of the 1951 Asch experiment. Sorry for the deception, Amanda, Ethan, Eliza and Zoe, but everyone else was in on the test. I primed them to give the same, but incorrect, answer to the maths question to see if you would conform to the majority's answer, even though you logically knew that it was wrong."

Ethan burst out laughing at his own gullibility and I'm

just pleased that Mrs Taylor is actually trying something different rather than giving us hand-outs, but Amanda's pride has obviously been hurt by the little experiment.

"That's so unfair, miss," Amanda huffs. "I was going to say forty-nine but then people kept saying forty-eight, and when *Jack* said forty-eight as well I didn't want to look stupid by disagreeing."

"Thank you, Amanda, you've just beautifully articulated the effects of normative social influence," Mrs Taylor says, looking smug.

*

It's nearly the end of the day and, luckily, it's been easy to dodge Jack as people haven't left him alone. I'm out of sight, behind a computer in the common room, and I watch as Jack sits with Ethan on the uneven wooden floor in front of the fireplace. More and more people are heading over and plonking themselves down in a semi-circle. Everyone's outraged on Jack's behalf and furious with Sherwood. I doubt Sherwood will risk coming back any time soon. People have been venting their anger online; naming and shaming him, saying that they don't want him at the college.

There's a palpable atmosphere of relief and excitement at having Jack back and exonerated. Everyone sounds like they're even more in awe of him than before. They can't believe Jack annihilated Sherwood in the fight and hardly lifted a finger. They're all talking about how cool it was he when he just walked back into the common room and took down Sherwood by posting the video.

I prick up my ears as Justine tentatively asks the question I've been dying to ask. "But how did you get that video? Who was filming?"

"It was me!" Jack laughs. "To be honest, it was pure luck. I'd been doing a bit of filming with people on the dance floor to post on my Instagram and I mustn't have turned it off. So, when I was walking past the cloakroom and saw you, I'd put my phone in my front pocket, still filming without even knowing."

There's laughter and a buzz of approval at Jack's good luck. Pete West joins in, telling Jack that it's great to have him back, but his main concern seems to be when they can play Underground Revolution against each other again.

"What about tonight?" Pete asks.

"Sure," Jack says. "Anyone else want in?"

I can't believe the number of people calling out. Since when did half the sixth form become gamers?

"Are you still OK for the match on Tuesday?" Aaron Lewis asks above the noise. "We really need you upfront."

"Yeah, I know you do," Jack says teasingly. "I'll be there. I don't want you crashing out of the league."

Helen Rogers half-jokingly protests that Jack won't have time to be playing computer games and football because they've all missed a week of fitness training.

Sonja's nose crinkles with disapproval as she says protectively, "Can everyone stop hassling Jack. He needs to take it easy."

Jack waves a hand dismissively. "Thanks, Sonja. I'm fine. I'm happy to continue the training, but only if everyone's sure that they still want me to run the sessions?"

There's a barrage of voices as people reassure him they can't do it without him.

"I've *got* to keep exercising, I've just spent a hundred and sixty quid on my Go-Getter," Helen says, holding up her wrist.

People agree with her, as more and more arms go up in the air to show their fitness monitors.

Eliza Trent waves her arm as she shouts above the crowd. "I've bought a Fit Friend. It's got loads of the same functions and it's half the price," she says proudly.

People turn to her, looking curiously.

"That's great, Eliza," Jack smiles warmly. "If anyone can't afford a Go-Getter then, Fit Friend is definitely an alternative. It actually hasn't got a lot of the features but, for *basic* fitness monitoring, it'll get the job done."

His words make Eliza shrink into the floor and I notice her subtly putting her sleeve over her Fit Friend to conceal it.

"Hey, let's grab a photo of all our Go-Getters," Helen says enthusiastically.

Everyone with the *right* fitness watch gathers around Jack, messing around as they do superhero poses and post their shots on Instagram – *#GoGettercrew #Getmotivated #Fit4life #HintonDaleCollege.*

The home bells rings and Jack makes to leave, but people are bombarding him with questions. I take the opportunity to avoid him by sliding out of the room. I make my way out of the college grounds and across the main road, head down, earphones in, but I'm walking through Fellfoot Park when I feel a tap on my shoulder.

Ethan and Jack are right behind me. I glance at Jack out of the corner of my eye. He's giving me one of his full-beam smiles. He doesn't *seem* to be holding a grudge.

"Hey, Zoe, you headed off quickly," Ethan says.

"Yeah, I've got a load of work to do," I half-lie.

We've reached the alley with the vicious dog and Ethan must notice my body tense because he gives a concerned look, and says, "I hate you using this alley with that dog down here. You know, I went to the station on Breck Road and told the policeman on the desk about it. But Jack was right, they weren't interested. All he did was say he'd note my complaint," Ethan says with disdain. "I told him that he'd be sorry if that dog attacked someone and they'd done nothing to stop it. He actually accused me of being disrespectful. Can you believe it?"

"Don't worry about it, Ethan, I'll be fine. I do battle with the beast every day and he's not got me yet," I say, like it's no big deal, although I feel sick every time I walk through here.

Ethan insists on escorting me and I find myself flanked by him and Jack. We hear Bullseye's barks as we approach the increasingly flimsy gate. The dog is there, desperately trying to squeeze himself through the splintering slates of wood.

"Come on." Ethan takes my arm, hurrying us along. But Jack just continues his casual pace, unfazed by the animal.

We reach the other end of the alley and I realize that my

hands are trembling. Embarrassed, I put them in the pockets of my biker jacket.

"Please don't go down there, Zoe. It's not safe," Ethan pleads.

I know he's right, but the detour takes for ever. "I'll see," I reply, being non-committal.

Ethan's frowns. He looks like he's about to lecture me but his phone rings.

"Hi, Dad ... yes, OK... Right. Yeah, I know, I'm wonderful ... what do you want?" Ethan rolls his eyes at us, listens for a minute, then hangs up. "I need to get home. Dad's been called into work. One of the other health-care assistants has rung in sick. Mum's already there doing her shift, so it looks like I'm on babysitting duty again."

"Thanks for your support over the Sherwood thing, Ethan. It meant a lot to me," Jack says.

"Well, it's brilliant to have you back, mate," Ethan replies with feeling. He presses his Go-Getter, grimacing. "I've really let things slide without you around. My step numbers are pitiful."

"Let's get you back on track," Jack says "How about a run tonight and work-out tomorrow? We need to do more weight-training and you need to keep your carbs up."

"Sure, that'd be great. Bye, Zoe. I'll see you later, Jack," Ethan says and starts to jog down the pavement.

My heart sinks as I watch Ethan go. I'm left alone with Jack. He's just standing there, letting silence hang between us, looking at me with those big dark eyes.

"Jack," I say, my voice coated with guilt. "I'm sorry for not being like Ethan and just supporting you over the cloakroom thing. It was just really difficult to know the truth because I didn't see what happened."

"I don't blame you, Zoe," he breaks in. "It made sense not to take sides when you didn't see what happened. Ethan just had faith in me. I suppose I kind of hoped that you would too."

I look down at the ground, fiddling with my earrings agitatedly. I feel terrible.

"Can we just forget about it?" he says, putting me out of my misery.

I nod silently. Him being so nice about it makes me feel even worse. What's wrong with me, anyway? Why *couldn't* I just believe Jack over a vile person like Harry Sherwood?

We walk side by side in silence as I desperately think of something innocuous to say.

"So, your mum and dad . . . I met them outside the club." I glance at him. "They were pretty cool. They really took control of the situation."

"Yeah, they're fantastic." He gives me lightning-quick smile that drops as fast as it appeared.

I can't make him out. He's not like anyone I've ever met, and I wonder if his life can be as perfect as it looks in all his posts and photos. Everyone does it. Everyone has at least two versions of themselves and we all know that most of it on social media is bullshit, but we still buy into it. That's a big reason I keep off it now; I don't want to waste my time worrying that my life isn't as good as everyone else's.

I picture how young his dad looked that night outside the club. His mum must be a total cougar. I know that I'm just being nosy, but I'd love to know what the story is there.

"So, your mum and dad? Have they been together long?" I ask casually.

"Yeah, years."

God, Jack's dad must have been a kid when she met him. "How old are they?" I ask.

"Dad's forty this year, and Mum's forty-five."

"Wow, your dad doesn't look forty."

"He has good genes. I'm hoping that I take after him," he says with a grin.

"And your mum, she must be super fit with you two training for a marathon together."

"Yeah, she's amazing! She's my motivation." His voice is full of affection. "We love running together. It gives you a natural high. I guess that's why I'm always trying to get everyone else on the fitness bandwagon." His pride in his mum is so sweet that I can't help smiling at him.

"Listen, Zoe, I've been thinking. . ." Oh, no, what's he going to say? I've never heard Jack sound nervous before. "This may not appeal to you, but I'm a big fan of Baz Luhrmann movies."

My eyes widen. "I love Baz Luhrmann," I murmur. "I can never persuade Ethan or the girls to watch his films."

"Don't go telling Aaron and the team about my guilty pleasure. They made me go and see some gross horror the other week." A single perfect line forms on his forehead in mock-disgust. "But, to be honest, you can't beat Baz Luhrmann. His movies ooze style and the soundtracks are always amazing."

I nod ardently. I can't believe it – I haven't met anyone who loves his movies as much as me.

"Anyway," Jack continues, "the Art House cinema is showing a special double-bill tomorrow night. *Romeo + Juliet* followed by *Moulin Rouge*. Would you like to come with me?"

I freeze. Did I hear him right? Is Jack Cartwright asking *me* on a date? To see a Baz Luhrmann double-bill?

He's looking down at me expectantly. "Well?"

I don't know what to say. Jack and I have never spent time together on our own. I'd love to see the films and I can't deny that I'm flattered. After all, he could ask any girl at Hinton Dale to go to the movies and they'd jump at the chance. So why am I hesitating? I'm nervous, for sure, but it's more than that. I don't think I can do this. I have to get out of it.

"Thanks for the offer, Jack, but me and Ethan have already arranged to go to the multiplex tomorrow night," I mumble.

"No worries," he says easily. "What are you going to see?"

Oh, god, what *am I* going to see? I picture a trailer that keeps popping up on my laptop. "The latest X-Men movie." I can hear the hesitation in my voice; I've never been a convincing liar. I feel awful.

"I wouldn't have guessed you were a Marvel fan," he says teasingly.

I'm blushing now. He can see right through me.

"Yeah, me and Ethan love all that stuff. But thanks for asking me to the films. Some other time, perhaps? I'd better get going," I say, rushing away. I hurry around the corner and quickly phone Ethan.

"Hey, Zo, everything OK?" he pants. He must still be jogging.

"How about going to see the new X-Men movie on Saturday?"

He laughs incredulously. "What? I can't pay you to see a superhero film normally. I thought you didn't like them?"

"Well, *you* like them, don't you? You can show me what all the fuss is about."

"Sure," he says cautiously. "Who else is coming?"

"Just you and me. Is that OK?"

"Just you and me?" he echoes in happy surprise. "Brilliant, yeah!"

"And if Jack happens to ask when we arranged it, could you just keep it vague?" I say, feeling terrible.

"Why?"

"It's just . . . easier," I say evasively.

OK," he says without further question.

I hang up. He sounded so excited about it. Why do I feel like I've just made things worse?

CHAPTER 11

Warm, damp air fills the over-bright foyer of the multiplex. It's always busy on a Saturday night. Groups of friends carrying giant buckets of popcorn and slurping Coke from gallon-sized cups make their way into the screens, couples queuing for tickets are still arguing over what they want to see, and there are loads of people sitting in the diner, watching trailers on the overhanging screens as they dip their chips into ketchup.

I watch the long row of glass doors, waiting for Ethan to appear, and glance again at my phone. I've already bought our tickets and the movie started ten minutes ago. I've tried his mobile again and again but it's turned off. I've emailed him, messaged him, but still no reply. This isn't like Ethan. I hope he's all right. He's probably just forgotten; although why would he forget when he seemed so excited about seeing this movie?

I try him one more time, then sigh and give up. Stepping

out into the hammering rain, I wish I'd brought an umbrella. Once I leave the well-lit car park, the streets seem dark. I'd hop on a bus but I've spent all my cash on the tickets I haven't even used. "I'm going to kill Ethan," I mutter under my breath.

I wrap my arms around myself, shivering as the rain rolls down my neck and makes my top and jeans stick to my skin. There's no one around. The weather is keeping people indoors. I quicken my pace. I don't like this stretch between the multiplex and the town. It's a no-man's land, cut off by the ring road. I find The Killers track on my phone and sing along to "All These Things That I've Done" to keep my mind from dwelling on the dark and wet – I stride along the narrow pavement in time to the beat, trying to avoid the grassy slope on one side, as cars rocket by on the other.

I don't hear him. I don't see him. I just feel the dull pain of something smacking into my shoulder from behind. I stumble forward as a hooded figure grabs hold of the strap of my bag. He pulls me along as he tries to wrench it off my shoulder. I'm unbalanced but I hold tightly on to the strap with white-knuckled hands. *I'm not going let him take my stuff!* I try to stop myself being dragged into the road. My hands burn as the leather cuts into the skin. His face is shrouded in shadow but there's a glint of a gold front tooth and, as he yanks at the strap, I notice that both of his hands have a tattooed line at the base of every finger, making it look like he's wearing a row of black rings.

I'm grunting with the strain. I feel my grip slipping as I see a flash out of the corner of my eye and someone sprints up from behind and launches themselves at the hooded man, rugby-tackling him to the ground. The mugger releases the strap and hits the pavement with a deep groan – all the air knocked out of him. I flail backwards, clutching my bag and rolling down the grassy slope into a muddy ditch. The rain blurs my vision as I look up to see the mugger wrestling out of the other person's hold and scrambling away. My rescuer doesn't run after him, instead he slides down the slope and stretches his hand out to me.

"Are you OK, Zoe?" His voice is familiar.

I squint to see more clearly. "Jack?" I splutter.

He gently pulls me out of the ditch and up the slope, but I wince as I feel an ache in my ankle.

"Is your ankle all right?" He frowns, sweeping his wet hair off his forehead.

"I'm not sure," I say, still dazed.

"I should check. You shouldn't walk if there's damage," he says, kneeling in front of me like he's about to propose. "Tell me if this hurts at all."

I stare straight ahead, trying to steady my breathing as his hands cup my ankles one by one, gently pressing and kneading. Any ache I may have had disappears under his tender touch.

"Does that feel OK?" His voice sounds like melting chocolate.

I swallow hard. I'm thankful that the dim street lights and pelting rain hide my blushes. "Yes."

He rises up. We're standing so close that raindrops from

his face fall on to mine. I can smell his heavenly aftershave; the one that Ethan and half the boys in the year seem to be wearing now.

"No broken bones and you don't seem too shaken up. You're a very strong character, Zoe. I've noticed that about you." The tone of his voice sends a delicious shiver through me. I look up into his eyes. I swear I can actually see his pupils dilating; they're mesmerizing.

A car speeds past, spraying us with water; breaking the spell. I shake myself. "I can't believe you saved me from that mugger *and* I've still got my bag."

"I'm just sorry he got away. I couldn't keep hold of him." Jack sounds disappointed in himself.

"You were brilliant. Thank you." I fish my phone out of my bag. "I'll call the police."

"Maybe we should get you home first," he suggests. "Call them from there, when you've had a chance to get dry. Otherwise you could be waiting around for ages."

I nod. He's got a point. A failed mugging without a weapon isn't going to be a priority for the police on a Saturday night.

"Did you see his face? Would you recognize him again?" Jack asks.

"I didn't see his face, but he's got these black tattoo lines across every finger. That's got to help, hasn't it?" I say hopefully.

"Yeah, well spotted." He sounds impressed. "Why don't you call your mum and get her to pick you up?"

I hesitate. Mum is on her first date with a match from

the website and I don't want to disturb her. "No, I'll be fine," I say.

"Well, we'll get a taxi, then," Jack says firmly.

"I haven't got any money," I say, embarrassed.

"I'll pay," he says, taking off his coat and wrapping it around me.

"But you'll get soaking," I protest.

"And you could get pneumonia," he replies, matter of fact. He sticks out his arm and flags down an approaching cab. It slows and pulls into a lay-by. Jack takes my hand, as if it's the most natural thing in the world, and we make our way to the waiting cab. I'm no one's damsel in distress but I'm more shaken up than I want to admit and it feels good to have his hand around mine.

"I don't understand, Jack," I say, buckling up in the back of the cab. "How come you were there?"

"Well, I decided it wouldn't be much fun seeing the Baz Luhrmann double-bill without you, so at the last minute I thought I'd come to the multiplex and watch the X-Men movie with you guys. I guessed that you and Ethan wouldn't mind. I mean, it's not like you two were on a date or anything, was it?" He lifts his eyes to mine.

"No, no. It wasn't a date," I say too quickly. "Me and Ethan have been friends for ever."

"That's what I thought," he smiles. "Anyway, when I arrived, you were making your way down the road. I called out, but you mustn't have heard me. I was catching you up when that guy came out of nowhere and tried to snatch your bag."

I shiver at the thought of it, rubbing the welts on the palm of my hand where I grabbed on to the bag like my life depended on it.

"Where is Ethan, anyway?" he asks.

"I don't know. He didn't turn up and his phone is turned off," I say, picking up my mobile and trying Ethan's number again. "It's so weird. Not like him at all."

"I saw him today – we did a work-out at the gym. He mentioned he was seeing you tonight – he was looking forward to it." Jack shakes his head. "Strange."

"Yeah, I hope he's OK." I feel a twist of anxiety.

The cab turns into the warren of car-lined streets. We pass the rows of semi-detached houses, some scruffy student accommodation, others rented and in need of repair and a few, like mine, prettified with hanging baskets outside the porch and pots next to the driveway.

"It's just the house on the right here," I say to the driver as we crawl along my street.

Before I can even open the door, Jack has gone around the side and opened it for me. He offers me his hand to help me out, but I can't help chuckling as I wave it away. "Jack, you were born in the wrong era. If this was a horse and carriage, you'd be Mr Darcy."

"It looks like there's no one home," he says, ignoring my comment and gesturing to the darkened house.

"Mum will be in later." I make sure I sound upbeat. "And I've got my key . . . thanks to you."

He frowns. "I'm not sure you should be on your own after

all that. I don't mind staying with you until your mum gets home."

"That's nice of you, Jack, but she'll be back soon. I'll be fine."

"Well ... OK. At least let me call you when I get home and check that you're all right," Jack says.

"Sure," I say softly. I lift my eyes to his, transfixed by them

The cab driver leans out of his window. "Hey, is one of you getting back in this cab or what?"

I turn, flustered. "Quick, get in, Jack, the meter's running."

"No. I'll wait till you're inside," he says chivalrously.

I head up the driveway and open the front door. I do an overdramatic step to show him that I'm inside the house and give a cheesy wave. He nods in response and gets into the cab.

Despite the trauma of the night, I find myself grinning. As I stand in the hallway peeling off my coat, I remember that it belongs to Jack. I hang it carefully on the peg; it's about a hundred times nicer than anything I own. I inspect it – apart from being wet from the rain, it looks pristine. It's still got a discreet price tag on the inside – three hundred pounds. Wow! Jack and me definitely don't shop in the same stores.

I check my phone. Nothing from Ethan. I double-check that all the doors and windows are shut, and I leave lights on downstairs. I hate this feeling of being vulnerable. I tell myself to keep strong as I get dry and into my PJs.

I'm exhausted suddenly. I know that I should report what

happened to the police but I just want to get into bed; I'll ring them in the morning. I try to settle but I'm too on edge to get comfortable. I reach up to the bookshelf over my bed with its selection of Jane Austen and Brontë sister novels and I pick out my dog-eared copy of *Jane Eyre*. If ever I need to feel braver and more confident, then Jane is the one I always turn to. She's my kind of heroine. I love her quiet determination and self-assurance, following her own path and never feeling inferior or intimidated by wealth or power. I turn to my favourite chapter and soak up the words of Jane's speech to Rochester.

> *"I tell you I must go!" I retorted, roused to something like passion. "Do you think I can stay to become nothing to you? Do you think I am an automaton? – a machine without feelings? and can bear to have my morsel of bread snatched from my lips, and my drop of living water dashed from my cup? Do you think, because I am poor, obscure, plain, and little, I am soulless and heartless? You think wrong! – I have as much soul as you, – and full as much heart! And if God had gifted me with some beauty and much wealth, I should have made it as hard for you to leave me, as it is now for me to leave you. I am not talking to you now through the medium of custom, conventionalities, nor even of mortal flesh; – it is my spirit that addresses your spirit; just as if both had passed through the grave, and we stood at God's feet, equal, – as we are!"*

I sigh at the beauty and power of those words. Jane's passion leaves me awestruck every time I read it. I know that it's a story, but how must it feel to have that spiritual connect with someone ... to find your soul mate? The ringtone of my phone blurs, jolting me out of my musings. I lunge for it, hoping it's Ethan, but Jack's name flashes on the screen. I'm flustered before I even say a word.

"Hey, Jack." My voice is all over the place. I don't know what tone to take.

"Hey, Zoe," he says quietly. "Just checking you're all right."

"Yeah, fine. Did you get home OK?" That's a stupid question. Of course he must have or he wouldn't be calling.

"Yeah. Has your mum turned up?"

"Not yet, but she won't be long." I have no idea how long she'll be.

"Did you call the police?"

"I'm going to do it in the morning. I'm feeling a bit wiped out, to be honest. I'm in bed, just about to go to sleep." I feel myself flushing. It feels suddenly weirdly intimate to be speaking to Jack while I'm in bed.

"Oh, I'm sorry, did I disturb you?"

"No, not at all. It's good of you to check up on me. By the way, I've still got your coat. Can I give it to you on Monday?"

He hesitates. "Actually, I was wondering – why don't we hang out tomorrow, if you're free? We could go through that psychology assignment that's due in. At my house. What do think?"

No one has been invited to Jack's house, not even Ethan.

I am curious. But it's more than that. The thought of being alone with Jack makes me nervous still – but now it's more of an excited kind of nervous.

"Yeah, OK, that'd be great," I reply. I switch off the light and lie there with a ridiculously big grin across my face that I'm glad he can't see.

CHAPTER 12

I wake to the sound of my phone ringing. I knock it off the bedside table as I grope for it, still more asleep than awake. I lean out of bed and scoop it off the carpet.

"Hello," I say groggily.

"Zoe! It's Ethan."

I check the time: eight a.m.

"What happened to you last night, Ethan?" I lever myself up in bed.

"I don't know." He sounds confused. "I'd got ready to go out with you. I had half an hour before my bus and I'd been feeling completely washed out . . . and I mean *exhausted*. I could hardly keep my eyes open, so I just thought I'd lie on the bed and close my eyes for *ten* minutes . . . just ten minutes and, you'll never believe it, Zoe. . ."

"You fell asleep," I sigh.

"Yeah, but not just any sleep, it was the sleep of the dead. Guess what time I woke up?"

"I don't know, Ethan," I say coldly.

"Five minutes ago! I can't understand it. How could I sleep that long? *And* I've got the most evil headache. I can hardly move."

"You'd done a big work-out with Jack, hadn't you?" I say unsympathetically. "He told me last night. You probably pushed yourself too hard trying to keep up with him. No wonder you were knackered."

There's a silence. "You saw Jack last night?" he says finally.

"It's a long story, but after I'd been *stood up* by you, I was walking back towards town and this guy tried to mug me and luckily Jack came to the rescue – you know he's basically a superhero, right?" I say, only half-joking.

"What? You got mugged? Jack saved you?" Ethan sounds shocked. "God, Zoe, I feel terrible. How are you? Were you hurt?"

"No, just a bit shaken up, but Jack looked after me."

"What was he doing there?"

"He decided to join us at the last minute."

"Oh, I thought it was just going to be me and you." He sounds disappointed.

"It was. I didn't invite him, but thank god he turned up anyway."

"Yeah . . . sure. I'll give him a ring to thank him."

"You're not my dad, Ethan. You don't have to ring him to thank him for saving me."

He laughs nervously. "Yeah, sorry. Anyway, let me make it up to you. How about I take you for a big Sunday roast dinner at that café on the high street? They do a mean banoffee pie. You'll love it."

I'm about to accept when I remember that I have plans, and my heart leaps in my chest. "Sorry, I can't. Jack's invited me around to his. We're going to look at that psychology assignment on free will and determinism." I try not to sound too excited.

"Really? To his house? No one's been to his house."

"Yeah, it's just to do college stuff. He's just being kind," I reply, not convinced that I'm telling the whole truth.

"Sure." Ethan sounds gutted. "Well, believe me, Zoe, I feel *so* bad about missing our date."

I grimace to myself. Did Ethan think the movie was a *date* date? I remember how he kissed my hand in his bedroom; the way he looked at me. The way *I* looked at him. It's not how best friends behave with each other. I shake it out of my head. I can't dwell on it.

"I can't explain why I slept for hours like that," he says, all in a rush. "I just want you to know that I was looking forward to seeing you so much, and now I feel a thousand times worse knowing that you were mugged. It wouldn't have happened if I'd been there."

I soften towards him; I can't help it. "Forget about it, Ethan. You didn't let me down on purpose. The mugger didn't get anything and I'm absolutely fine. We're cool. I'll see you tomorrow."

"OK, see you Monday," he replies quietly.

I pull the warm covers up to my chin and feel myself nodding off when the beeping of my phone jolts me awake again – it's a text from Dad.

> Hi Zoe, I'd like to take you somewhere special for your birthday next week. If you're free, please pack an overnight bag for Friday. I'll pick you up from the house at 6 p.m. Could you let your mum know? Love Dad xx

I raise my eyebrows in delighted surprise. Dad must be feeling guilty about cutting short our pizza outing. He's never taken me away. I wonder where were going? Is it a spa? Do I need to pack a swimming costume? Hmm, do I want to go to a spa with my dad? *Come on, Zoe, it doesn't matter where it is, the important thing is that you'll get to spend some proper time with him.*

I wander across the landing in my PJs and poke my head around Mum's door. The shape in the bed stirs and calls out to me.

"Zoe, love. How was the film?" she asks sleepily.

The evening flashes in front of me; Ethan not turning up, that guy trying to mug me, Jack. . . I look at Mum's eager face and decide not to tell her, in case she gets paranoid about me going out at night.

"It was fine. What about you? Was it a good night?"

She puts her head in her hands and gives a mortified

laugh. "Not really, love. He wasn't quite what I expected. All he wanted to talk about was fly-fishing and his ex-wife."

"Oh, no." I cringe for her. "I'm so sorry, Mum, but at least you've done the hard part . . . you've got out there again," I say, trying to sound wise and mature.

She squeezes my hand, looking determined. "Exactly. I'm not going to let one disappointing experience put me off. There's bound to be someone for me out there."

"Of course, there is," I say. "There's someone out there for everyone." And, for some reason, Jack's face comes into my mind.

CHAPTER 13

Jack's house looks impressive; a new-build on a private estate in a quiet cul-de-sac, where everyone's front gardens are immaculate and the cars on the driveways scream "money". I haven't seen one bit of rubbish floating round or dog muck on the pavement. Everything's clean and fresh, not like my scruffy street, and certainly not like Ethan's estate, where stepping in dog muck is the least of your problems.

I look at my reflection in the shiny brass letter box of the duck-egg blue door, checking I don't have lip gloss on my teeth and that my lilac bob is still sleek. There's a fluttering in my stomach as I ring the bell and straighten my shoulders.

Jack's mum opens the door with a broad smile. Not surprisingly, she seems a lot more relaxed than the first time I met her outside the club. She looks effortlessly chic in leggings and a colourful tunic top. Her white-blonde hair is piled high on top of her head and a chunky necklace dangles from her neck.

"Well, hello, Zoe. Come on in." She ushers me into the spacious, warm hallway. There's a lovely mahogany piano near the front window and an ornate coat stand by the door. I feel my shoulders relaxing as I inhale lavender-scented air.

I put down my rucksack with my laptop in and Jack's mum helps me take off my biker jacket; this is where Jack must get his manners from.

"Nice jacket," she says, putting it on a coat stand. "I used to have one of those back in the day." She gives me an impish smile. "Not going to tell you how long ago that was."

"Here's Jack's coat," I say, holding it out. "He lent it to me . . . last night." I hesitate, suddenly unsure whether he'll have told her about it, but she nods sympathetically.

"Oh, yes, the mugging. Just terrible!" she says, her ocean-blue eyes widening. "He said that you were really very brave, standing up to that awful mugger."

How sweet is Jack, telling his parents that? I bet he played down what he did. "That's very kind of him, but *he* was the brave one. He jumped on the guy . . . got my bag back."

There's a look of pride on her face. "Well, I'm glad he could help you; after all, you're the one who saved him the night he had that dreadful fall. We owe you such thanks, Zoe. You really were wonderful." She seems to tremble. "I dread to think what might have happened if you hadn't been so quick-thinking."

"Oh, no, Mrs Cartwright, please – I don't even think he needed CPR. I feel a bit stupid actually."

She smiles kindly and puts her arm around me. "Call me Annie; and, either way, you jumped in and helped my son. Rob and I will be eternally grateful to you."

"I'm just glad he's OK. Have the hospital given him the all-clear?" The memory of his head smashing against the road makes me go cold.

"Yes. He's absolutely fine."

"But he had to stay over a couple of nights in St Monica's, didn't he?"

"Just on the observation ward because of the concussion, then I insisted he stay home a few more days but, to be honest, he was desperate to get back to college. He's enjoying it so much. He says that everyone's lovely."

Jack mustn't have told her about Harry Sherwood and all the trouble he tried to cause. He mustn't have wanted to worry his parents.

"Yeah, well, he's very popular, Mrs . . . I mean, Annie. Everyone thinks he's great."

"I'm glad to hear it. We were worried about moving him from Somerset. It's difficult being the new boy and having to start again, but he seems to have settled in."

She opens the door of the living room, where music is playing. Jack's dad is on the sofa on his iPad. He jumps up as soon as he sees me. He looks just as young as I remembered. He has a kind of eternal student vibe going on – relaxed and cool. He's shorter and less well-built than

Jack, with round glasses and big brown eyes. His slim, pale face is topped off with dark hair that sticks up and is ultra-short at the sides.

He shakes my hand in a firm grip. "Nice to meet you properly, Zoe. I'm Rob. I feel like I know you already – Jack can't stop talking about you."

Jack can't stop talking about me? I repeat his words in my head.

"What's the music? She's got a beautiful voice," I ask, trying to focus. The singing is extraordinary; at once strange and beautiful, tragic and uplifting.

He looks pleased. "This is Nina Simone. We love her, don't we, Annie? She was the greatest jazz singer that ever lived . . . in our humble opinion." He taps his iPad and the music swells, her voice filling the room.

"Yes, we're big jazz and blues fans," says Annie, dropping on to the sofa next to him. "We actually met in a jazz club *years* ago. I was the singer in a band called The Purple Rose – not that I could hold a candle to Nina."

"You sung like an angel, Annie . . . you still do," Rob says, looking at her adoringly. I feel a lump rising in my throat. In the old days I would have cringed at hearing adults saying stuff like that, but now I'd give anything to have Mum and Dad just talking to each other.

"How's the marathon training going?" I ask.

Annie looks at me blankly for a moment and then shakes her head, laughing. "Oh, Jack told you about that, did he? To be honest, Zoe, sometimes I wish he'd never talked me into it, but I've got to admit I'm a lot fitter now than a few months ago."

"Well, I think it's amazing."

"Thank you. Now make yourself comfortable. I'll go and tell Jack you're here," Annie says warmly.

"And I'll get you something to drink," his dad says cheerfully. "What will it be?"

"Coffee, please."

"Americano, espresso, latte, cappuccino?" he asks.

I hold in a laugh. In my house it's a choice of instant coffee or instant coffee. "A latte would be lovely, thanks."

He disappears, and I sink into the soft sofa with a sigh. The carpet is so thick and has that brand-new smell. A cast-iron log burner glows orange, making the room sleepily warm. A massive TV hangs high above the fireplace and an oak bookcase full of hard-backed novels stands against one of the walls. The room is stylish and uncluttered – minimal, even. I wonder whether that's their taste or whether they have boxes still to unpack from their move.

My eyes are drawn to the conservatory, which is off the living room. I wander in and pick up the framed photos displayed on the window sills. There's one of a dark-haired baby that I guess must be Jack, and another of him at primary school, looking super-cute. French doors lead out to a tranquil, Japanese-style garden with a water feature and ivy clad pagoda. There's a lovely atmosphere of calm about this place.

I hear a rattle of cups and walk back into the living room,

sitting down on the sofa again. Rob enters carrying a tray laden with snacks and coffee that he places on the glass coffee table. Jack and Annie follow him in.

"Hi, Jack," I say, trying to sound casual, but my voice comes out too eager.

"Hi, Zoe, glad you could make it." He drops on to the sofa next to me. "Have my parents been talking your ear off about music?"

"Hey," says his dad, laughing. "She asked!"

"I love it," I say, and I mean it.

"Yeah, it's a rare 1965 track recorded at the Village Gate," Jack says, holding his hands up. "I admit it – I've been indoctrinated by them."

I smile. It's so cute that Jack is into his parents' taste in music.

"Zoe, we've got amaretto biscuits, stuffed olives, black pepper bread sticks, all kinds of dips – help yourself," Annie says with a flourish.

I delve in, before passing the plate of biscuits to Jack, and he takes one.

"No, Jack!" his mum says sharply. Jack doesn't even look at her as he obediently puts the biscuit back on the plate. She must see the surprise on my face as she says apologetically, "Jack's allergic to some nuts. We have to be careful."

"Have some water, Jack," his mum suggests. Jack takes a swig from the red water bottle he always has at school.

"Jack's not a caffeine junkie like us," his dad says teasingly. "Always on some health kick."

I drink my coffee as the conversation flows between us all. His parents seem genuinely interested in me. They're making a big effort. I get the impression that they think I'm someone important to Jack and I admit that I'm flattered.

"So why did you move here from Somerset?" I ask, finally fitting in a question of my own.

"Nothing very exciting, just for jobs," Rob replies, shrugging. "I got an offer I couldn't refuse from a rival insurance company in town and Annie got a HR management position in the same firm, so it worked out nicely for us."

"Is that the company with the flash offices opposite the town hall? What's it called? I pass it all the time . . . Midas Insurance?"

"That's the one," Rob replies.

Jack surprises me by standing up abruptly. "Zoe and I have work to do. See you guys later."

"Of course, darling," Annie says, squeezing his hand.

As Jack leads me into the hall I can't help being impressed at how lovely and respectful they all seem to each other. I mean, I love my mum but we have been known to have the odd shouting match.

"Who plays the piano, Jack?" I ask.

"We all do."

I sigh inwardly. I bet they're the kind of family who gather around the piano at Christmas to sing carols. I love the idea of that. I picture myself joining them, Jack's arm around me as we sing.

"Would you play something for me?" I ask

"What would you like me to play?" he says, sitting on the stool.

"Anything . . . you choose." I stand at the side of the piano with growing anticipation.

"OK." He plays the first few bars and my face lights up. He's playing "Mr Brightside"! I *adore* this song. I watch in awe as his fingers glide gracefully along the keyboard. All the while he looks straight ahead, concentrating. I'm singing along in my head, too embarrassed about my voice to sing out loud. His fingers skitter across the keys faster and faster, the tempo of The Killers' anthem gaining pace until I can't keep up. The music becomes frantic as his fingers move in a blur. My heart races . . . it's exhilarating.

Annie appears behind him and lays a hand on his shoulder. "Enough now, Jack," she says softly.

His hands shoot off the keyboard and hover in the air.

"Think of the neighbours!" she says, rubbing his back. "Let's not get carried away."

"That was incredible!" I say breathlessly. "How can you play like that?"

"Practice! Lots and lots of practice, isn't it, Jack?" Annie says, her voice gentle. "Jack is very . . . determined. He can do most things he puts his mind to."

They smile at each other, but Jack's doesn't reach his eyes. "Come on, Zoe," he says quietly.

Jack's room is, predictably, perfect. It's large and *so* tidy, not like mine. His double bed is neatly made with the duvet tucked into the corners and his pillows plumped. There's a massive beanbag sofa under the window that looks brand new. He hasn't piled all his dirty clothes on top of it like I'd do. The room smells fresh and clean; no trace of boy's sweaty armpits or stinking trainers. There's a poster of an ecstatic Mo Farah crossing the winning line at the London Olympics and another of Arcade Fire on stage at Glastonbury. On the desk his college books are methodically ordered by subject and different-coloured ink pens and highlighters are lined up in a row. I do a double-take as I spot the framed poster for *Romeo + Juliet* above his desk. It's the same one I've got in my bedroom; Leonardo DiCaprio and Clare Danes looking so young and beautiful. Jack really is a fan of Baz Luhrmann movies. Regret niggles at me. I wish I'd gone with him to watch them. I would have loved seeing it on the big screen with him.

"I've got that poster," I say. "I'm sorry I didn't come to see the movies with you last night."

"Ah, you don't need to apologize," he says breezily. "You were already going to the movies with Ethan."

I cringe inside. I feel terrible that I lied to him.

He picks up his psychology books and puts them on the bed. "Do you mind if we work on here? It's just more comfortable than the floor," he asks with his unfailing politeness.

"Sure," I say, leaning on a mountain of pillows and spreading my books out.

"OK, so how far have you got with the question on free will versus determinism?"

I look at my jumble of notes and dozens of question

marks. "To be honest, I don't know where to start. I've read it again and again but can't get my head around it."

"Well, tell me what you think it means," he says gently.

I exhale deeply, feeling self-conscious. When me and Ethan study together at least we're as ignorant as each other. Jack is just going to think that I'm stupid.

"OK, well, I think the debate is about whether we can freely choose how to behave or whether everything we do is influenced by other forces."

"Yeah, that's a decent summary," he says.

"But it's way more complicated than that, isn't it? What about all the different approaches – psychodynamic, biological, cognitive, behaviourist, humanistic." My head is spinning just listing them.

"Well, which one do you think applies to you the most?"

"I'd like to think it was the humanistic approach, just because I'd love to believe that I had free will and was in control of my own behaviour and decision-making."

"Sure, it would be nice to think that," he says slowly, "but, in reality, I'd say that human behaviour is more on the determinism side of the debate. Outside influences will always affect our decisions, so that makes determinism the logical theory."

Thoughts of my dad suddenly surface. If Jack's right, does that mean Dad's decision to have an affair and leave Mum for Petra was somehow beyond his control? Was he actually at the mercy of his genes, his subconscious, his environmental conditioning?

A sense of injustice grips me. That can't be right. That theory just lets him off the hook. Gives him an excuse not to take responsibility for his actions.

"But what about Erich Fromm's theory?" I say, my mind fired up, piecing together all I've read. "Didn't he argue that all of us have the potential to control our lives, but that many of us are too afraid to do it, which means we give up our freedom and allow our lives to be governed by circumstance, other people, political ideology, society? So, Fromm didn't believe that determinism is inevitable," I declare, surprising myself at how passionate I sound. "We just have to hold on to our free will and resist outside influences. And I agree with him . . . yes, Fromm is right . . . well . . . that's what I think, anyway."

I come to a faltering stop, suddenly feeling embarrassed. I glance at Jack out of the corner of my eye, expecting him to be smirking or looking unimpressed, but instead he's nodding enthusiastically.

"You see, Zoe, you know so much more than you think, and you've already come to your conclusion. So now we need to get all that down in summary, so you can write it up later," he says, leaning across and typing into my laptop. I should be looking at what he's typing but instead I find myself watching him, soaking in his flawless skin, the firm line of his jaw, the sloping groove between his nose and his cupid's-bow lip. I've never seen someone so perfect.

His dog-tags swing gently in front of me. One of them has his name and date of birth, but I sneak a look at the inscription on the other – *"You must be the change you wish to see in the world." Gandhi.* I smile to myself; that doesn't sound like a quote a determinist would choose.

"So, what do you think? Have I got all your points down?" he says, startling me out of my reverie.

"Sorry . . . yes. That all looks great. Jack, could you please be our teacher instead of Mrs Taylor?" I say teasingly.

He smiles and leans back. "Zoe, you'll be fine. You're more than capable of getting a top grade, you just need to be confident in your own ability." He speaks like he really believes in me. I feel a rush of pride.

I've been in the sitting in the same position too long. I stretch out my arms and legs and put my laptop on the bedside table.

"Oh, *Wuthering Heights*!" I say, picking up the book lying on his table. "Where are you up to?" I open it at the bookmark and start to read: *"He neither spoke nor loosed his hold for some five minutes, during which period he bestowed more kisses than ever he gave in his life before, I daresay: but then my mistress had kissed him first, and I plainly saw that he could hardly bear, for downright agony, to look into her face!"*

Jack looks into my eyes, continuing the quote without missing a beat. *"The same conviction had stricken him as me, from the instant he beheld her, that there was no prospect of ultimate recovery there – she was fated, sure to die."*

"That's word for word," I whisper, my gaze locked with his. "How can you do that?"

He shrugs. "Because I've read it so many times," he says,

running his fingers over the duvet. "I think that Heathcliff and Cathy are the most romantic lovers in all of English literature."

I hesitate. I adore the book but I'd say their love was more toxic than romantic. The truth is that I'll always prefer Jane Eyre and Rochester to Cathy and Heathcliff. Rochester may have been arrogant and made terrible mistakes, but at least he learns from Jane in the end and they have a relationship based on love and equality, not the destructive obsession in *Wuthering Heights*. But I keep my mouth shut. I don't want to spoil things when it's obvious that he's so passionate about the book.

I love everything that I'm discovering about Jack today; all his different tastes and talents, how he is with his parents, how lovely it feels to be with him in his home. How did Ethan's dad describe him – "comfortable in his own skin"? Yeah, Jack's his own person. He's a leader, not a follower. No wonder people are so drawn to him.

"Have you ever been to Howarth Parsonage?" Jack asks as he shuts his laptop and tidies up the scattered text books.

"The Brontës' home? No, but I'd love to go. They were all incredible, especially Charlotte."

"I went a couple of years ago, but it was a school trip so there wasn't time to really explore the place." He pauses then says, "We should go, Zoe. We could walk on the moors, see what inspired such vision and passion." He glances at me and a wave of heat rises up my neck. "I'd love to be there with you."

I can't deny it this time. He's not just being polite. I'm not reading the signals wrong, am I? Jack Cartwright likes me.

"Well?" he says tentatively, watching my face. "Would you like that?"

My heart is hammering so hard I'm sure he can hear it. I'm hesitating, but I don't know why. He's gorgeous, clever, thoughtful and we've got so much in common. He could date any girl he wants, but he's asked *me*! What am I waiting for?

"Yes, I'd like that." I try to sound calm, though I can feel my mouth sliding into a massive grin.

"Good." The seductive tone of his voice sends a shiver of delight down my spine.

I swallow hard and start to gather up my things. "I'd better get going."

"Are you sure you don't want to stay a bit longer?"

I'm too flustered to stay. I'm bound to say something stupid and ruin the moment. "No, I've got to get home, but thanks, Jack. Thanks for helping me with the essay and, you know . . . saying what you did," I bumble awkwardly.

"It was a pleasure. Bye, then, Zoe. I'll see you tomorrow." He bends down and kisses my cheek sweetly.

I nod dumbly. I close his bedroom door behind me, walk down the stairs and stand very still in the hallway, my hand fluttering over my kissed cheek, but then I realize; I've left my laptop charger on his floor.

I turn around and climb back up the stairs and tap on Jack's door, half-embarrassed and half-excited to see him again.

"Sorry, Jack." I stick my head round the door. "I left my charger."

He doesn't reply. He's sitting, straight-backed, on the side of his bed, his head is bowed.

"Jack?" I crouch down at his feet and look up at his face. His glazed eyes are open, but he's just staring at the carpet.

"Jack!" I say in alarm. "Are you all right? What's the matter?"

Suddenly Rob is in the room. "Is everything OK here?"

"It's Jack. It's like he's in a trance."

Rob drops to his knees and touches his son's back gently. "Jack?" he says quietly.

"Dad!" His head jerks up and his gaze slides past his father to me. "Zoe?" he says wonderingly. "Great to see you."

I stand up . . . bemused. "Are you OK, Jack?" I ask gently.

"Yeah. Why do you look so worried?" He frowns.

I don't know what to say.

His dad escorts me out. "He just needs some rest," he whispers to me. "The hospital warned us that this might happen. He's been overdoing it lately." He smiles, but I can see anxiety in his boyish face. "He doesn't know when to slow down."

"Will you take him back to the hospital?" I push.

"Yes," he says slowly. "We will."

CHAPTER 14

People are giving me funny looks as I walk past them singing in my tuneless voice. I need to shut up, but this playlist Jack has made for me is packed with bands that I love – The Killers, The Cave Dwellers, Florence and the Machine, and beautiful tracks from Nina Simone. He sent it last night when he should have been resting. It came with a message saying, *Thinking of you*.

I didn't tell him, but I was thinking of him too. In fact, he's *all* I can think about. I couldn't sleep because he was going round and round in my head. I'm worried about him. I'm excited and confused by him.

I pause at the entrance to the alleyway, finding a song to pump me up for my encounter with Bullseye – the theme from *Rocky* – perfect. I brace myself and stride onwards, but Bullseye doesn't come running to the gate to snarl at me. In fact, all seems quiet and there's no sign of him in the garden.

And that's when I see it; tied to the gatepost there's an A4-sized poster in a plastic wallet.

I step closer to read the poster. The top half is filled with a coloured photo of Bullseye and underneath, in big red letters, it reads:

Have you seen Bullseye? Bullseye went missing on Friday 9th November. He's a five year-old black Staffordshire Bull Terrier. He's wearing a collar with his name and my number. Any information, please phone Barry on – 07700900951.
£50 reward for Bullseye's safe return.

I go cold at the thought of a vicious dog like that out on the loose. I see Ethan in the distance by the entrance to Hinton Dale. Just like at the club, he's more groomed than his usual, endearingly-dishevelled self. He's ditched his slouching jeans and baggy T-shirts for a sharper, hipper look. He seems less like the boy I've grown up with. As I get closer, though, I notice his sheepish expression, even though he's apologized to me a dozen times already about Saturday night.

"Hey, Ethan," I call to him. "You won't believe this, you know that dog, Bullseye? He's gone missing! There's a poster on the gate."

He doesn't look too surprised. "Good, I'm glad. At least he won't be able to terrorize you any more." We start walking up the marble steps into college. "How did it go at Jack's house? Did you get any work done?" He stares at me intently, like he's looking for clues.

"Yeah, loads." I'm not going to tell him about Jack basically asking me out. I'm not sure how he'd react. It feels weird not to tell my best friend, but then things between us *have* felt weird lately. "I'll go through it with you in our free this morning." I catch his arm. "Listen, Ethan – I'm worried about Jack. I think he's still not right after the accident. Yesterday he looked like he was having a mini seizure. His dad is going to take him back to St Monica's."

Ethan whistles. "Oh, man. He seemed fine on Friday night when we went for a run *and* on Saturday when we were working out."

"Yeah, it's *you* who wasn't fine," I lecture. "Ethan, it's great that you're getting fit, if you want to, but if it's making you *that* exhausted then you need to slow down. You passed out for twelve hours straight."

"I can keep up with Jack," Ethan protests. "Sort of. I've never felt that tired – I felt rubbish all day as well. I don't understand what happened to me. There's no way I should have slept like that. I even had this energy drink Jack made for me. It's like rocket fuel. I should have been buzzing."

"It's very simple – Jack pushed you too hard and you flaked out. Just . . . pace yourself, OK?"

His head drops, making his soft curls droop. "I wasn't there for you, Zoe. I'm so sorry." He looks up at me, his blue eyes full of regret. "I would never have forgiven myself if something really bad had happened to you."

"Ethan!" I yelp in frustration. "For the last time, stop apologizing. You're driving me insane. There was no harm done. I had Jack."

"Yes. You had Jack," he echoes slowly.

We meet Jodie in the hallway and she's sticking her chest out at me comically, to draw attention to the dog-tags attached to a silver chain around her neck.

"Do you like it? I thought I'd go for the whole army vibe," she smirks, pointing to her khaki shirt.

I lift the two dog-tags between my fingers and read what's written on them. One is engraved with Jodie's name and date of birth, and the other is a quote: *"Fashion fades, style is eternal." Yves Saint Laurent.*

"I love it," I say genuinely.

"You two should get one. People are going crazy for them since they saw Jack's."

Ethan shakes his head. "I'll pass, thanks."

"How much are they?" I ask.

"Well, it's the *proper* vintage one. . ."

"OK, but how much was it?" I ask again.

"Three hundred and fifty, plus the cost of engraving," she says rapidly as she squirms.

"Wow!" Ethan says. "Isn't there a cheaper version?"

"Yeah . . . imitations, but what's the point of that? Everyone will be able to tell it's not the real thing. Anyway, it's an early Christmas and birthday present from my mum and dad, so everything's good," she says defensively.

"I thought you were having a weekend in Paris with your

mum for your birthday. You've been talking about it for ages," I say.

Regret flickers across her face, before she says merrily, "I'll do that when I'm eighteen. It'll be better then, anyway. I'll be able to drink champagne on the Champs-Élysées."

"Good plan," I say supportively. "But don't ever forget, Jodie, *you're* the fashion icon. You set the trends and others shall follow." I say it jokingly, but I mean it and she high-fives me, saying in her best American accent, "You're damn right, girl!"

We walk down the packed corridors and see Jack deep in conversation with Mr Dunn outside his office. I don't want to disturb them, though I'm desperate to check that Jack's OK. We go to walk past but Jack ushers us over to him.

"Guys, don't you agree with me that people are getting fed up with the common room?" he says, dragging us into the debate. "Surely by now the governors have made a decision about the things we need? We did what you asked . . . we had a fund-raiser."

"Yes, a club night that ended up with you being hospitalized," Mr Dunn scowls.

"But, sir, Jack's right. It would be great to have a proper chilling space," Ethan says quickly.

"The common room is like a morgue. It's depressing," Jodie sighs.

"Having fun things in it would incentivize us to study even harder," I say disingenuously.

Mr Dunn narrows his eyes at Jack. "These things take time."

"But life is too short to let bureaucracy slow decisions down, and, Mr Dunn," Jack says, pointing to the head's nose, "you should get that mole checked. Make an appointment today. It's changed shape over the last few weeks – that's not a good sign."

Mr Dunn's hand shoots to his nose. "Are you being serious?" he says, half-angry, half-shocked.

"Absolutely, sir," Jack says. "Now, if you'll excuse me, I must go. I don't want to be late for class." He heads off down the corridor and we follow him, speechless.

*

Playing pat-a-cake with Sonja is making our icy palms smart as they slap together. We get faster and faster until we're completely out of sync and our hands flap around. We collapse in a fit of giggles, our bursts of breath like tiny clouds in the freezing air. We really should be inside, sitting around the clanking radiators in the common room, but we like coming to the stadium at lunchtime. It gets busy straight after college when Jack runs his training sessions but, at this time, it's usually all ours. We can relax here, especially now that Harry Sherwood isn't around. He didn't dare return to college and he's had to come off social media because of all the online abuse he was getting from people.

I've noticed that it's not just Ethan who's changed his style. Recently Sonja seems to have ditched her office-like clothes for a softer, glamorous look. Under her new black velvet coat, she's wearing an emerald-green silk blouse and high-waisted culottes with shiny patent leather court shoes. Her white-blonde hair flows freely instead of being tied back in a tight plait. She has the air of a forties movie star.

"I'm loving your new look, Sonja," I say admiringly.

"Oh, thanks, Zoe," she beams. "I can't take complete credit for it. I have a fashion adviser."

"Ah, I bet Jodie has been enjoying herself," I laugh.

"No, it's not Jodie. I was having one of my discussions with Jack."

"About clothes?" I ask curiously.

"No, about business. He likes to hear about my plans for the future and he's always sending me articles about inspirational entrepreneurs. Anyway, he showed me a feature on this amazing millionaire business woman in New York. She's only twenty-seven! She's so elegant and chic that I realized I was getting it all wrong."

"How?"

"With my style. I need a cool, retro look. This entrepreneur has her own clothing range for young business women, it's not cheap, but I persuaded Mama to put it on one of her credit cards. I've told her that it's an investment in my future. I'll be going on work placements . . . having job interviews, and," she says fervently, "if you want to succeed in business you have to project the right image."

I nod unenthusiastically. I know that Sonja's mama is willing to sacrifice a lot for daughter, but I'm not sure this is the best use of their money.

I wrap my biker jacket around me and pull my red bobble hat over my cold ears, suddenly feeling self-conscious about what Jack must think about my *style*.

I watch them as they do squat thrusts down on the track. Ethan is laughing, his arms quivering with effort, but Jack is powering away. I wish Jack would slow down. He shouldn't overdo it after what happened in his bedroom yesterday.

It was a mistake to tell Jodie and Sonja about Jack saving me from the mugger; they're lusting after him even more. I haven't told them about Jack's suggestion that me and him go on a day trip together; I don't want them to be jealous and they'd make it into such a big deal that I'd be even more nervous. It's too soon to know how I really feel about him. It's best to keep things quiet for now.

Jodie is on the language app that Jack found for her. She makes us chuckle as she paces between the rows of benches repeating phrases out loud. At first she was only learning Polish to impress Jack but now she's really into it and loves trying to speak with Sonja.

"*Czy moge kupic twoja swinie?*" Jodie announces with a flourish.

Sonja bursts out laughing. "Jodie, you've just asked whether you can buy my pigs."

"And that's exactly what I wanted to say," Jodie shoots back. "At least I'm trying."

"Yes, you are, and if you keep this up my mama has told me she's going to adopt you," she cackles, and jumps up to give Jodie a hug.

The boys climb the stadium steps and drop down next to me. Ethan's cheeks are flushed in his Union Jack hoodie but Jack looks unruffled in his tight black T-shirt. Jack takes a gulp from his red water bottle and then, to my surprise, drapes his arm around my shoulders.

I freeze. I glance at Ethan's shocked face. Jodie and Sonja nearly drop their phones. Only Jack behaves like it's nothing out the ordinary.

Sonja and Jodie exchange a loaded look.

"Excuse us," Jodie says. "We just need to speak to Zoe for a moment."

I brace myself. I know what's coming. They take a hand each and pull me off the bench, away from Jack. They march me along the row of benches and when we're out of earshot they begin their interrogation.

"Right, Zoe," Sonja says firmly. "Exactly how long has *this* been going on?"

"What?" I reply, fidgeting nervously with my earrings.

Jodie wags her finger at me. "Don't play games, Zoe. You and Jack Cartwright! I mean . . . *Jack Cartwright*!"

"Nothing's happened. We haven't been sneaking around behind your backs, or anything," I say, sounding like a defendant in court. To tell the truth, I'm as confused as them. I know that Jack likes me – but I didn't realize he thought we were *definitely* more than friends.

"But how did this happen?" Sonja asks in disbelief. "*When* did this happen?"

I shrug. "The day after the mugging – yesterday – I went

round to his house and I met his parents but it's *nothing* yet. I think Jack likes me, I like Jack. He just asked if I wanted to spend more time together, that's all."

"What I wouldn't do to *spend more time* with Jack Cartwright, you lucky, lucky cow," Jodie says, grinning with admiration and envy.

Sonja's mind is whirring. "We should post a photo of you and Jack on Facebook and tag in that loser you met on holiday. What was his name?"

"Matt Gillingham!" Jodie answers.

"Yeah, then he'll see the kind of man you *really* deserve," Sonja says adamantly.

"No way! Would you two calm down? Me and Jack aren't even going out, and it might be nothing, so let's just keep this between ourselves," I plead. "I don't want everyone talking. We're just getting to know one another."

"Sure," Jodie says, her eyes dancing. "As long as you keep us informed. We want to know *all* the details." She gives me an ostentatious wink.

"Not going to happen, Jodie," I say, tight-lipped.

"Spoil sport," she laughs.

Jack calls over to us. "Guys, I've got an idea I want to run past you!" Sonja and Jodie walk over to him eagerly, but Ethan is keeping quiet, looking at the ground. I wish I knew what he was thinking.

"So, people have been asking me to sort out another fundraiser for the common room. Basically, I think they just want an excuse for another club night." Jack grins. "But seeing as Mr Dunn has banned us, I was thinking it would be great to get everyone involved in a sponsored football match instead."

Sonja's eager face disappears. "I can't play football. I hate football."

"This would be worth it. I've been making a few calls and I've got a promise from the makers of Voltage that they'll donate jackets to everyone who plays. It's good publicity for their brand to help teenagers in the community. In return we just give a bit of a shout-out to them on Instagram."

"Voltage! I love their clothes, but I can never afford them," Jodie says excitedly.

I shift uncomfortably. Jack and Jodie seem so pleased that I don't want to spoil things, but I've got to tell them. "Listen, I'm not sure Voltage is a brand we should be promoting. I read online recently that they use child labour in South-East Asia to manufacture their clothes."

"It's probably a rival company putting out fake news," Jodie says hopefully.

Sonja is busy looking it up on her phone. "Hard luck, Jodie," she says. "Look at all these links to articles. It looks genuine to me."

"No!" Jodie cries. "Does this mean I have to pass up the chance to get one of their jackets for *free*?"

"Not necessarily," Jack says, to my surprise. "You'll find that most companies do this kind of thing, but only a handful are ever exposed. Obviously, now Voltage would have stopped using child labour and their offer to us is probably part of them trying to make amends. Personally, I feel we shouldn't be too judgemental and accept it."

"*Really*?" I say. "I know that you must have gone to a lot of trouble to get their sponsorship, Jack, but I don't think I want to be wearing their jackets."

"OK." He shrugs. "Well, the fairest thing to do would be to give anyone who plays the choice. We'll explain the situation and then it's up to them."

"I think that sounds like a good plan," Jodie says, trying not to look too pleased.

"Great!" Jack says, keen to move on. "Let's have a match between our year, mixed teams – boys and girls – and it doesn't matter how good or bad you are, everyone can join in. What do you think?"

Sonja has her arms crossed defensively.

"Come on, Sonja," Jack coaxes. "No one will be laughing at you. It's just for fun, to raise a bit of cash and show that sport is for everyone. Would you do it for me, *please*?"

Sonja throws up her arms in surrender. "OK, but only because you asked so nicely."

"Thanks, girls, you're wonderful. Now what I need you to do is to recruit our teams. Could you go around college signing up students? We're looking at next Thursday after school. Tell them about the offer of the free Voltage jackets, *and* the situation, of course," he says, looking to me compliantly. "And I don't mind you telling them that I'll be accepting mine, just so they know. Ethan, could you do a bit of recruiting too?"

"What, now?" Ethan sounds unwilling.

"Yeah, now would be great."

"Come on, Ethan, we need you." Sonja and Jodie link arms with him.

"Are *you* coming, Zoe?" Ethan asks.

I hesitate. I really want to stay here with Jack. I can tell that he's been looking for a chance for us to be alone all day. "I'll be along in a minute," I say casually.

Ethan's eyes shift from me to Jack. He seems reluctant to leave us, but the girls drag him away.

Jack moves closer to me; his shoulder touching mine. I tense with excited anticipation. "Hang on," he says, and opens his rucksack.

He gets a plastic container out of his rucksack and gives it to me. "I made you a beef and bean burrito. You like them, don't you?"

This isn't quite the romantic move I was expecting, but then Jack is never predictable. "They're my favourite. How did you know?" I say, baffled.

"You told me the other day, remember?"

"Did I? Well, thanks, that's lovely of you." I take it gratefully. "Have you made one for yourself?"

"Yeah, I ate it early. It's a pain but my training programme means that I stick to weird mealtimes, but don't worry, I'm fine." I can't disagree as he slaps his taut stomach.

I pick up his jacket from the bench and drape it around his shoulders, worried he'll get a chill in just his T-shirt

"Thanks." His huge pupils swallow me up. "I don't really feel the cold."

"You've got to look after yourself, Jack. I don't want to interfere," I say tentatively, "but have your parents made an appointment at St Monica's?"

"Yes. Dad told me that I've got an appointment in a couple of weeks."

"That's so far off! Couldn't he get one sooner?"

He takes my icy hand in his cool palm. I feel a jolt of something that makes it suddenly hard to concentrate. "Thank you for worrying about me, Zoe. I've never met anyone so lovely."

I stare at my feet, bashfully. "I'm sure that can't be true." I don't know what to say next, so I wave the burrito lamely at him. "Thanks for lunch. Your burritos are even better than the ones my mum makes."

"How is your mum?" he asks thoughtfully.

"She's good," I say, trying to sound convincing.

"It must be tough on her being on her own," he says gently. "Just the two of you."

There's something about the concern in his voice that nearly tips me into tears. I think of the contrast between my mum and dad, and Jack's parents, still in love and happy.

"Yeah, I mean, she does *so* well," I say, my lips starting to quiver. "She's just started going on dates again. She's trying to look to the future. But it's been hard on her since Dad left. They don't speak, only ever text, or use me as a go-between, and now he's gone and got married to Petra, the woman he left Mum for." My jaw clenches at the mention of her. "Petra doesn't seem to want Dad to spend any time with me alone. I can't stand it." I take a deep breath. I have no idea where that came from, it's stuff I mostly just talk to Ethan about.

"So, what do you think needs to happen to make things better?" says Jack.

I hesitate. No one's asked me that before – we've always just accepted that we have to muddle through as best we can. "Well, Mum needs to keep moving on – not that she needs a new man for that. I just want her to be happy again. And, as for Dad. . ." I let out a deep sigh. "Well, it's too late for him. He's married Petra. And she wants him all to herself."

"Petra may change, now that they're married. She might feel more secure and so be happier about him spending time with you." Jack sounds infinitely wise, but I know better.

"No." I shake my head vehemently. It's like all the effort of keeping it together for Mum has worn me down and now I can't pretend any more. "My guess is that she'll get pregnant soon and when they have a baby together, she'll be even more possessive of him . . . trying to write his 'old' family out of his life." I feel bile rising in me. I kick, kick, kick at the bench in front of me. A silence hangs between us. I wonder if Jack is going to come out with some platitude to try and make me feel better; but instead he says,

"I dreamed about you last night." His comment stops me in my tracks. I sit very still, staring straight ahead across the stadium but I feel his eyes on me. Heat is creeping up my neck. My head suddenly too hot under my bobble hat.

"And what was your dream?" I whisper.

"We were on a train travelling through Europe. There

was beautiful countryside rolling past the window. It was so sunny and bright. We'd only just met, but we got talking and there was this incredible connection between us. Our destinations weren't the same, but I asked you to get off with me in Vienna, and you did. And then my dream was full of us having the most amazing day in this gorgeous city. But the most wonderful thing about it was just being with you, and we talked and talked and talked, until we felt like we'd known each other all our lives. It was the most incredible feeling. Like we were destined to be together."

My erratic breathing is being exposed as bursts of icy clouds. I pull my hat off, feeling suddenly overheated, and the cold air prickles my skin.

Slowly, very slowly, Jack reaches over and cups my face gently between his hands. "Close your eyes and don't move," he murmurs. My heart is in my mouth.

"Hi!" I hear Ethan's voice and my eyes shoot open. As he gets nearer I see his brow crease as he glances between us. I pull away from Jack's hands, riddled with a confusing guilt.

"Everything OK?" Ethan asks, subdued.

"Yeah, Zoe has something in her eye. I was just about to get it out," Jack says calmly. He puts a hand under my chin. "Close your eyes." My eyelids flutter with nerves as he gently plucks something from my lashes.

"See?" he says, holding a piece of red fluff between his fingers. He opens his fingers and it floats off in the breeze.

CHAPTER 15

Jen keeps disappearing from my phone screen as she leans into her mirror to apply more lipstick. I don't know why I bother to FaceTime her as I hardly ever get to see her face. She's always multi-tasking, always in motion.

"So, Dad is actually going to take you away somewhere?" her disembodied voice says. "Just the two of you? Amazing. He'll probably have to lock Petra in a room first, then make a run for it."

"Yeah, can you believe she's letting him take me somewhere alone?" I say.

"To be honest, no!" She dabs gold eyeshadow on to her lids. "But you make sure you have a good time and let him spoil you, because he owes you, big time."

"Thanks, I will, though I still don't know where we're going."

Her luminous face framed by deep-auburn hair looms into the screen. "It had better be somewhere special. Now listen, I haven't forgotten your birthday. I'll email you a voucher – then you can buy whatever you want. If I choose something, I'll only get it wrong. What presents have you got so far, anything worth mentioning?"

"Well, Sonja and Jodie got me a set of brilliant make-up brushes, and Mum got me these," I say, picking up the hair straighteners to show her. "She's obviously hoping I'll grow my hair."

"She's not very subtle, is she?" Jen laughs. "Where is she, anyway?"

"We had a little celebration when I came home, but then I insisted she went around to Karen's from work for a Prosecco and pamper evening. She's going to stay over."

"Good on her. It's about time she started enjoying herself," Jen says. "So come on, any more gifts?"

"Well, Ethan … Ethan gave me a gorgeous present," I say, suddenly feeling a lump in my throat.

"Show me, then."

"I can't show you. You'll have to listen." I press "Play" and Ethan's voice rings out, deep and menacing:

"*Little pig, little pig, let me come in. No, not by the hair of my chinny chin.*"

"What the hell was *that*?" Jen says, her face puzzled.

"It was Ethan reading *The Three Little Pigs*," I laugh.

"Why?" she says, and I laugh harder.

"Because I told him that I like hearing him read bedtime stories, so he's recorded himself reading different fairy tales for me. He does all the different voices. I absolutely love it!"

"When did this happen?" Her voice is full of surprise.

"When did what happen?" I frown at her.

"When did Ethan start fancying you?" I stare at her; she means it.

"Oh, god, don't say that! Me and Ethan are just mates!" I can hear my voice getting shrill and take a deep breath. "OK . . . listen, a few weeks ago I thought that maybe he wanted something more and it was all just too confusing. I don't know how I felt about it . . . about him, but now. . ." I duck my head, embarrassed. "Well, now there's Jack."

"And who's Jack?" she asks

"The new boy at college. He's. . ." I don't know how to describe him. "He's not like anyone I've ever met before."

"Have you got a photo of him? I need to see him," she demands.

"You can look him up on Instagram; he's Jack Cartwright101."

"Hang on." She puts me on hold and a few seconds later her face is dancing in front of the screen. "Oh my god, have I got the right one? Tall, dark, gorgeous? *He* fancies *you*? No offence, Zo, but are you sure?"

"Thanks a lot," I reply sarcastically. "I know it may be hard to believe, but some boys are a bit deeper than just wanting to date prom queens like you."

She can't stop grinning. "Well, what are you waiting for? Go out with him before he changes his mind."

"For your information, he's already asked me to spend more time with him," I say, trying to contain my glee.

"What the hell does that mean?"

"I *think* it means we're going out. He put his arm around me in front of the guys the other day."

"He put his *arm around you*? He sounds like a right Casanova!" she laughs, wandering away from the screen to pick up her jacket from the floor.

I hear a horn honking from the street and at that moment a text comes through from Dad. "I've got to go. Dad's waiting for me outside."

"Well, have a brilliant time and remember to keep me updated on your love life. If it works out with that gorgeous specimen of a boy then I might even have to come home to meet him," she cackles.

I blow her a kiss and switch to check my "Amigos" WhatsApp group that's started buzzing like mad. There's a string of messages with a link to Matt Gillingham's Facebook page.

Sonja: Zoe! Check out the video on Matt Gillingham's FB page.

Jodie: Now everyone can see what a scumbag he is

Sonja: He's been trying to delete it and he can't 🤣

Jodie: Look at the comments from his girlfriend and her mates. He's going to need police protection.

Ethan: Who posted it?

Sonja: Can't tell. So many people tagged in, it's got loads of shares.

Ethan: Zoe, r u there?

I hurriedly click the link and Matt Gillingham's Facebook page appears. The video's title is *Who's Been A Naughty Boy?* The footage is less than thirty seconds long, but it's enough to show someone, who is unmistakably Matt, sitting on a bus with a girl – who is *not* his girlfriend. They are snogging the faces off each other. The comments are going mad. It's clear that Matt Gillingham had better go into hiding if he doesn't want to be lynched by his girlfriend and her furious mates.

I plonk down on the bed, grinning at the thought of all the grief he's going to get. I feel sorry for his girlfriend, but at least now she knows what he's really like. I reply to the Amigos.

Zoe: Well, guys, thanks for sharing. That's made my day! xx

A satisfied smile is still etched on my face as I grab my bag and run outside to meet Dad. He flashes his headlights in the dark and I wave, skipping up the street towards the Jaguar; bubbling with excitement about where he might be taking me, although anywhere will do, just as long as we get to spend time together.

As I near the car, I stop abruptly. There's someone in the shadows in the passenger seat. I peer closely and see her sleek blonde hair with brilliant white teeth shining out of her doll-like face. She gives me a little wave and my stomach turns.

No! No! He's not bringing Petra along with us. He can't. He wouldn't.

I knock sharply on Dad's driver-side window and it slides down soundlessly. He gives me a big smile, which doesn't reach his eyes.

"Happy birthday, honey. Pop in the back and we'll get going," he says, pretending nothing is wrong.

My eyes shift to Petra as she says eagerly, "Yeah, happy birthday, Zoe."

"Dad, would you get out of the car? I need to talk to you." I don't want to argue with him in front of her.

"No, Zoe. Please don't waste time. We need to hit the road," he says tensely.

I lean through his window and into his personal space. "I thought it was just the two of us. This is *our* time together . . . my birthday treat?"

He shrinks into the seat, his hands tightening on the steering wheel. "Of course it's our time together, Zoe, but I thought it would be good if Petra came with us." He fakes cheerfulness. "It'll give you two time to get to know each other."

Petra nods in agreement as she places her handbag on her lap.

I can't contain my anger. "No way! It's just meant to be us, not *her*."

"Don't be rude, Zoe." Dad bristles. "Things are different now that Petra and I are married. She's going to be a permanent part of your life, and she'd really like you two to get along."

Petra gazes up at me. "Zoe, I'm really looking forward to getting to know you. I realize that you may not have a great opinion of me, but I'm sure that there's been a lot of misinformation about what I'm *really* like."

"Misinformation? Like the fact that you had an affair with my dad and that he left his wife and kids to shack up with you – do you mean stuff like that?" I scowl.

"I hope that we can move on from that," Petra says, her voice small.

"Enough now, Zoe." Dad sounds exhausted. "Get in the car. We're going somewhere nice and we're going to enjoy ourselves."

I want to turn around and march back in the house, slamming the door on him and her, but even as I stand there seething, a part of me realizes that I can't ignore what's happened. Dad's right; this ridiculous woman is now permanently in my life. I've got to be grown up about this. Half the kids at college are in the same situation as me: parents split up, new partners come on the scene . . . step-mothers, step-brothers, merged families having to adjust, compromise, get along for the sake of everyone. I shut my eyes and try to absorb the blow. OK, I'll give Petra her twenty-four hours. I've no intention of ever being friends with her, but maybe I'll discover that she's someone I can stop wasting my energy resenting.

I sit in the back of the car and cross my arms in protest as Dad starts up the engine and pulls off. The journey feels like an eternity and he's only just reached the motorway. Petra is insisting on making small talk.

"How's school?" "What's your favourite lesson?" "What music are you into?" On and on she goes as I give her begrudging, monosyllabic answers.

Eventually Petra's questions dry up and she starts chatting to Dad instead. I'm relieved. I get out my phone and WhatsApp the guys, telling them I've been tricked into spending my birthday get-away with Dad's child bride and that they need to send a rescue party.

I stare at my phone and read my friends' responses. Sonja is outraged and Jodie's cuttingly funny remarks about Petra are making me feel better. Ethan is just upset for me.

Ethan: There's no way your dad should have done this to you. He's bang out of order. You should call your mum.

But that's the last thing I should do. I can't let Mum know. She'd be angry and hurt that Dad's brought Petra along. I can't let Mum and Dad's fragile relationship get any worse. I've got to get through this.

At last the car comes off the motorway and soon we're weaving along country lanes so winding that I'm beginning to feel queasy. I'm relieved when we turn off at a sign for Great Valleys Country House Hotel. We cruise up a driveway surrounded by parkland. Despite myself, excitement rises in me as the headlights illuminate deer among the oak trees and an elegant manor house comes into view. Maybe this weekend isn't going to be so bad after all.

The hotel car park is busy with men and women in business suits greeting each other with air-kisses. Dad parks up and struggles as he pulls Petra's ridiculously large case out of the boot. She supervises him, warning him to be careful with it, as she's packed a couple of bottles of champagne in with her clothes. As Dad wheels her luggage towards the grand entrance, several people come to say hello, calling him by his first name. I'm confused – how come they know him? My Doc Marten boots crunch over the gravel and up the steps into the ornate lobby, but as I walk towards the reception desk I spot the message displayed on the TV screen: *Great Valleys Country House Hotel warmly welcomes Bright Light Inc for their weekend sales conference.*

I grab Dad's arm. "Bright Light Inc? This is a *work* weekend?" My voice comes out high-pitched. "Have you brought me to your work conference for my birthday treat?"

"Listen, Zoe." He pats my hand as my grip tightens on his arm. "It makes perfect sense. I'll be doing a bit of work while you and Petra get to enjoy all this." He sweeps his arm around the lobby. "You've got an upgraded room, there's a top-class spa with a pool, and the grounds are beautiful."

"But this was meant to be about us spending time together. First of all, you brought *Petra* on our father-daughter trip, and now I find out that you're going to be working the whole weekend?" Tears are pooling in my eyes. Petra is looking uncomfortable. "You could have taken me away next weekend instead," I say.

“I haven’t got a free weekend for months.” He looks apologetic. I wipe angry tears away with my hand. “It was this weekend or nothing.”

“Well, I’m sorry for being such an inconvenience to you,” I hiss.

“Can I help you, sir?” The woman receptionist cuts through our confrontation as the queue lengthens behind us.

Dad composes himself and checks us in.

The receptionist hands over the key cards. “Enjoy your stay.” She flashes a sympathetic look at me, which makes me want to cry even more.

I discover that I’m on the first floor and they have a suite in the attic. There’s no denying that my room is lovely. The plump bed is huge and a picture window looks out on to the floodlit gardens at the back of the hotel. The sleek black-tiled bathroom is literally bigger than my bedroom. The walk-in power shower and Jacuzzi bath are pure luxury and I immediately plan to take home the bottles of expensive lotions and potions sitting above the sink.

It only takes a minute to unpack my bag. I brought along my smartest jeans and top, just in case we came to a place like this. I envelope myself in the fluffy bathrobe hanging in the carved wardrobe. I hop on to the bed and switch on the TV, but despite the gorgeous surroundings I can’t relax. Dad didn’t say when we were meeting up and my stomach is growling with hunger.

Just then, a text comes through from Dad.

Order anything you want from room service. Petra and I have to attend the conference dinner in a minute. You'd be bored silly. Use the pool. Enjoy yourself.

And then a second text:

BTW, Petra wants to know what treatments you fancy. She's booking you both into the spa for tomorrow.

I throw the phone across the bed. I'm not even allowed to eat with him.

"Some birthday," I mutter at my reflection in the enormous gilt-edged mirror.

Right, if that's the way he's going to be, then I'll hit him where it hurts. I study the room-service menu and ring reception to order the most expensive food I can – steak and lobster with extra chips and the chocolate extravaganza with lavender ice cream.

"That comes to one hundred and forty pounds," the receptionist says. "Should I charge it to your room?"

"I'm with my dad. Sean Littlewood. He's in the attic suite. Please charge it to him," I say breezily.

My spirits are lifted at the thought of Dad's face when he gets the bill. I'm settling down to watch a movie when there's a knock on the door. I jump off the bed and open it to find Petra standing outside. She's in a shimmering gold skin-tight dress that reflects on to her sun-kissed skin. Her shiny blonde hair is strategically placed to fall around her cleavage. She's touched up her make-up so she looks even more flawless.

"Hi, Zoe." She smiles and my stomach turns. "Just checking in about those spa treatments for tomorrow?"

"I'm not into spa stuff," I say coldly. What I really mean is that I'm not into spa stuff if it involves her.

"Oh." She seems to flutter her eyelashes in slow motion. Is this meant to be her "disappointed" look? "Couldn't I just book you a facial? They're so good for opening the pores."

Who cares? I *so* want to give her a shove and watch her topple over in those skyscraper heels.

"No, Petra. I don't want a facial, but you go ahead. Knock yourself out," I say viciously.

"Well, you can still use the sauna rooms and pool. And there are gorgeous hot beds. We could chill on them and chat." I roll my eyes, but she pretends not to notice. "I want us to get along, Zoe. Please give me a chance."

I hesitate. She looks like she means it, but I feel like I'm betraying Mum even talking to this woman. "You'd better go. You don't want to be late for the *conference dinner*," I say bitingly.

I watch her baby-giraffe legs totter down the corridor, her heels getting snagged in the thick carpet. I swallow a bitter taste in my mouth knowing that Dad never once brought Mum to one of these weekends. She didn't get taken to posh hotels to be paraded in front of his colleagues.

I can just imagine the comments he'll get tonight – men secretly patting him on the back, asking him how he bagged someone like Petra. Telling him that he's punching way above his weight. Dad will lap it all up and Petra will play the beautiful young wife to perfection. Will anyone even be bothered about the way he treated Mum? I doubt it. She's been airbrushed out of his life and now Dad's forcing me to play happy families with the woman he left her for.

I shut the door and fling myself on the bed, burying my face in the cloud-like duvet. I can't stop the torrent of tears and sobs.

I don't know how long it is before I'm all cried out, but when I eventually sit up I'm woozy. Shuffling to the bathroom I splash water on my face, staring at the reflection in the mirror – a puffy, blotchy, sad-eyed image stares back. A horrible sense of loneliness descends, but I can't let it overwhelm me. I'm not alone! I have people who care about me . . . love me. I grab my phone and WhatsApp the Amigos, praying that one of them will pick it up.

Zoe: This is all bullshit! He's got me here to babysit Petra while he has a work conference. It's not a birthday treat at all.

Ethan: Come home. You can't spend your birthday like this! Phone your mum and get her to pick you up or tell your dad to pay for a taxi.

Zoe: I can't phone Mum. She can't ever know and I'm not asking Dad. He'll make me stay.

Ethan: I wish I could help but Dad has our car at work. How far away are you?

Zoe: It's a good hour away. Don't worry about it, Ethan. I'm being a drama queen. I'm stuck in a four-star luxury hotel so don't feel sorry for me. I just needed to rant at someone.

Ethan: I'll ring you.

Zoe: No. Go to bed. I'm fine. I'll call tomorrow. Xx

"Room service," a voice calls out from the other side of the door. The young man wheels in a trolley piled with plates covered with domed lids. I scramble around in my purse and find a tip for him.

"Is everything all right, miss?" he asks, obviously noticing my tear-stained face.

"Yes, everything's great. Thanks," I say, shutting the door behind him. I lift the lids off the dishes. They should smell delicious but I've lost my appetite. I force a piece of steak down my throat, hoping it will make me feel better but it just sits like a stone in my belly.

I don't know what to do. Maybe I should get a shower and try to sleep. I'll work out how to get a lift from someone in the morning. My phone rings and my stomach flutters as Jack's name flashes up.

"Jack?"

"Hi, Zoe, how's your weekend away going?" Just the sound of his lovely voice is going to start me crying again.

"Not so great," I say tearfully. I'm too exhausted and

miserable not to be honest.

"Tell me what's happened," he says in that calming, reassuring voice of his, and I do. I tell him everything.

He listens without interrupting then asks, "What do you want to do, Zoe?"

"I want to go home," I whisper. "But I'm stuck here."

"Where are you?"

"It's called the Great Valleys Country House Hotel. It's miles away," I say despondently.

"OK. I've got it up. It'll take us about sixty-five minutes to get to you."

"Oh, no, Jack. You can't come and fetch me. I'm fine," I say, startled.

"Hang on a minute." There's the sound of muffled voices then Jack says, "That's settled. Mum insists we come and collect you. She'll be more than happy to."

"No, I can't let you do this. It's too much."

"We want to. We'll meet you in the hotel lobby. I'll let you know when we're nearly there. Make sure you tell your dad that you're leaving – I don't want him to think you've been kidnapped," he says.

I'm speechless. Jack and his mum are really going to do this for me. I garble an inadequate thank you, but he's already gone.

*

The doors to the Banquet Hall are shut, but I can hear all the chatter and laughter coming from Dad and his work mates.

I *could* march in and announce that I'm going home in front of them all, but even though I'm furious, I don't want to humiliate him; I just want him to be a good dad.

I ask for a pen and paper at reception and write a note to tell him that I've got a lift home with a friend. I tell him that I wanted to spend my birthday weekend with him, not at a work conference playing happy families with his new wife.

I ask the receptionist to give it to him once the meal has finished and then I zip up my jacket, sling my rucksack over my back and wait on the steps of the hotel, looking out for Jack's parents' car.

The white four-wheel drive cuts through the darkness as it glides down the drive. Annie stops right outside the entrance, her engine still running, like a getaway driver ready to whisk me away.

"Hello, Zoe," she calls out, her hair falling around her face. "Hop in the back with Jack and we'll get you home."

I'm gushing with thanks as I climb into the warm car next to Jack. Despite it being nearly midnight, Jack is as fresh-faced as ever. I envy him. Some people are just lucky like that; it's in their genes. They can party all night and still look amazing in the morning, not like me. If I don't get my full eight hours, dark circles appear under my eyes like a partial eclipse.

"How are you feeling?" Jack asks, gazing at me with his doe-eyes.

"Much better now I can go home," I smile. "This is so kind of you and your mum. I feel embarrassed. It was a really nice place, it's just. . ." I swallow. "Anyway, thank you."

"Well, I wasn't going to leave you there, having a miserable time on your birthday."

"Oh." I hadn't realized he knew.

"I didn't forget your birthday," he says, like he's just read my mind. He passes me a beautifully-wrapped package. It's the shape and size of a book. I can't stop grinning at him. I've got a feeling it's going to be a copy of *Wuthering Heights*, but as I rip the paper off, the title reveals itself and I fight to keep the smile on my face.

"Wow," I say, hoping I sound genuine. "*The Clean Eating Bible*."

"Do you like it?" He seems eager for my approval. "That book is changing people's lives, Zoe. The woman who wrote it is an inspiration. I wanted to share it with you."

"Yeah, right, well, that's good news." I flick through it, pretending to be interested, but the artistically-photographed plates of food don't look enough to feed a mouse. "Thanks, Jack, that's very thoughtful of you."

"I've got you something else as well," he beams.

"Oh, no, Jack. You shouldn't have." He hands me an envelope and I pull out a ticket – a ticket for The Cave Dwellers gig! The one that I was desperate to go to with Sonja and Jodie. Jack remembered! It must have cost him at least sixty quid.

"Oh my god!" I say breathlessly. "Thanks so much – but this is too much. I can't let you buy me this."

"Of course you can, Zoe. I'll be upset if you don't. I know how much you wanted to see them." He smiles at me. "And I just want you to be happy."

I swear that my heart misses a beat. I look towards his mum. Can she hear how romantic he's being? I wonder what she's thinking; but she keeps her eyes on the road in silence.

"Should we take a photo? I'd like us to remember this," he says.

"Yeah, sure." It'd be great to have a photo of us together. He leans in to me and puts his face close to mine.

"Why don't you hold up the book?" he suggests, angling his phone.

I give my best toothy smile and hold the book under my chin as he takes The Cave Dwellers ticket and we try out different poses, taking shot after shot.

He fiddles with his phone before saying, "I dreamed about you last night."

"You're making a habit of this," I say shyly. "Are you going to tell me?"

"Sure," he says, looking into my eyes. "We were on a train travelling through Europe. There was beautiful countryside rolling past the window. It was so sunny and bright. We'd only just met but we got talking and there was this incredible connection between us..."

"I know this one," I interrupt, laughing nervously. "Does it have a different ending this time?"

"I think you're getting muddled up, Jack," his mother says. Her voice is soft, but it makes me jump.

"Sorry for repeating myself, Zoe. I got muddled up," he

says, like a little kid.

I reach across and touch his arm. "That's OK." His expression is blank. Poor Jack. I'm so worried about him. Two weeks is too long to wait for his appointment at the hospital. The thought of him being affected by the head injury is unbearable.

For the rest of the journey, I do my best to keep the atmosphere light. We play tracks for each other, sitting close, the earphones stretched between us. I hum along to the music, taking sneaky looks at Jack as he beats out the rhythm on his knees with impeccable timing. A dull ache builds in my chest as if my heart is swelling. I want to know how it would feel to kiss this boy who's gorgeous inside and out. This incredible boy who cares about me so much.

I let my hand rest next to his so that our little fingers touch. He gives a nod. A stupid grin spreads across my face. I love his little quirks, all those things he says and does that make him like no other boy I've ever met. But as we sit so close to each other, an uneasy sensation creeps over me. I feel like I'm being watched. I raise my gaze and see Annie's eyes on us in the rear-view mirror, a strange, unreadable smile on her face.

CHAPTER 16

I was surprised when Ethan texted this morning and said he'd call for me, so we could walk in together.

"Where's Jack?" I ask him. "Why aren't you two power-walking into college today?"

"I just thought it would be nice to spend some time together … just the two of us," he says as we skid along the frozen pavements towards Hinton Dale. "I saw the photos of you on his Instagram."

"Really? Which photos?"

"The one in the back of the car with you holding up the presents he bought you. Tickets for The Cave Dwellers!" His cheeks flush. "I'm sorry that the only thing you got from me were those stupid recordings."

"Ethan, I love your present. It's gorgeous … unique," I say, fumbling for my phone and bringing up Jack's Instagram.

I stare at the photos Jack took on Friday. I didn't know he was going to post them. I read the caption:

Got my best girl, Zoe, a couple of birthday treats. We're aiming to live for ever (well, almost) with a little help from @CleanEatingBible. Managed to grab her last available tickets for the awesome #CaveDwellers @GoGig.co.uk Happy (Birth)Days!

It's got a ton of likes and comments. They're all nice enough . . . enthusing about clean eating or saying how lucky I am to get tickets for the gig and what an awesome site GoGig is. There are comments from people saying that they wouldn't mind living for ever if it was with Jack, and even more declaring stuff like:

Zoe must be one special girl! Not jealous (much) 😉

My stomach churns. I know that for Jack it's natural to put everything on Instagram, but it makes me feel exposed. I thought that moment was just between us. I swipe the page and try to forget about it as we enter the alleyway leading to the park.

"Still no sign of Bullseye," I say, as we pass his empty garden, the lost-dog poster tied to the gate now soggy and unreadable.

Ethan doesn't respond. He seems deep in thought. As

we approach a sheet of black ice on the ground, he offers me his hand.

I wave it away, laughing. "Thank you, but I don't need a knight in shining armour."

"Unless his name is Jack Cartwright," Ethan says under his breath.

I pretend to ignore his comment and change the subject.

"How many steps have you done today?" I ask, pointing to his Go-Getter monitor.

"I don't know," he says abruptly. "Who cares?"

"Well, I thought *you* cared. Look how fit you've got," I say enthusiastically. "If you keep training with Jack, you'll be running marathons soon."

"I don't want to train with him any more," he says coldly.

"Why? I thought you enjoyed it, and you and Jack are such good mates."

"I'm not so sure about that," he mutters, kicking a block of frozen soil down the park path.

I give him a playful shove. "What do you mean?"

He shakes his head, picks up the pace. "Nothing ... ignore me."

I grab his arm to slow him down. "No, you can't say something like that then shut down on me. I want to know."

"You're going to think I'm being stupid." He stares at the ground.

"I won't ... I promise." I'm bursting and dreading hearing what he's got to say.

He takes a deep breath. "OK, but you'll think I'm crazy."

"Try me."

He stops and turns to face me. "That night we were meant to be meeting at the multiplex ... it wasn't normal, Zoe, I've never slept like that before."

"Yeah," I say, hanging on his every word.

"Well, remember I told you that me and Jack did a work-out?"

"Yeah."

"I practically had to crawl home after. I was *so* exhausted that I fell asleep and missed our date."

I shake my head, bemused. "You're not suggesting that Jack made you do a massive work-out, just so you'd fall asleep?"

I'm laughing but Ethan isn't. "I think he did more than that. I think he might have drugged me."

My mouth drops open. "Please tell me you're not being serious?"

"I know it sounds totally bizarre, but I can't think how else it happened. At the end of the work-out he gave me this energy drink and straight away I started to feel weird ... woozy. I thought it was because I was knackered, but the more I've been thinking about it, the more I'm convinced that there was something in it. I basically collapsed on my bed and woke up all those hours later with the most massive headache."

I take a step away from him, my hands on my hips. "Let me get this straight. You think Jack drugged you? Why would he do that?"

Ethan chews on his lip before saying, "So I'd miss the movie date with you and he could step in."

I hold my heads up in disbelief. "Jack's your friend, Ethan. *I'm* your friend, your best friend, so believe me when I say please don't ever repeat to anyone what you've just told me, or you'll get yourself sectioned."

"I knew you'd react like this."

"Ethan, stop!" I dread saying it, but I can't ignore it now. "Is all *this* because you're jealous of Jack?"

He recoils like my words are an electric shock. "I don't know what you're on about," he says weakly.

"I'm sorry, Ethan. I know that things got a little . . . weird between us the other week but we're best friends and I don't want anything getting in the way of that. Your friendship is too important to me. You understand what I'm saying, don't you?"

His head drops, his voice is thick as he struggles to speak. "I've imagined telling you how I *really* feel a hundred times, but never like this. It wasn't meant to be like *this*. I know it's pathetic, but I only agreed to let Jack train me because I was so desperate. I thought if I got fit . . . bulked up, you might start seeing me differently, as someone you could fancy, not just a scrawny, lanky boy who'll only ever be your friend."

My heart aches. To actually hear Ethan confess his feelings is so strange and confusing. He's opening up. He's putting everything on the line.

"Oh, Ethan," I say, tears brimming in my eyes. "I don't want you to *bulk-up* . . . to change. You're perfect just the way you are."

"But as a friend," he says, his voice full of trepidation. "You mean that I'm perfect as a friend?"

I can't answer. I'm not sure what I mean, but the one thing that *I am* sure about is that I don't want to jeopardize our years of friendship for what could be some short-lived, misguided romance and, anyway, there's Jack now and he's changed everything.

"Listen, I get it. You don't feel the same way," Ethan says quietly, sorrow etched on his sweet face. "But I'm worried about you and Jack. I'm not making it up – I really think he gave me something that day to make me pass out. All to get closer to you." He looks me in the eye, swallowing down his emotion. "I think you need to be careful. Don't get involved with him."

"Stop it, Ethan. I know you're hurt, but you're out of order."

"You can't trust him. Give me a bit more time and I'll prove it," he says urgently.

I turn and march away, sad and worried about him. He's acting paranoid, crazy. I thought I knew Ethan inside out, but I don't recognize him when he's behaving like this.

*

Sonja, Jodie and I are leaning on the noisy radiator in the common room. Ethan is in the corner, working. He's obviously trying to avoid me. I hate that we're like this.

"What's up with Ethan?" Sonja asks.

"Don't know." I shrug, not wanting to get into it with them; hoping that if I give Ethan some space he'll come to his senses and everything will be OK.

I'm aware that I'm getting stares from other students, particularly the girls. Eventually, one of them comes over, a girl called Tanya who hangs out with Pete West and the partying crowd.

"Hi, Zoe, guys," she says. "Listen, a few of us were thinking of having a night out in town next Saturday. If you guys want to come, just let me know."

"Thanks," Jodie replies, amused.

"We'll have a laugh." She looks directly at me. "And, Zoe, if you want to bring Jack along, that's fine by us."

I try not to smirk as I thank her, and she strolls off.

Jodie digs me in the ribs. "I think she was trying to be subtle. I hope you've got your diary ready for all the invitations you're going to get now everyone's seen on Instagram that you're Jack's 'best girl'."

I grin but cringe a little inside. I don't want people to suddenly think I'm worth knowing just because I'm with Jack.

"I still can't believe him and his mum drove all that way to rescue you in the deep of night," Sonja says dramatically.

"He's like some romantic hero," Jodie chimes in. "It's a wonder he didn't arrive on horseback and whisk you away."

"*And* he bought you The Cave Dwellers ticket! He's just . . . he's just *perfect*," Sonja swoons.

"Yeah," I whisper. "I think he might just be."

"Speak of the devil!" Jodie announces as Jack heads our way.

We watch as he stops by Ethan's desk. I don't hear what

they're saying, but Ethan quickly packs his rucksack and heads out.

"What's wrong with Ethan?" Jack asks when he reaches us.

Jodie and Sonja shrug.

I can't tell him about Ethan's drugging accusation, he'll think that Ethan is insane. But I should tell him something at least. I take Jack's elbow and lead him to a quieter spot in the hall.

"Listen, Jack, I know that you and Ethan are good mates, but if he's behaving a bit off with you, then maybe you just need to give him a bit of space. He'll come around eventually."

"It's because of me and you, isn't it? He jealous," Jack says suddenly.

My eyebrows raise in surprise. I hadn't realized that Jack had picked up on Ethan's jealousy.

"You do know that Ethan is in love with you," Jack says matter of factly.

How does he know that? Did Ethan confide his feelings about me to Jack? If that's the case, then no wonder Ethan's angry with him and making up bizarre accusations; he's had to watch as Jack has got closer and closer to me. He must feel so betrayed.

"Did Ethan actually tell you how he felt?" I say tensely.

"No, but it's obvious."

"How's it obvious?"

Jack leans towards me, saying gently, "Have you never noticed how protective he is of you? How his pupils dilate when he looks at you? How he mirrors your body language, watches your mouth when you talk?"

I struggle for words as my chest tightens with a thrilling tension. Is Jack talking about Ethan or himself? He does all those things. He must be aware of that.

A gradual silence descends on the hall and I realize that Mr Dunn has entered and is poised to give his weekly assembly. I lean against the wall, my arms crossed. Jack does the same.

Everyone seems to be paying Mr Dunn more attention than usual. Heads sway left then right, trying to get a better view of him. I go up on my tiptoes and see why. Mr Dunn has a dressing across his nose. The strip of white bandage is stuck down on either side with plasters.

"About time he had that nose job," Jason Caston stage-whispers to discreet laughter.

"Good morning, ladies and gentlemen," Mr Dunn says. "I come bearing good news." No one can quite believe how animated he sounds. "Student welfare and satisfaction is of paramount concern at Hinton Dale College and, therefore, I'm delighted to announce that the governors and stakeholders of the college have agreed to provide students with the equipment requested for the common room."

Mr Dunn goes for maximum impact as the common room door opens and the caretaker and his team wheel in a table tennis and pool table and plump plastic-covered sofas. There's rapturous applause as all the goodies are set up.

"The vending machines and air hockey will arrive next

week. Enjoy, but treat this equipment well, or it will disappear as quickly as it's appeared. And no playing for money!" Mr Dunn looks almost jolly as he trots out of the hall.

Everyone clambers excitedly around the games, rushing to have a go, but Jack stays in the background.

"Why's Mr Dunn suddenly become Father Christmas?" I ask, sensing Jack knows something about this.

"It's confidential," he whispers. "But, as I advised, Mr Dunn had the mole on his nose checked out and it was cancerous."

"No way!"

"They removed it all the next day. It hadn't spread. He's in the clear, but as you can imagine, he's very grateful."

I shake my head, awestruck. "You really are something else, Jack Cartwright."

"So are you, Zoe Littlewood," he says, causing that exquisite dull ache in my chest again.

CHAPTER 17

I stand in my bedroom. Staring into space, deep in thought. God, I hope Ethan is all right – that crazy accusation against Jack and the look on his face when I said we would only ever be friends – it was like I'd destroyed him.

My instinct is to call him, but my head is warning me not to. I'd only make things worse because I can't say anything that he wants to hear. He needs time to come to terms with it. Maybe then we can get back to how we were. I sigh despondently. Who am I kidding? Even if Ethan can move past his feelings for me, he'll never accept me going out with Jack. They were such good mates, but now Ethan seems to have developed a special kind of resentment towards him.

How would a psychologist label Ethan's behaviour, a "displacement of anger", "a fixation" or maybe it's simply powerful, poisonous jealousy? I never could have imagined that Ethan would act this way.

Jack will be here soon and, despite my concern for Ethan, I can't help being excited.

I *had* invited Jack around for dinner. Mum volunteered to cook and was even going to use recipes out of *The Clean Eating Bible* to try to impress him. It was so lovely of her. She must have picked up how happy I was about him coming round. But in the end Jack said he had training and would come after dinner instead, which has worked out better because I need time to tidy this room. It's a mess!

I grab an armful of dirty clothes from the corner of the room and I shove them in the washing basket. I gather my pots of foundation and bags of make-up off the floor and stuff them in drawers. My college notes are littered all over the place, but I put them in piles on my desk to give the illusion that I'm organized. I look down at my carpet and grimace. Now that I've cleared the floor, I've exposed all the stains. I frantically vacuum, but the machine is spitting out more dust than it's picking up. Opening a window, I cough up dirt into the cold air.

My sequinned duvet is hanging off the bed. I straighten it and plump the pillows and then strategically move my *Romeo + Juliet* poster over a peeling patch of wallpaper. I light my orange blossom candle to mask the slight damp smell that pervades the whole house, then I stand in the middle of my bijou room, surveying my efforts – it's not looking terrible, but what will Jack think? His bedroom was immaculate. In fact, the whole place was like a show home; everything stylish and pristine. I take a deep breath to put a brake on my stupid worries. I've got to stop stressing! Jack likes me for *me*. He won't care whether the house is a palace or a hovel, but maybe I'll keep the lighting "subtle", just in case.

I stifle a squeak at the sound of the doorbell. What is wrong with me? I've got to calm down. I race down the stairs, but Mum gets to the door before me.

She opens the front door with a flourish. "Welcome, Jack!"

Jack gives a little nod and presents her with an elegant bouquet of flowers. "For you, Emma."

"Well, how gorgeous! Thank you," she says, her nose in the bouquet. "Let's go through to the living room." She leads him the few steps down the hall.

I give Jack a little shove, whispering playfully in his ear, "You creep."

He looks at me, confused. "I thought it would be a nice gesture."

"It is . . . they are. I was only joking," I say reassuringly.

When we enter the living room I can tell that Mum's been busy tidying too. "What would you like to drink, Jack?"

"Nothing for me, thanks, Emma."

"I'll have a cup of tea, please, Mum," I say.

"OK, I'll join you," she says. "And I'll put these beautiful flowers in a vase."

As soon as she leaves the room, Jack beckons me to sit next to him on the sofa. He takes my hand. "I've missed you," he says.

"Don't be daft. I only saw you a few hours ago at college," I say.

"I know, but I miss you every minute that we're not together."

"Ha, ha," I respond sarcastically, though he looks completely serious. He means it! My cheeks fire up. He's not holding back about his feelings. I'm completely flattered but also disconcerted. Mum walks back into the room, carrying a tray with two china cup and saucers. I smile inwardly. She's using the best crockery.

She hands me a cup and sits, straight-backed, on the other sofa. "So, Jack, do you feel settled here? Are you enjoying college?"

"Yes, it feels like home. And college is great. I've met the best people there," he says, turning to me.

Mum tries to stop herself grinning. "Zoe told me that your parents moved because of work," she says, doing that adult small talk thing all parents feel they have to do.

"That's right. They both work for an insurance company in town." He smiles politely.

"And have *they* settled in? It must be so hard moving into a new area and not knowing anyone."

"I think they're fine. They don't need to go out much. They're happy to just hang out as a family."

Mum's eyes soften, and I see sadness in them. We were a family once.

"You've got a lovely house, Emma," Jack says, looking around the tired room with its woodchip wallpaper. I want to tell him to stop trying so hard.

"Thanks," Mum says uncertainly.

"Mum, me and Jack are going upstairs, OK?" I beckon him to get up, before he starts complimenting our horrible patterned carpet and electric fire.

I shut the bedroom door behind us and quickly kick a stray bra under the bed as his eyes scan the room. I put on some Cave Dwellers to distract him.

"I've got something for you," he says, delving into his rucksack. I wait, feeling apprehensive. I hope it's something small, something silly, but it's not. It's an iPad, brand new in its box. This is so awkward.

"But . . . but these things cost loads," I splutter, knowing that me and Mum would never be able to afford one.

"Look, it was a freebie," he says. "Dad got it at work and we have enough of them at home already."

"No, Jack, this is just too much." I push it away. "Thank you, but I can't accept it."

"Please take it, Zoe." He cocks his head on one side, looking adorable. "It'll make me happy if you take it."

I waver, looking from the iPad to his pleading face. "OK, thank you."

"Great! Let me help you set it all up."

We sit next to each other on my narrow single bed, his legs dangling off the side. It feels so intimate. I keep stealing glances at him, but he's absorbed in tapping at the screen.

"Here," he says at last. "I've installed all these apps. Now let's set up these accounts for you."

"What accounts?" I ask.

"For Twitter, Snapchat, Instagram, Facebook and a couple of new platforms that everyone is going to be moving on to soon. It's good to have all the options and then you can try them out and see which of them suits your style best," he says, handing me the iPad.

"Oh, thanks, but I'm not really bothered."

"Oh," he says, obviously disappointed. "I was hoping that you'd want to post photos of us together. I want the whole world to know about you and me."

I feel bad. He's being massively romantic. He must think I'm so ungrateful. "I know that this makes me sound like a weirdo, but I've tried it and all the social media stuff really wasn't working for me, so I deleted my accounts," I say apologetically.

"But nothing on the internet is ever really deleted." He says it like it's a good thing, but the thought of it unsettles me. "Someone with the right skills could always retrieve it."

"Well it wouldn't be worth retrieving my stuff. I just posted my favourite music videos and clips of movies. The best thing on it was Jodie doing a tour of my bedroom using her David Attenborough voice." I start laughing, remembering how much fun we had making that stupid video.

"It sounds like you gave up because you weren't getting the most out of it. It's an amazing way to connect with people," Jack persists.

"Maybe that's because people actually follow you and you don't have to worry about getting no likes for every comment you make," I reply sighing.

"Come on," he coaxes, giving me a playful shove. "Give it another go. I'd be able to tag you in my posts and it'll send people your way. People will start following you too."

I hesitate. There's no denying that it's tempting, but I'm not sure I want to get sucked into it all; I'd waste so much time trying to come up with witty and interesting posts to try to keep any followers that came to me just because I'm with Jack. It could just be a stress.

"Do it!" Jack says, grinning. "How else are you going to leave your mark on the world? Get your message out there about something that's important to you?"

I shrug, confused by his intensity. "I don't really have a message for the world; even if I did, I doubt anyone would be interested in hearing it. Anyway, most people just use it to talk about *stuff,* which is fine by me, but I can talk about that with my mates."

"OK." He puts the iPad down and I see that he is frowning. "Maybe another time, then."

My phone beeps with a message from Dad arranging our next meet-up. I'm in no rush to answer him.

"Anything important?" Jack asks.

"Just my dad."

"What did he say about you leaving the hotel?"

I exhale deeply. "He refuses to see what my problem was. He thinks I was just being an ungrateful, stroppy teenager." My voice wobbles and I bite my lip; I can't cry in front of Jack. I won't.

Jack takes my hand and I find I keep talking.

"But it's not all Dad's fault. Petra must have insisted on coming along. *Petra* is the one taking up all his weekends so that he couldn't rearrange." I grit my teeth. "I'm sorry. You must think I'm all bitter and twisted."

"No, I don't. I understand why you're angry with her and you're worried that Petra will get pregnant soon and try to write you out of his life."

My eyes widen. Has Jack remembered every single word that I've ever said to him? "Yeah, but still . . . I shouldn't be laying my problems on you."

"I need to know, because anything that makes you unhappy, makes me unhappy and I want to make things better for you."

Oh my god, he is so sweet. I instinctively wrap my arms around his neck and lay my head against his chest. The blood is pumping so hard in my skull that I can't even hear his heart beating, but I'm distracted by a cloying smell. It's getting stronger. What is it?

I sit upright and look at Jack. "Can you smell that?" I ask him, scrunching up my nose.

"No, what?" he asks.

I start to cough as acrid fumes crawl into my throat. It smells like . . . like . . . a burning tyre? I jump off the bed and see the flame from my orange blossom candle licking the soles of Jack's trainers as they dangle over it.

"Move, Jack! Your trainers!" I shove his legs out of the way and blow the candle out. Covering my hand with my sleeves, I pull his trainers off his feet and rush to throw the windows open to let the fumes escape.

"Oh my god, are you all right? Are your feet burned?" I splutter.

He's inspecting the trainers calmly. "No, I'm fine. The flame has only scorched the soles."

I look at where the rubber soles had begun to melt and twist in the heat. I feel wobbly at the thought of what could have happened if it had lasted a minute longer; the flames taking hold and burning him.

"I'm so sorry, Jack. I shouldn't have put the candle on the floor! It was so stupid of me. I'll buy you a new pair of trainers," I say, feeling terrible.

He wraps his arms around me and kisses the top of my head. "There's no need. Although, to be fair, it *was* your fault. Because I can't concentrate on anything else when I'm with you."

CHAPTER 18

I turn up the dial on the electric fire. The fake coals glow orange as it heats the living room. Mum wraps her hand around her mug of tea as she keeps one eye on the television.

"Even the local news is depressing. What happened to all the feel-good stories they used to show?" she sighs, nodding at the screen.

"Turn it over, then," I say as I settle at the opposite end of the sofa and stretch my legs out. Mum lifts my sock-clad feet on to her lap and absentmindedly rubs my toes. It brings a smile to my face.

"Is your dad going to rearrange your weekend away?" Mum asks, sipping her tea.

I feel a twinge of guilt. Mum had spent that Friday night at Karen's from work, so when she got home on Saturday and found me in the house I'd told her that I'd cancelled the weekend away with Dad at the last minute because I had a stomach bug. She didn't question it, and she's still none the wiser, because I knew Dad wouldn't tell her what happened. Anyway, I shouldn't feel bad about lying. I'm doing it to protect her. Mum would never forgive Dad if she knew the truth.

"Yeah, he will. I guess it's a busy time for him," I mumble.

"I'm sure he'll do his best," she says unconvincingly. "Anyway, tell me your news. How are your friends?"

I haven't told Mum about my falling out with Ethan. She'll be upset. She thinks the world of him.

"Everyone's fine, thanks, Mum."

"And how's Jack? He really does seem like a lovely young man."

"I'm glad you like him, Mum. He's great. I like him *a lot*." I'm blushing just thinking about him.

She grins, patting my hand and yawning. "Well, I'm happy for you, Zoe. He's welcome here any time. Listen, I'm going to get off to bed. Turn everything off before you come up."

"I'm going up myself now anyway." I step towards the TV to press the button, but the words of the local news presenter make every muscle in my body freeze.

"Police are looking for a person caught on CCTV disposing of a dog's body behind Arlington Row shops," the presenter says, her face solemn. "Please be warned that some viewers may find this footage upsetting."

I'm transfixed by the images on the screen. The grainy black-and-white footage shows a hooded figure illuminated from above by a security light, walking into the refuse area behind the local shops. He's carrying something in his arms that's wrapped in a sheet. The person struggles to lift the lid of one of the big dumpsters with just one hand. The sheet gets snagged on the edge of the container and peels away, revealing the inert body of a dog. The figure hurriedly tosses the dog inside, before leaning into the dumpster to cover the body with bags of rubbish and cardboard packaging. They keep their hooded head bowed as they close the lid and hurry away.

I feel for the sofa as I stagger back, the words of the presenter floating in the air.

"The dog has been identified as a five-year-old Staffordshire Bull Terrier called Bullseye, who had been reported missing by his owner in the Hinton Dale area. The CCTV footage was recorded at 9.05 on the night of Friday the ninth of November. The police are asking the public to help them identify the figure in the video. If you have any information, please call the number coming up on the screen . . . and now let's see what the weather has in store for us."

"Zoe, you look like you're going to be sick. What's the matter?" Mum's face looms in front of me.

"Did you see that?" I whisper.

"Yes. Horrible! Who'd do such a wicked thing to an animal?"

"What was he wearing?" I hold my breath, praying that I'm wrong.

She looks at me in surprise. "As far as I could see it looked like joggers, trainers and a hoodie with a Union Jack on."

*

Mum fusses over me as I make my way up the stairs, gripping the rail.

"Is it that dog report that's upset you?" she calls after me. "Or maybe you've picked some bug up at college? Get straight into bed and if you're still feeling unwell in the morning then take the day off."

I shut the door and stand in the middle of my bedroom in a daze. It can't be Ethan . . . it can't be!

My phone buzzes. Jodie's face fills the screen, all wild-eyed and agitated.

"Did you just see the local news?" Her voice is strained.

I nod.

"Tell me that wasn't Ethan."

"It could be anyone. Loads of boys could have that hoodie." I try to sound confident.

"Agreed, but how many of them have threatened to sort out that exact dog?" she says.

The hairs on my arms stand up as goosebumps erupt on my skin. "Ethan would never do something like that," I say firmly.

"I know, but he was so wound up about Bullseye. Don't you remember how angry he was when he tried to attack us? And he said he would sort him out. He said he didn't want you to be scared of him ever again."

I remember. I conjure up his expression when I told him that Bullseye had gone missing. He hadn't seemed surprised.

"That figure in the video didn't seem like Ethan. He didn't walk the same. He was taller," I say desperately.

"You couldn't tell how tall he was," Jodie replies.

"But this is *Ethan* we're talking about. He isn't capable of killing an animal," I protest.

"Yeah, but here's what I think happened; Bullseye got over the gate and jumped at Ethan and he killed him by accident, defending himself."

"I'm not sure," I sigh.

"Think about it; Ethan just panicked and tried to hide the body. No one could blame him. Would you want to tell that thug of a man you'd just accidentally killed his dog?"

"Well, no, but..."

"We need to know the truth," Jodie says urgently. "We can help him. Will you talk to him, Zo? You're his best mate."

"Things are sort of . . . weird between us at the moment," I say weakly. I know she's right, though; if Ethan will open up to anyone, it'll be me. "OK, but listen, Jodie; only you, me, Sonja and Jack know that Ethan threatened to sort Bullseye out, so we keep it to ourselves. We give Ethan a chance to clear this up."

"I won't tell anyone," she says. "Just let me know what Ethan says."

I take a minute before I get up Ethan's number, but I can only stare at it. How can I ask him whether he did such an horrendous thing? I've got to think straight . . . I'll phone Jack, talk it through with him. He always keeps his cool in situations; he'll be able to help me see things clearly.

I feel such relief when he picks up.

"Hi, Zoe," he says sweetly. "I was just thinking about you."

"Jack, did you watch the local news just now?" I say abruptly.

"No, why?"

I tell him about the footage and he listens without interrupting.

"He was wearing Ethan's hoodie," I finish, and he doesn't respond. "So, what do you think?" I ask anxiously. "There's no way it's Ethan, is there?"

"No," he says at last. "Of course not." There's something hollow in his voice, though.

"Really?" I push.

Silence again. Then he says, "Look, I've got to be honest with you; he was really worked up about the dog. When we walked to college he'd mention it most days. He said more than once that he'd make sure the dog could never harm you."

"But that was just talk, wasn't it? Just Ethan sounding off."

"Of course it was! You know how he feels about you. He was just being protective."

"The news report said it happened on a Friday night, the ninth of November." I rub my forehead, trying to remember what happened that day.

"Friday the ninth?" Jack says ponderously.

"Yes, why? Does that date mean anything to you?"

"Absolutely," he says cheerfully. "You can stop worrying. That was the day before the cinema. It couldn't have been Ethan. We went for a run that night. He *was* wearing his Union Jacket hoodie; he usually does, but I was with him."

I let an enormous sigh of relief. "I knew it couldn't have been him."

"Yes, we'd gone for a late run. I felt bad because we hadn't been going for long when I realized I was meant to be online, playing Underground with Pete and the others. So, I had to abandon Ethan, but he kept going; said he'd do a few more kilometres."

"What time was that?"

"Hmm, I probably left him around eight-thirty," Jack says.

My hand tightens around the phone. "Eight-thirty? But the footage was filmed at five-past nine."

There's silence from the other end of the phone.

"Jack?"

"Listen, it wouldn't be Ethan. He'll have an alibi. Don't worry about him." His voice drops slightly. "I can't wait to see you tomorrow."

"You too. Thanks. Goodnight," I say distractedly, ending the call.

I tell myself that everything is going to be OK. Ethan was probably home by nine o'clock. His parents will be able to vouch for him. Yes, I won't call him now. I'll wait and see if he mentions something in the morning. I have faith it wasn't him. He wouldn't have done this. I know Ethan. He wouldn't.

CHAPTER 19

Sonja, Jodie and I sit anxiously on the seats in the stadium as we listen to Jack.

"The police called me before I left for college. They must have spoken to Ethan already. They were asking me whether I was with him that night and what time I left. I had to tell them the truth," Jack says.

"Of course you did," I say, picking the varnish off my nails in agitation. "But how did they know it could have been Ethan? None of you gave them his name, did you?"

"As if we would!" Jodie says crossly.

"Sorry . . . sorry. I know you wouldn't," I say guiltily. "I'm just so stressed about him. He's missed all his classes this morning. He's not answering his phone."

Jack rubs my back reassuringly.

"Ethan!" Jodie suddenly shouts over my head as he makes his way up the steps, his head bowed.

"We've been worried about you," Sonja says, hurrying towards him.

He stands in front of us. He looks dreadful, exhausted, his eyes bloodshot, his face deathly pale.

"The police have been around." His voice falters. "That dog – Bullseye – has been found dead in a dumpster. They obviously think I did it." He runs his hands down his weary face. "Apparently they've got CCTV of a figure dumping the body. He's wearing a hoodie like mine. Someone saw it on the local news last night and gave them my name."

"Sit down, Ethan," I say, guiding him on to the bench. "Tell us what happened."

I sit next to him while Jack keeps his distance. Sonja and Jodie loom over us, the tension crackling as we wait for him to explain.

Ethan stares at his hands. "They interviewed me this morning. I told them that I was out running with Jack that night."

Jack moves towards him, saying gently, "Yes, they called me. I told them there's no way it was you, but I had to say that I left you around eight-thirty. I'm sorry I couldn't tell them any different, mate."

"Well, what time did you get back from your run? Can your parents vouch for you?" Jodie asks.

"No, I didn't get home until after nine-thirty. I'd got into a good rhythm and Jack wanted me to keep it up, so I just kept running. They said the dog was put in the dumpster about nine o'clock. They said that I was in the area and would have had time to abduct Bullseye from the garden in Hinton Dale and dump it behind Arlington Row shops."

"But why would they even think you'd *want* to kill Bullseye?" Sonja asks. "The police don't know that you have any connection to him. As far as they know he's just some random dog."

"No." Ethan bites his lip. "They know the connection. They have a record of my complaint about a dangerous dog, about how I thought Bullseye would escape and attack someone. They sent the officer round who I'd dealt with. He said that he remembered how angry I'd seemed when he'd told me the police couldn't do anything about the dog. He reckoned it was too much of a coincidence that the CCTV showed a figure wearing the exact clothing that I own. He bagged up my hoodie to put through forensics. He said this was a serious crime and did I have anything I wanted to tell him before things got a lot worse." Ethan's voice trails off and he drops his head into his hands.

An ominous silence hangs in the air.

Jodie breaks it, her voice small and nervous. "But you didn't hurt that dog, did you, Ethan? Even by accident? You could tell us – we're your friends."

Ethan sits bolt upright. "Wait – you think I did it?" He jumps up. "You think I killed that dog?"

"Sit down, Ethan." I hold on to the sleeve of his coat. "Let's talk this through. We can help you sort this out."

"Sort what out?" His horrified gaze rakes over me. "You

think I did it too! Do you *all* think it was me?" He searches our expressions.

"You did keep threatening to sort out the dog," Jodie say softly.

"Once! I was angry and worried about him hurting Zoe, but I wouldn't *kill* him."

"It was more than once, Ethan. You used to talk about it all the time," Jodie says. "On your way to college."

Ethan's mouth drops. He glares at Jack with pure hate. "Is that what *he's* been saying?" He jabs a finger at Jack. "He's a liar!"

"Calm down, Ethan," Jack says. "We're on your side."

Ethan turns to me. "Zoe, you don't believe him, do you?"

The truth is I don't know what to believe. "Ethan I . . . I. . ." My words trail off.

He walks down the steps and out of the stadium. I get up to go after him but Jack puts his arm around me.

"Leave him, Zoe," he says gently. "He needs some time to calm down. Maybe you can persuade him to still play in the match later? It'll do him good, take his mind off things."

"OK," I mumble. "I'll talk to Ethan when he's calmer." But I don't know what to say to him. I want to believe him, but my head is ruling my heart.

*

Thanks to Jack, Mr Dunn has already supplied us with what we asked for in the common room, but people were still keen to play the football match, especially if it meant getting a designer jacket thrown in. Everyone but me seems to have convinced themselves that accepting the clothes is OK, particularly once they heard that Jack was going to. As I stand in my thin cagoule, getting wet through, I try not to doubt my decision. I hope people don't think I'm just being self-righteous.

One of the PE teachers is meant to be supervising, but the driving rain has made him retreat to the shelter of the dug-out where he waves us on encouragingly. Everyone's milling round, comparing their Voltage jackets, but Amanda Parry is monopolizing Jack's attention; anxious that he looks at an Instagram picture of her dinner.

"It's a recipe I made from *The Clean Eating Bible* but I put my own twist on it. I bought some of that spirulina you mentioned. I was so pleased with it," she trills.

"Wow, Amanda, that looks delicious. Did you get the spirulina from the Super Foods website?"

"No, I found it in a health food shop in town."

"Well, it's up to you, but I'd go to Super Foods next time," Jack says enthusiastically. "I can get you a discount code too."

"Yeah, sure." Amanda beams at him.

People jostle her out of the way as Jack gathers us round for a group photo. He waves me over to him, wrapping his arm around me. I'm bursting with pride, but I notice Amanda trying to hide her bitterness with a rictus smile. It's obvious that she can't work out why Jack is with me.

He gets one of the team to take a ton of pictures. Jack uploads them on Instagram and we all pull out our phones to look at them, reading his caption:

#Voltage jackets mean rain never stops play #Sports4all #HintonDaleCollege

Jack looks gorgeous and I look like a drowned rat, my hair plastered to my face, my eyeliner running down my cheeks. I can't believe how many followers he has; the number just keeps growing and growing. I guess people can't get enough of looking at a fit, handsome boy. I swipe through his recent pictures. There are no drunken antics or laddish behaviour. Each photo oozes health and positivity. He gets endless questions from people asking him where he gets clothes, how he gets his teeth so white, what diet he recommends, whether they can meet up with him. He's full of fun lifestyle tips and each post has links to products to help you achieve them. Just looking at his photos and videos makes you want to look after yourself more; resist that packet of crisps, go for a jog, help someone out . . . just be better.

I peel off my soaking jacket and wander around the pitch, vaguely guessing where I should stand, while Jack tries to direct everyone. Jack's certainly got his "inclusive" game. Some players are a lot sportier than others, but even Jodie and Sonja have invested in the tracksuits that Jack wears for his after-school training sessions. I'm distracted as, all over the pitch, I keep hearing famous voices coming from Go-Getters encouraging people to "keep going" and informing them that they've earned money off this and that. It can't be just me who thinks it all sounds bizarre.

I look towards the college, there's still no sign of Ethan.

I hate to think it, but maybe it's best if he doesn't turn up for the match. I can't work out how people got to know, but everyone's been watching the footage shown on the local news. All afternoon I've heard talk about it, in the common room, in the corridors, even in the girls' toilets. Then, in our psychology class, I saw Eliza Trent nudging the girl next to her as Ethan took his seat at a table on his own. He obviously wants to let me know that he feels I've let him down.

I heard Eliza whispering that the police had charged Ethan with killing a dog. I looked across the room and scowled, hoping to shut her up, hoping that Ethan hadn't heard. If he did, he didn't show it. He just kept his head down and then quickly left the classroom when the bell went. I guess he probably went straight home. I'll call him later . . . when I figure out what to say.

Jack has taken off his jacket and stands in the middle of the pitch in his black-and-white referee strip. He couldn't find a whistle, so he holds up a mini foghorn to start play, but I wave at him to wait, as I spot Ethan walking towards the pitch in his kit.

Ethan looks so serious as he takes up his position in attack. My stomach starts to churn as I hear mutterings from around the pitch.

"What's *he* doing here? Dog killers aren't welcome," Aaron Lewis says loud and clear for Ethan to hear.

Ethan ignores him and starts jumping up and down to warm up.

"Hey, what kind of sicko kills an animal?" Pete West shouts out.

Jack calls for everyone's attention and then blasts the foghorn for kick-off.

To my relief, things seem better once the game gets started. Everyone's too busy chasing the ball and panting to waste their breath insulting Ethan. Jodie and Sonja are meant to be on opposing teams, but they've both gravitated to the side-lines, chatting. Suddenly the ball sails over and rebounds off Jodie's head. She squeals in protest as me and Sonja fall about laughing. Despite water dripping down my top and my lungs bursting with the exertion of running, I can feel myself beginning to enjoy the game.

I try to stay focused as there's a throw-in and the ball rockets towards me. I put my left foot out but it sails straight past. Pete West gets it and starts dribbling it up the pitch. But then I see Ethan sprint towards him. He's surprisingly skilful as he intercepts the ball. Players rush towards him, so Ethan crosses the ball to Amanda and then runs into the penalty box, calling for her to pass. Even I can tell that their goalie is way too far off his line. It's practically an open goal and Ethan is in the perfect position to knock it in. Ethan waves and shouts at Amanda but she ignores him and kicks the ball back in my direction instead. I boot it towards Ethan but as he rushes towards it Jason Caston rams into him, felling him to the ground.

I look to Jack, waiting for him to respond, but he doesn't seem to have noticed. Ethan picks himself off the grass, muddy and dripping wet. He narrows his eyes at Jason, though he keeps his mouth shut.

"Hey, ref," I shout. "That was a foul!" None of my team are joining in my protest.

Ethan signals to me to let it go. I shake my head at Jack but he just rushes the game on, giving the other side a free kick. Seconds later the ball glides into the back of the net. My team mates are grumbling.

"Get Ethan Mansfield off. They wouldn't have scored if he hadn't given away that free kick," Aaron Lewis complains loudly.

"That's crap," I shout. "Ethan was fouled."

I look over to the PE teacher, but he's walking back towards the college with his phone to his ear.

Jack seems oblivious to all the tension on the pitch. He blasts the horn and Helen Rogers kicks the ball from the centre. I keep an eye on Ethan, worried about him. He seems more determined than ever to prove he can score. He flies towards the ball, but a boy comes at him from behind and slide tackles, taking Ethan's legs from under him. He lands face-down with a thud as water sprays up around him. I hear laughter from a couple of girls on the other team. I glower at them but one mouths at me, "He deserves it."

I sprint over to Ethan and offer him my hand, but he waves me away, embarrassed. He clambers up and shakes himself down, but there's watery blood flowing from his mouth where his lip has split.

"Ethan, your lip's bleeding. Maybe you should go off," I say quietly.

"No!" He wipes his bloody chin with his sleeve. "That's what they want . . . to make me go. To shame me. Well, I'm not going anywhere. I haven't done anything wrong."

"I'll get you some water," I say, running to the dug-out where Justine sits on the bench engrossed in playing Roulette on that casino app.

"Where's sir gone?" I ask her.

"He got a call. His kid has thrown up at nursery, he's got to collect her," Justine replies, not even looking up from her game.

"Play on!" I hear Jack call. I throw my arms up at him. How can he *not* have noticed that foul? Why doesn't he book that boy? He could have broken Ethan's leg. Jack needs to get them in order. Everyone respects him; one word from him would calm people down, stop them picking on Ethan.

I search for water on the bench, but the only one around is Jack's red bottle. I hand it to Ethan, who tips it to his mouth, before shaking his head.

"Empty," he mutters, looking determined to keep playing.

I go over to Jack, trying to be discreet. "Jack, can't you see that Ethan is being fouled?" I whisper. "People are targeting him on purpose. You've got to protect him. Book people, send them off. Show them it's not OK."

"I haven't noticed any fouling, Zoe," he replies, taking his water bottle from me. "It's just all part of the game." He unscrews the top and seems to take a swig.

I look at him, baffled.

"What's wrong?" he asks, as he takes another gulp. There is no water in there.

I tear my eyes away, my heart thumping in confusion. "Nothing." I can't get distracted from helping Ethan. "Just please look out for Ethan," I say, as I run back to the left wing.

There's a throw-in and a mad scramble for the ball. Two boys from my English class clash into Ethan, one on either side. His body is crushed like a nut shell being cracked. Ethan falls to his knees, gasping in pain.

"Stop the game. Ethan's hurt!" I rush over.

Jack marches towards us and tells me to give Ethan some space. He lifts Ethan effortlessly, holding him tightly for a second, but Ethan pulls away, his face is contorted by fury.

"What did you say? What did you say?" Ethan roars.

Jack frowns and turns his back on him, walking away calmly. But Ethan charges and shoves Jack to the ground. Jack quickly rolls over, and Ethan straddles him, pinning him down.

Ethan pulls a clenched fist back. Blood-stained spit sprays out of his mouth as his chest heaves.

"'Zoe will never love a dog killer' – that's what you said, isn't it?" Ethan snarls. His nostrils flare as his knuckles turn white. I've never seen Ethan like this.

"What are you talking about?" says Jack. "I know you're under stress, Ethan, but don't take it out on me."

Ethan isn't listening. He aims his fist at Jack.

"No, Ethan, don't!" I plead.

He draws back his arm to strike, but, at the last second, he slams it into the ground instead. Jack just lies there passively, the drizzling rain falling into his eyes.

"Enough!" Aaron Lewis says, grabbing Ethan by the shoulders and dragging him off Jack.

Ethan staggers back, looking startled, disorientated.

"Zoe?" He stares at me, his eyes full of tears, his fist raw and swollen, but I can't bear to even look at him. I'm ashamed of him.

"Go away, Ethan." My voice quivers with anger

"Piss off, you psycho. Killing dogs, attacking people who are trying to help you. You've got problems, mate. You need locking up," Aaron shouts.

Ethan stands there for a moment, looking utterly lost and alone. Everyone forms a protective circle round Jack. Shutting Ethan out. I'm scared for him. The mood has turned ugly.

"Please, Ethan, go," I say bitterly.

His eyes meet mine and I see the hurt in them. Then he backs away, and, turning, he sprints out of the college grounds like a fox being hunted.

Jack gets back on his feet, surrounded by people checking he's OK. He has that blank look on his face again. The same look he had in his bedroom.

I signal for Jodie to take Jack's hand and I take the other. We lead him towards the college, leaving behind the worried crowd on the pitch.

"Give me your phone and I'll call your mum. She can pick

you up," I say, taking his phone from him. He doesn't resist, just stares ahead.

"We'll let the nurse check you out. Just to be on the safe side, isn't that right, Jodie?" I say, trying to sound upbeat.

"Yeah. We just want to give the nurse something to do. She gets bored in that little cupboard of hers," Jodie laughs nervously.

I grimace as Annie's number goes to voicemail. "Hi, Annie, it's Zoe. Nothing to panic about. I'm probably being way too cautious, but Jack had a fall playing football and, well . . . I'm a bit worried, so we're just taking him the college nurse to get checked out. Could you come and pick him up?"

The college corridors are practically empty. There's just the odd teacher who's stayed behind after the last bell, so I'm relieved when I see the door of the nurse's office is open and I hear her chattering voice.

I knock and we shepherd Jack inside the disinfectant-smelling room where posters of vile diseases cover the walls.

"Must go, Bev, I've got students here," Mrs Bracknell says, ending her phone call and putting down her biscuit. She looks Jack up and down and then asks him to sit on the chair next to her desk as me and Jodie hover anxiously at his side. "Well, young man, you look a bit *dazed*. What have you been doing?"

To our relief Jack speaks, but he's staring right through her. "I'm fine. I'm OK. I need to go home."

"Hmm, I'm not sure that you are OK, my lad," Mrs Bracknell says, taking her notepad out. "What's your name?"

"Jack Cartwright. I'm sixteen. My parents are Annie and Rob Cartwright. I live at 32, Horton Drive. I came here from Somerset in July. It was a big move, but I like it here. I like Zoe Littlewood. She's very special to me."

His words melt my heart but it's too odd to be saying that here ... now. I fiddle nervously with my earrings, keeping quiet so the nurse can do her job.

"What happened to you?" Mrs Bracknell asks casually, though I watch her eyes assessing him.

"Ethan killed Bullseye. Ethan isn't well," he says, and a shiver goes down my spine.

"Jack had an accident a few weeks ago. He hit his head and ended up in hospital and now he's just been pushed over on the football pitch. He didn't seem to hurt his head again, but since he got up he's been like *this*," Jodie explains to the nurse.

"Right, then, well, let's check you out, young man," Mrs Bracknell says gently as she leans over and gets a small torch out of her drawer. "Let me just have a quick look in those eyes of yours." She turns on the light and raises it to Jack's left eye. Without warning his arms seem to spasm uncontrollably. They knock the torch clean out of Mrs Bracknell's hand, causing it to fly across the room and smash into the wall.

Mrs Bracknell tries to hide her alarm. We all hold our breath until Jack's arms come to rest.

"Sorry, sorry, sorry." Jack's voice sounds like machine-gun fire.

"Oh, you mustn't apologize, Jack. You've done nothing wrong." Mrs Bracknell smiles to mask her concern. "Has that happened before . . . the spasms?"

Before he can answer, the office door is flung open and his mum and dad rush in.

"Jack, darling, are you OK?" Annie says. She's flushed and wet from the rain.

"Mum, I'm fine. Don't panic. I'm fine . . . I'm fine."

Jack's dad bends down to him, trying to make eye contact. "Stop, Jack!" he says firmly. Jack's head bows as his dad's words seem to calm him.

Annie sighs in relief. "Thank you all for looking after him," she says to us. "Was it a bad fall?"

"No," I answer. "But he seems quite dazed . . . disorientated. Like the other day in his bedroom." I look at Rob knowingly.

Mrs Bracknell rises from her chair. "Hello, Mr and Mrs Cartwright. I'm Mrs Bracknell, the college nurse. Would you mind if we all sat down for a moment? I was just assessing Jack."

Annie takes Jack's hand and leads him towards the door. "This is no disrespect to you, Mrs Bracknell, but I feel Jack may require more expertise than you can provide," she says abruptly, walking out.

Mrs Bracknell straightens her blue uniform as she calls after them. "I quite agree, Mrs Cartwright, and I strongly advise you to take Jack to A&E. He's disorientated, his speech is impaired and he's just experienced significant spasms of the arms."

Jack's mum and dad buffer him as they escort him down the corridor. Me and Jodie follow behind.

"Annie," I call after her anxiously. "Please let me know how he is."

She turns to me and kisses me on the forehead, taking me by surprise. "Of course I will, Zoe. You're very special to Jack."

We watch as they hurry out of the building, Jack's voice echoing down the corridor, "She's very special to me."

CHAPTER 20

My stomach twists as I ring the bell of number 814. Ethan didn't come into college yesterday and he isn't answering his phone. I can't just do nothing. If he's at home, I'm going to make him talk to me.

I'm worried about Jack too – he stayed home today. We've been messaging each other and he's behaving like it was no big deal, but he must realize that things aren't right. When I asked him what the doctors in A&E said, he replied they checked him out and thought it was fine to wait for his appointment with the neurology department. I didn't want to stress him, but I said he shouldn't wait that long. I think I may have overstepped the mark, as his reply was uncharacteristically frosty. He said that the medics knew better than me and I was to stop worrying. After that I thought it best to let the subject drop, for now.

Lily opens the door of their flat with a harassed smile.

She looks exhausted. Jimmy, Amy and Reece are running in circles around her, playing chase. They greet me with a chorus of hellos and grab my hands, leading me into the living room, where I find a creation made of cardboard boxes in the middle of the room.

"We've built a monster's cave. Amy lives in it 'cos she's the scary, ugly one." Jimmy falls into fits of giggles at his own joke.

Amy puts her hands on her hips. "You're the stinky, disgusting monster and I'm the princess coming to *kill* you with my sword." She pokes him in his belly with her finger and Jimmy pretends to collapse on to Reece, who squeals as he pushes him off.

"Stop it, all of you. I just need you to play nicely for ten minutes without upsetting or hurting one another. Can you do that?" Lily sounds at breaking point.

The kids obviously pick up that she's stressed, and nod their heads, saying angelically, "Yes, Mum."

"Lily, is Ethan in?" I ask, trying to sound more casual than I feel.

"No, he went into town," she says.

"OK, then," I say, disappointed. "I'll let you get on."

"No, stay," Lily says, patting my hand. "We should talk." She leads me into the kitchen. I've known Lily most of my life, and she's always so easy to chat to, but I sense this is going to be different.

"Tea, coffee?" Lily says, putting the kettle on. Lily is usually bustling around the place, multi-tasking, full of energy, but today she seems so drained.

"Tea, please." I look at her apprehensively as her eyes fill with tears. "Are you OK, Lily?"

"Not really. It's this awful business about the dog," she says, struggling not to break down.

"Yes, it's terrible."

"It's ridiculous," she says, her voice rising. "I don't believe for one second that my son is capable of killing an animal and dumping it in the trash."

I shift uncomfortably on the kitchen chair.

She looks at me, upset. "Zoe, you don't believe it, do you?"

"No, of course not," I say, crushing down my doubt. "It's just . . . he was really wound up about the dog . . . and he has that exact hoodie. It could have been an accident."

"It's all circumstantial," she snaps. "They took his clothes away and told us that forensics could take up to two weeks. But it won't show a thing, anyway, as they'd all been washed."

"When?"

"That night. Ethan came home, had a shower and put them straight in the washing machine."

I look at her unsurely.

"You're being as bad as the police. They tried to make out he was getting rid of evidence when, in fact, it's perfectly normal for Ethan to put on a wash; you know how helpful he is."

I lower my gaze, embarrassed. Of course I do. That sounds just like Ethan, but still. . .

"How's he meant to prove he's innocent when they've

already decided that he's guilty?" she says despondently as she pours out our mugs of tea.

I steel myself for what I need to say. "Lily, to be honest, I've been worried about Ethan for a while. He seems . . . not himself. That night we were meant to meet at the cinema – did he tell you why he didn't come?"

She piles dirty breakfast bowls into the sink and starts washing them vigorously. "Yes, I know why – he fell asleep after training with Jack. He was devastated that someone had tried to mug you and he wasn't there to help you."

I pick up the tea towel and start drying the breakfast bowls. I've got to tell her. She needs to know all the facts. "But did he tell you that he blames Jack for that? He's saying that Jack drugged him to make him miss the date and yesterday, he – well, he almost punched Jack when we were playing football."

Lily freezes. The bowl that she's holding hangs, dripping in mid-air.

"Lily?" I say gently.

She lets out a stuttering sigh and sits down at the kitchen table, her head in her wet hands. "That's awful. I didn't know. He hasn't said anything to me or Simon. All we knew was that he'd stopped training with Jack. He told me he was bored of it. We were disappointed, I suppose. The training had been great for him. But – well, I thought I knew the real reason why he'd stopped." Lily looks at me knowingly.

"Why?" I ask tentatively.

She takes my hand. "Zoe, Ethan isn't one to shout about

his feelings. He hasn't discussed this with me, but I wouldn't be a very good mother if I couldn't tell how my own son felt about you."

My cheeks burn.

"You've been best friends since you were little, but for so long now I've seen how Ethan behaves around you, how he looks at you, talks about you. And now he's jealous, Zoe. He's jealous because he sees any hope of you two getting together fading away when he sees you with Jack."

My face crumples. "I'll always love Ethan, but he's changed the rules and I don't know what to think and now . . . there's Jack," I mumble, trying to articulate something that I've not worked out myself yet.

"You don't need to explain. Neither of you can help how you feel. What I'm more concerned about right now is how he's dealing with all this. Unless. . ." She rubs her forehead deep in thought. "Unless there is something in what he says."

"You don't believe what he's saying about Jack drugging him, do you?" I ask in disbelief.

Lily stares at the table. "It sounds too outrageous to be true – but I saw him that morning, Zoe, and it wasn't normal. He complained of a terrible headache, he could hardly move. He was so groggy that I thought he might be coming down with flu. It took him the rest of the day to recover."

"Couldn't it have been exhaustion?" I ask.

"Maybe . . . probably," she says, shaking off her doubts. "Simon and I will talk to Ethan. We'll ask him about his accusations against Jack. We'll listen and try to get to the bottom of it – but he needs your support, Zoe." She looks at me beseechingly. "I know that you're in a difficult position, but I'm asking you, as his dearest friend, to stick by him through this. Once we clear his name over this dog being killed, Ethan will be in a better place."

"Of course, Lily." I meet her eyes squarely. "I'll always be here for Ethan."

"Thank you, Zoe." She checks her phone. "I'd better get ready. Simon will be home in an hour and then I'm on until eleven."

A thought hits me. "Lily, are you and Simon still working on the healthcare of the elderly wards?"

"Yes, it's non-stop. We're understaffed and there are always people waiting for beds." She shakes her head in frustration.

"Do you know anyone in the neurology department at St Monica's?" I ask eagerly.

"Not the surgeons, but I know their secretaries quite well. We liaise over patients' appointments and I sometimes go up to the department."

"OK." My excitement is growing. "Well, Jack has an appointment there in ten days or so. But something is really wrong and he needs to be seen now. He's not been right since he hit his head outside the nightclub and he's been having these strange episodes, like mini seizures. I'm so worried about him, and his parents . . . well, they're really nice, but I think they need to get things moving. Could you go and see the secretary and check if his appointment can be hurried up? Maybe they'll find an earlier day, or a cancellation."

"I can't do something like that, Zoe, that's up to his parents," she says apologetically, but I'm not giving up.

"Please, Lily. Please! What harm can it do to just try?"

Lily sighs. "All right, Zoe. I can't promise anything, but I'll see what I can do. I'll have a word with the secretaries on Monday."

My shoulders drop as relief washes over me. "Thank you, Lily. Thank you! Everything's going to be OK. We're going to sort out Jack *and* Ethan, and put all this behind us."

CHAPTER 21

I'm walking around The Brontë Parsonage with Jack Cartwright. And I can't believe it.

I woke up this morning expecting to spend Sunday completing assignments and doing a grocery shop with Mum, but before I'd even had my breakfast, Jack called and asked me whether I'd like to go to Haworth.

"Haworth? The Brontë sisters' home? Today?" was all I could manage to say.

"Yeah, like we talked about, remember?" he'd said in that dreamily-smooth voice of his.

Of course, I remembered. I seem to remember every word that he utters. I should be giddy at the thought of this trip with him – but I can't stop thinking about Ethan.

Jack's mum insisted on driving us. Jack apologized, saying his mum was being cautious and didn't want him to go far without her in case he had "one of his funny turns". I'm just happy that Annie wants to keep an eye on him. Maybe she's realized how serious this could be. I still want to talk to her about it. So, when we parked up in Howarth, I took my chance while Jack put money in the meter.

"Annie, I know that they said in A&E you could wait for Jack's neuro appointment, but aren't you worried that he needs seeing straight away?" I said boldly.

She flashed me a sharp look. "I *had* him seen straight away and that's what we were advised. I think the medics know better than you, Zoe."

I cringed, suddenly feeling rude, like I was doubting her care for her own son.

Annie put an arm around me, softening. "I know that you're worried, Zoe. It's lovely that you're so concerned about him, but it's all under control. To be honest I'm worried too – about the boy Jack was so close to . . . Ethan, isn't it? He attacked Jack on the football pitch, didn't he? And aren't the police investigating him for killing a dog?" She shakes her head sadly. "He sounds like a very troubled young man. I've warned Jack to keep his distance from him and – well, maybe you should do the same."

Tears sprang to my eyes. Poor Ethan. But I couldn't blame Annie for wanting Jack to stay away from him.

"I didn't mean to upset you, Zoe," she said gently.

"No, it's OK," I sniffed. "I understand. It's just . . . Ethan isn't really like that." Even as I said it I realized it certainly didn't look that way. I saw Jack coming towards us and summoned a cheerful smile. I didn't want anything to ruin our day together.

We all walked to the centre of the village and Annie announced that she was going to stay and look around the shops, so me and Jack headed up the cobbled street to the Parsonage Museum and here we are, standing in the very dining room that Charlotte, Anne and Emily wrote their incredible novels.

It's pleasant enough with all its Victorian features and furniture, but it's not grand or showy, and I wouldn't want it to be. I think it's just perfect that in this unremarkable room, remarkable stories were written by young women with boundless imaginations and passion. I feel quite emotional as I inspect the shiny wooden table with the sisters' writing desks on it, surrounded by everyday things: cups and saucers, plates and candles, embroidery boxes and lace handkerchiefs, boring stuff that they were expected to do when inside their heads they were living other, much more exciting, lives.

"This is the original table, not a replica," says Jack in a reverential voice, as if we're in a church. "Every evening the sisters would walk around and around this table discussing their stories."

I picture them in my head. I hear them discussing their work, feeding off each other's ideas. It's awe-inspiring. I can feel the creativity pulsing around this table.

"After Emily and Anne died, Charlotte continued to walk around it every evening. She had to, or else she couldn't sleep," Jack says.

I bite my lip. "How sad. She must have missed them *so* much. They had such an incredible connection to each other."

"I know that feeling," Jack whispers to me.

My eyes widen. I turn my back on him and inspect the book-lined shelves so he can't see my blushing face. "How come you know all this? You're like the tour guide."

"I've been here before. I'm good at remembering things," he says matter of factly. "For example, Emily died in this room on the blue sofa over there."

I turn, staring at the velvet sofa. "That's horrible."

"I don't think so. She died in a place she loved, leaving an incredible legacy with her novel. They all died young. All the sisters, apart from Anne, are buried in the family vault beneath their father's church." He points out of the window to the graveyard and church beyond the small walled garden.

"Imagine writing in here and looking out at the dead every day," I muse. "Do you think Emily was influenced by it when she wrote about Heathcliff having Catherine's grave dug up so he could gaze upon her corpse?"

"Possibly; people are inevitably affected by their surroundings."

"It's such a disturbing scene," I say, picturing Heathcliff violating the grave of his lover.

"No," says Jack slowly. "It's an act of a man who's so passionately in love that he won't even let death part him from his soul mate. I think it's beautiful. It's what real love is all about."

"But he had no right to do it," I reply, surveying the bleak graveyard.

"Catherine wanted him to. She haunted him. Beckoning Heathcliff on to the moors after her death. When he died he wanted to be laid next to her with the sides of their coffins opened up so that he could 'absorb' Catherine's corpse into his and they could dissolve into each other. Don't you think that's romantic?"

"I think it's creepy," I whisper, not wanting to offend the room full of Brontë fans. "*You* must remember the rest of the quote? Heathcliff wants them to dissolve into each other, then Edgar will not be able to distinguish Catherine from him. I think Heathcliff wanted to do it as much for revenge on Edgar, as any act of love for Catherine."

"This is not my understanding of the text," Jack says so formally that I chuckle.

"Did I make a joke?" he asks seriously.

"No! I'm not laughing at you, honest," I say quickly. "Let's go upstairs. I want to see where they slept." I hope I haven't upset him. I've got to remind myself that Jack and I are still getting to know each other. It's not like talking to Ethan where we know each other inside out and don't need to explain things – at least that's how we *used* to be.

Jack takes my hand as we go upstairs, his palm smooth and cool. We climb the elegant staircase and he points out one of the bedroom doors off the landing. "That was their father's room, although he ended up having to share it with his son, Branwell."

"Was that normal, to share with your son?" I ask.

"No, but Branwell was an alcoholic and opium user. One night when he was drunk, he set his bed on fire. Emily saved him but after that they all kept a close eye on him, so he ended up sleeping in his father's room."

"I knew there was a brother, but you never hear that much about him," I say.

"He is written about, but only as a failure," Jack says. "Branwell was mentally weak, the three sisters were mentally strong. They used their talents, he wasted his. They're the ones who'll always be remembered."

He's right, but I can't help feeling sorry for Branwell. For people like Jack, being mentally strong and using your talents comes naturally; it's not so easy for someone like me . . . imperfect, unsure if I even have a talent. I let my hand slip out of his as we enter the main bedroom off the landing.

I'm surprised. I didn't expect it to be so bright, with its light blue walls, it gives it quite a modern feel but then, in the centre, is a large glass cabinet displaying one of Charlotte Brontë's outfits. I study her full-length, long-sleeved, high-necked dress. It's pinched in at the waist and at the foot of it is a matching bonnet, white stockings, gloves and a fan. It makes me claustrophobic just looking at it. It must have felt like being bound up every day, not able to let your body breathe.

Jack wanders over and stands next to me. "Their stories seem even more of an achievement when you see how restricted they were; young Victorian women in a countryside parsonage."

"But just look at the view from up here." I point to the window and the sweeping moors outside. "That's where their imaginations could run wild."

"Did you know what Charlotte said about Jane Austen's world? That it was limited as 'one sees there only a highly-cultivated garden and no open country'."

"Ouch, that's a bit bitchy," I say, disappointed at her lack of sisterhood.

"Charlotte didn't like the narrow, repressed world Austen wrote about," Jack says. "But we live in better times. Soon no one's experiences will be limited by where they live or their social class."

"That's a big claim. How come?" I ask curiously.

"Because everyone will be using virtual reality and, without even leaving your bedroom, the world, even other worlds, will be opened up to you. Any experience you can ever imagine can be shared by you and your friends together and all you'll have to do is connect to a VR system."

I frown at him. He's talking like a salesman. I didn't know he felt so passionately about this, but then there's still so much I've got to learn about him. I love his infectious enthusiasm and knowledge about so many different things, but I kind of hope he's not right about virtual reality. I don't like the idea of everyone getting hooked on it.

"That sounds incredible, in theory," I say carefully, "but the problem is we could become immersed in a fantasy life instead of spending time with people in the real world. It would all be fake."

"Why does it matter if it's fake, as long as the effect is the same? What you *feel* will still be real," he says with his usual certainty.

I haven't got an answer for him. I haven't got a mind like his to work out an instant argument. I know what my instincts tell me, but not how to explain it. So I keep my mouth shut.

We explore the rest of the parsonage, Jack filling me with facts and quotes that I can't even see on the information boards. It's all really interesting, but I'm starting to feel like I'm on a trip with a teacher not a boyfriend. As we make our way out of the parsonage and into the garden, we find a green-bronze statue of the three sisters. The expression on their faces, their loose clothes and even the way they stand, transforms them from their repressed Victorian era. Charlotte looks downwards pensively, but Emily has a wildness and passion about her as Anne stares skywards, as if breaking free from this world. I'm so engrossed in their images that I jump when Jack taps me on the shoulder.

"I've bought you a gift so that you'll remember our trip." He hands me a paper bag.

"Thanks, but it should be *me* getting *you* a gift for bringing me here," I say. I hope it isn't something expensive. I know that Jack can probably afford to keep buying me gifts, but I can't afford to reciprocate and it's making me feel bad.

I open the bag and slide out a trendy cardboard jewellery box. I open it tentatively and inside I find a silver-beaded chain with vintage dog-tags attached. I give Jack a sideways look, unable to stop my smile. I pick the tags up and, on one I see my name and date of birth, and on the other the engraving reads, *I am Heathcliff.*

"I had it inscribed last week, but I thought that here was the perfect place to give it to you. You'll know the quote. It's Catherine's declaration of how they are one and the same person." He takes the chain and gently turns me around as he places it around my neck and fastens the clasp, saying in his deep, smooth tone, "*I am Heathcliff. He is more myself than I am.*"

I can hardly breathe as that dull ache fills my chest again. It's so exquisitely romantic and thoughtful. "I love it. Thank you," I mutter inadequately.

"Should we walk to Top Withens? It's only a ruin now but they say it was the inspiration for the Earnshaws' home, Wuthering Heights," he says keenly.

I don't want to spoil the moment, but I'm aware of my stomach growling. "Can we grab something to eat first?" I ask. "It's way past lunchtime."

"Why don't we wait until after we've seen it? It's not far and we don't have to stay long." He gives me an irresistible smile. How can I say no? "We don't need to follow the path. We can cut across the moor," he says, taking my hand and leading me through the pretty Parson's Field behind the house. The field is strewn with meadow flowers struggling to survive in the cold. I stop and bend down to inhale them and tug at Jack's hand to do the same.

"Smell that violet one. It's gorgeous," I say.

Jack puts his nose to the flower obediently.

"The scent reminds me of something," I muse. "What do you think?"

He shrugs.

"Maybe it smells of those peardrop sweets you get in the big jars in some newsagents. You know, the pinky-white ones covered in sugar?"

"Let's keep going before we start to lose the light," he replies, obviously uninterested in discussing flowers and peardrops.

"Don't you ever eat sweets?" I say teasingly. "I bet before you became this health and fitness guru you loved to stuff your face with a packet of Minstrels, or was it Snickers bars? Come on, Jack, what was your favourite sweet when you were little?"

He looks at me blankly, and then says softly, "I'm sorry but I don't remember."

"Oh, OK," I say, feeling slightly awkward.

As soon as we step outside Parson's Field, we're on the rugged moors, and within minutes I feel like we could be the only people for miles. A vast slate sky hangs above us as we traipse past clusters of spindly purple heather springing from the uneven earth. Rocky crags of dark stone loom out of the landscape like gargoyles, weather-beaten trees stand proud against the elements and a sudden, biting wind, all combine to gives this place a beautiful bleakness. I grin with satisfaction. This is just how I'd imagined it. These moors can't have changed from when the sisters walked them two hundred years ago, letting the landscape fuel their imaginations.

I look across to Jack who is striding at such a pace that I'm struggling to keep up with him. His jacket is flapping madly in the wind, but his face is fixed. He seems like a man on a mission as we rush onwards. The pace and wind are making it hard for me to catch my breath, but it's exhilarating as we race towards Wuthering Heights.

I spot it on the higher ground, a naked lone tree beside crumbling stone walls. I'm glad that Jack told me it was a ruin, or else I would have been disappointed not to see the Wuthering Heights in my mind's eye. Still, the roofless walls show the outline of the house and the stone-carved plaque embedded in them explains that, even when complete, this farmhouse bore little resemblance to the house Emily describes in the novel, though the setting is more likely to be what she was imagining. I stand at the front of the ruins and look out across the never-ending moors; not one sign of civilization in sight. Yes, the setting is what this place is all about. A place with such a wild and brooding beauty, where you feel a world away from the restrictions of society. The perfect setting for a passionate, obsessive love to flourish and a twisted revenge to be played out.

"So, what do you think?" Jack stands at my side. He's looking at me, not the view. My skin prickles with anticipation but I keep my gaze on the moors.

"It's awe-inspiring. I can see why Emily chose to set *Wuthering Heights* here. It makes you feel alive. It shakes up all your senses."

"You don't know how much it means to me to be here with

you." He's bending his face down to mine. He's so close that I see his pupils flare. He has that delicious aftershave scent in his hair . . . on his clothes. I want to touch his impossibly flawless skin. My eyes keep flitting to his bow-shape mouth and plump pink-red lips. He's leaning in even closer. He puts his hands gently on my shoulders. It's finally going to happen – our first kiss.

Our lips touch; feather-light to begin with, as if we're testing each other, then slightly harder as they press together and I lean my body into his, my hands gripping his arms. I shut my eyes and lose myself in the softness of his mouth, and wait – for the heat, the spark. And I feel . . . I feel . . . nothing.

My lips don't tingle on his, my body isn't responding with yearning for him. It just feels strange . . . clinical. Like kissing someone you're not meant to kiss.

I pull away slowly, pretending the kiss has come to a natural end. What's wrong with me? This boy is gorgeous. I've wanted to kiss him; daydreamed about it. So why was there no passion, no connection? He must know it too. I drop my head. I can't bear the awkwardness, the disappointment. He must feel the same.

"I love you, Zoe."

My head shoots up, and I meet his eyes, startled.

"Did you hear me, Zoe? I love you."

I make an unintelligible noise. I can't find my words. He takes my hands and kisses them. He stands in silence, waiting for me to regain my senses. I say the first thing that comes to my mind, and it surprises both of us.

"But you can't."

"Why not?"

"Because . . . because. . ." I splutter. I don't know why not. Except that it's too soon.

"It's just all a bit sudden," I say tentatively.

"I understand," he says quietly. "You've been let down by Ethan. You're probably feeling like you can't trust anyone right now. But I'm not like him. You can depend on me."

My temper is pricked. I don't like him saying that. "Ethan hasn't *let me down*. He's just struggling at the moment."

"You're being too loyal to him," Jack says firmly. "After all these years you thought you knew him, but he's shown you that you don't. We've got to stop making excuses for Ethan."

Is he right? Am I so desperate to believe Ethan didn't kill Bullseye, that he isn't losing control of his senses, that I can't face the truth?

"Anyway, falling in love isn't about how long you've known someone, it's about the connection between two people, and I've never felt so close to anyone in my life. I love you, Zoe, and I'll always be here for you." He says it with such conviction, holding my gaze.

"But how do you know that you love me?" I ask in disbelief.

"I can't stop thinking about you. In college I can't concentrate because I'm counting down the minutes until I can see you. At night I can't sleep because I'm dreaming about you. I physically ache to be close to you; to hear your voice and see your face. The truth is I can hardly eat; my stomach is so churned up about you. I feel like we're part of each other and when you find your soul mate you can't let them go."

His words take my breath away. I stand, speechless, as the wind howls around us.

"Do you love *me*, Zoe? Please tell me that you feel the same."

His pupils seem to fill his eyes as he stares at me. His urgency is overwhelming. It's as if his life depended on it. But I can't say it. The meaning of the words is so enormous, and there's that kiss . . . that kiss! It felt wrong.

I need him to slow down. I summon all my confidence and say, "If you do love me, Jack, then you'll wait and give me time."

He pauses and then gives a little nod. "OK. I'll wait for you, Zoe."

I'm relieved. That was so intense. I feel that I can breathe again now. "Thank you, Jack, and thank you for what you said. I'm flattered you feel that way about me."

I wonder if he's really taken in what I've said as he gets out his phone and wraps an arm around my waist. "I don't ever want to forget this moment," he says, taking photo after photo of us as my face begins to ache with holding my fixed smile.

*

A silver bell tinkles above the door as we enter the quaint teashop off the cobbled street. I feel my bones warming up immediately after the bitterness of the moors. It's so lovely and cosy in here with a roaring fire and the smell of delicious cakes and coffee in the air. I spot Annie at a corner table with her back to us. We weave our way through the maze of tables and chairs filled with chattering customers. As I get nearer I see that Annie is on the phone so I signal to Jack not to disturb her. He waits patiently behind me. Annie hasn't noticed us and I'm so close that I can't help but overhear her conversation.

"OK, darling," she's saying. "Be good for your daddy. I'll see you next weekend. Bye. Love you." She lets out a sigh as she puts down her phone.

I stop, confused, and at that moment Annie turns her head and sees me. She jolts, gasping,

"Oh my god, Zoe! You gave me a fright."

"Sorry, Annie." I say distractedly, as I notice her iPad, which is lying on the table. Its screen is showing a video of this teashop. It seems to be filming her – us – right now. Annie tracks my gaze and switches the iPad off. She gathers up her things and stands too quickly, knocking the rest of her coffee over the tablecloth. She looks increasingly flustered as she struggles to get her coat on.

"I was just calling my niece, Maisy. She's my brother's girl . . . a total sweetheart. He's on his own with her at the moment, so I'm going to visit next weekend and help out."

"Oh, that's nice." I turn to Jack. "Are you going to help as well, Jack?"

Annie answers for him. "No, Jack will be staying at home."

"I'll be staying at home," he echoes.

Annie leaves some money on the soaked tablecloth and bustles us out of the café. I could really do with some food but she seems anxious to get out of there. As we head towards the car park, she seems to regain her composure. Jack slips his hand into mine.

"So, Zoe, how did you like Top Withens?" Annie asks eagerly.

"How do you know we went there?" I ask, surprised.

She pauses for a split-second before answering. "Jack told me he was planning to take you."

"Oh." I wonder what else Jack discussed with his mum before this trip. Did he tell her what he was going to say to me once we got to Top Withens? Is she waiting until they're alone to find out how I reacted to his declaration of love? I suddenly remember the way she looked at us in the rear-view mirror of her car on the way back from Dad's hotel; that strange smile.

"Yes," I reply, trying to mask my uncertainty. "I loved Top Withens. I love the whole place. Thanks for bringing me." I feel the pressure of Jack's fingers against mine. "It's been an unforgettable day."

CHAPTER 22

My fingers caress the engraved dog-tags hanging around my neck and Jack's playlist fills my head as I walk down the high street to college. Now each track is even more loaded with significance as I pay attention to every lyric. The Beach Boys' "God Only Knows" starts to play. Why hadn't I noticed that this song is like a poem of undying love? It's so obvious now that Jack has been trying to tell me how he feels even before his declaration yesterday.

Last night, when I got back from Howarth, my mind wouldn't shut down. It replayed every minute of that scene on the moors, every word Jack said, every gesture, every second of that kiss. How can two people kissing each other experience it in completely opposite ways? He'd obviously been swept away by it and I'd been left cold. Empty.

I check his Instagram and my heart sinks as I see photos of us at Top Withens:

Unforgettable day at most romantic spot on earth with Zoe Littlewood, my very own Cathy, at #WutheringHeights #IAmHeathcliff @ BronteParsonage

There are already so many likes and comments. I die a little inside as I read them – some are saying that I'm no Cathy because Cathy was meant to be beautiful, others tell Jack that he can do loads better than me. There are a few nice ones saying we're a cute couple, more asking where I got my dog-tag necklace and there are even a few saying they like my "look". But mostly the comments are just lusting after Jack, saying he can be their Heathcliff any time.

Even as I look at it the number of comments is growing. I wish Jack wouldn't post photos of me for the world to see. I thought that trip was about us; why does he have to turn everything he does into *content*? I don't want to be judged by a load of strangers and I don't want my love life on display, particularly when things are so new between us.

I quicken my pace, but as I pass the betting shop on the corner I see a man huddled up in a sleeping bag in the doorway. He calls out to me, "Any spare change, miss? It's freezing."

I pull one of my earphones out to speak to him. "I can buy you a bacon sandwich or something?" I nod to the café next door.

He pulls back his hood and gives me a crooked smile. A gold tooth glints in his mouth. "You're an angel. An egg and bacon bap and black coffee, three sugars, would be a life saver."

He stretches out his hands to clasp mine in thanks, and as I take them my eyes are drawn to the line of tattoos at the base of all his fingers, like he's wearing a row of black rings. I've seen them before. The man who tried to mug me had exactly these tattoos *and* a gold front tooth. How many people can there be with the same markings? My heartbeat quickens as I pull my hand out of his. It's him. I'm sure of it.

I know that I should phone the police but I'm so outraged that, before I can stop myself, I blurt out, "You tried to mug me." I step back, pointing my finger at him. "I was walking along the ring road by the multiplex, Saturday night, a few weeks ago and you came up from behind and tried to drag my bag off me."

His dirt-ingrained face looks startled. He puts his hood back up and retreats into his sleeping bag. "No, I didn't!" he growls indignantly.

"I'm sure it was you. You didn't get anything because my friend stopped you. He rugby-tackled you to the ground but you managed to get away."

His crumpled eyes show a flicker of recognition, but it's instantly replaced by hostility. "You can piss off if you're going to accuse me of crap just because I'm homeless."

"If it wasn't you, then you won't mind me calling the police to come and ask you a few questions," I say, getting out my phone.

"Don't call the police! They're looking for any excuse to

lock me up. You seem like a nice girl. Why don't you just give me a break?" he says, suddenly sounding vulnerable.

"Tell me the truth and I'll think about it." I'm feeling out of my depth.

"Fine," he says resignedly. He leans closer. "It wasn't a proper mugging – I don't do that kind of thing. I was never going to take your bag or hurt you, so there's no need for the cops to get involved."

I narrow my eyes at him. Does he really expect me to believe this? "You attacked me when I was walking alone at night," I rumble.

"Yeah, but it wasn't proper . . . it wasn't real. It was a set-up."

I stare at him, stunned as I struggle to find my voice. "What do you mean?" I'm trying to sound calm, but my heart is thumping.

"Listen, I was in the park one day, having a few cans, minding my own business, when this guy came up and asked if I wanted to make a bit of money. He said it would just be pretending to mug a girl but not hurting her or anything."

"What? Who was he?" I ask in disbelief.

He shifts in his sleeping bag, mumbling into the ground. "I don't know. He never gave me his name. He was a skinny white guy with round glasses, spiky hair. He told me where to be and when. He said just to grab your bag, make like I'm robbing you, but to not actually take it. He didn't tell me that some big lad would be jumping on me and nearly crush me to death," he says bitterly.

My mouth is dry. "Would you recognize this man if you saw him again?"

He takes on a sly look. "Doubt it. Doubt I'd even remember this conversation, to be honest."

"Why did he want you to do that to me?" I half-whisper.

The man shrugs. "How should I know? He gave me fifty quid; I didn't ask questions. It weren't a real mugging. I didn't hurt you or anything."

I shake my head in confusion. This must be a pack of lies.

"Don't call the cops, angel," he says, sounding sickly sweet. "I've told you all I know. And no harm was done. If I were you – " his eyes meet mine and there's a warning in them – "best leave this alone and forget all about it."

I'm too dazed to answer him as I back away and rush down the street.

*

As I walk into the common room, my head is still swimming. I can't think of anyone who'd want to do this to me, and his description of the man – if there even *was* a man – could describe thousands of people.

My stomach lurches as I see an animated crowd around Jack. My first thought is that he's having another seizure but then I notice Amanda Parry standing in the centre of the circle. Her eyes are encased in sci-fi-looking goggles. She's shrieking and howling, her arms raised, her legs wobbling.

Jack lifts the goggles off her and she collapses on the

floor, panting and laughing euphorically. "I've just jumped off the Statue of Liberty!" she rasps. "It was awesome!"

People clamour around Jack, wanting to be the next to try the VR goggles. Everyone's bombarding him with questions. They want to know how much they cost, where's the best place to buy them, what's the craziest thing they'll be able to experience.

Jack spots me over the crowd and politely excuses himself as he makes his way towards me. He cups my face between his hands. "What's the matter? You don't look very happy."

"I'm a bit shaken up, to be honest. I had a really weird encounter on the way here."

"Sit down. Tell me what happened," he says, shepherding me to an armchair and wrapping an arm around my shoulder. I relax against him. He's always so calm, cool, and in control; like he can sort anything out.

"Well, I came across the man who mugged me."

His eyebrows rise. "Zoe – are you OK?"

"Yeah, I'm fine – it was just . . . so freaky. He's a homeless guy. He was in a shop doorway and I was going to buy him some food but then I recognized him. Anyway, when I accused him. . ."

"What, you didn't ring the police first?" Jack interrupts in disbelief.

"Well, no. I realize it was stupid, but I couldn't stop myself. I was so outraged that I didn't feel in danger or anything and when I confronted him he swore that he was never going to properly mug me and that he'd been *paid* to do it."

There's a pause and then Jack says, "What? By who?"

"By some white skinny man wearing glasses who he met in a park."

I look to Jack for a response, but he seems to be staring ahead, deep in thought. A prolonged silence hangs between us, before he eventually says, "You didn't believe him, did you?"

I shrug. "No. I mean – well, I don't know what to think."

"But you didn't call the police?" he asks again.

"No – I needed some time to – well, think this over. See if there was anything in his story."

He sighs and rubs my back. "Oh, Zoe, how could you be so gullible? Who on earth would do something like that to you?"

I wince, feeling like an idiot. "OK, now I've said it out loud, I can see how ridiculous it sounds, but you've got to understand that he confused me. He sounded so convincing. Who'd make something like that up?""

"Yes, I bet he *sounded* convincing. He's taken advantage of your caring nature." He kisses my cheek like I'm a silly kid. "Call the police if you want, but I bet he'll be long gone by now. He won't show his face around here again."

Jack's right; I've just been conned by my own mugger. I feel ridiculous. I'm too embarrassed to phone the police. I need to forget all about it.

"Did you see the photos of us on the weekend?" Jack asks, showing me his Instagram. I take a breath; now's my chance to tell him that I'm uncomfortable with it. But I'm interrupted by Pete West.

"Hi, Jack, hi, Zoe." He smiles. He would have struggled to remember my name before I started seeing Jack. "Jack, can you show me how to unlock this new emote on Underground Revolution?"

It takes a second for me to register that he's talking about the computer game that everyone in the year seems obsessed with. I stare at Pete. He looks different somehow. It's his hair, I think. He's always worn it over his ears with a floppy fringe that he'd flick out of his eyes, but now it looks a lot like Jack's – short, glossy, neat with a side parting. I discreetly look him up and down. He's wearing a top and trainers that I've seen Jack wear a few times. I scan the common room. I'm taken aback by how many of the boys have started dressing like Jack; same brands, same style. It's almost as if Jack's clothing has become the college uniform. It's so strange. I didn't even notice it happening.

"Will you excuse us, Zoe?" Jack says, jolting me out of my thoughts. "I'm just going to sort this out for Pete."

Jodie and Sonja head my way with grins on their faces.

"Did you and Heathcliff have a nice time frolicking on the moors yesterday?" Jodie smirks.

"You've seen the photos, then?" I say joylessly.

"*Everyone's* seen them. Zoe, most boys' idea of a romantic date is a visit to Nando's; Jack takes you to *Wuthering bloody Heights*," Jodie coos, inspecting my dog-tags. "Oh my god, that boy needs cloning. We all deserve a Jack."

"But have you read all the nasty comments about me?" I whisper.

Sonja flaps her arms dismissively. "Ignore them, Zoe. They're just jealous."

"Have either of you heard from Ethan?" I ask, hoping that he's staying in touch with the girls, even if he isn't contacting me.

"No, he's not answering our messages. Have you been looking at the college message board?" Sonja says, stony-faced. "People have been posting angry stuff on there. They're all talking about the dog killing as if he's been convicted already. I pushed back, said he hasn't even been charged yet, and I got a load of abuse for just defending him."

"Yeah, and a few people want him kicked out of Hinton Dale. They're saying they don't feel safe with him around, especially after his attack on Jack," Jodie says gravely. "It won't be long before Mr Dunn gets to know."

My stomach twists with anxiety. I need to help Ethan and stop this hostility towards him escalating. "Maybe I can persuade Ethan to publicly apologize to Jack," I say. "Then Jack could tell people to lay off. He could say that Ethan is under a lot of stress, that he's not himself and that he needs their support. That he's innocent until proven guilty over Bullseye."

Sonja nods enthusiastically. "That would help. Everyone will respect what Jack says. They'll follow his lead."

Jodie looks less convinced. "The problem is getting Ethan to apologize. You saw him on that pitch. He wanted to smash Jack's face in. It looked like pure hate to me."

"Well, we're about to find out," Sonja says tensely, nodding at the figure walking towards us.

"Ethan!" I can hear the fake cheerfulness in my voice. I have to dial it down.

"Zoe, Jodie, Sonja," he says, with an unnerving smile on his face.

"How are you?" Jodie asks sympathetically.

"Wonderful, thanks, Jodie." He says it like he hasn't got a care in the world.

"Oh, well, that's great," she replies, exchanging a baffled look with me and Sonja.

"You know that we're here for you, Ethan," Sonja says gently.

"I know." His bravado starts to crack. "Thanks for defending me on the college message board, guys. You don't know how much I appreciate it. I'm sorry I haven't been returning your calls. It's been a rough few days."

I want to tell him that I would've defended him too, but if he's checked Instagram he'll already know I was too busy on a romantic day out with Jack.

"Don't let the bastards grind you down." Jodie punches him playfully on the shoulder.

"Sure, but it gets worse. There've been a ton of messages on Facebook from 'animal lovers' telling me I'm a murderer, hoping I get locked up, one message even threatened to break my neck and throw me in the trash." His voice is strained.

"I'm sorry, Ethan," Sonja says, squeezing his arm.

"I can handle it, but what I can't handle is people taking it out on my family." Tears well in his eyes.

"What's happened?" I ask in dread.

"Someone posted dog crap through our letter box this

morning. Reece saw it first. He tried to clear it up and he got it all over his hands and clothes." He swallows hard, holding back tears.

I picture little Reece trying his best to help, the vomit-inducing stink of it all over him.

"That's disgusting. We've got to put a stop to this. Listen, Ethan." I'm apprehensive, but plunge on. "You need all the support you can get. I think it would really help if you'd say sorry to Jack for what happened on Friday." His eyes meet mine with an unreadable expression in them. "I know he doesn't hold a grudge. He wants to support you and I'm sure that he'd tell the whole college to lay off you."

Ethan shakes his head defiantly. "No way. That's not happening."

"Please, Ethan. Help yourself," Jodie says, getting anxious as other students start to look over, realizing that Ethan is in the room. There's suddenly a palpable change of atmosphere. I instinctively step in front of Ethan in a pathetic attempt to shield him. And then I see Jack, coming through the crowd. Hope surges in me as I watch him stride towards us. There's an expression of calm determination on his face. I step aside so that the two boys can face each other.

"Ethan." Jack stretches out his hand. "Look, mate. I know that you're under a lot of stress. Let's forget about what happened on Friday? No hard feelings. Let's move on from this." His hand hovers there, waiting.

I feel the eyes of every student watching. I hold my breath, willing Ethan to shake it.

But Ethan doesn't. "No hard feelings?" he says in a mocking tone. He takes a step closer to Jack. "I *know* what you did. I know that you drugged me the night of the cinema and I bet you're framing me for killing that dog."

Jack shakes his head sadly. The room hisses with disgust as people start calling for Ethan to get out.

"Listen, *Jack*." Ethan is visibly seething now. "Your time is up. I *know*. So, you should enjoy all your little followers while you've still got the chance, because by the time I've finished, you won't find anyone who'll even talk to you."

The noise in the room rises to an outcry. People are swearing at Ethan, threatening him, telling him to leave and never come back.

I wait anxiously for Jack to say something to calm them down, to make them back off, but he doesn't. Instead Jack shrugs at Ethan, saying, "Have it your way. I'm not comfortable defending a dog killer, anyway."

Ethan smiles, a nasty smile, then pushes past Jack, knocking into his shoulder.

People jostle and heckle him as he heads towards the door.

I grab Jack's arm, saying urgently, "Jack, do something to stop them. Tell them Ethan isn't well. That he needs their support."

"Why should I?" he replies impassively. "He's brought this on himself."

I watch Ethan leave, watch the door slam behind him and I don't know what to do.

CHAPTER 23

Jack closes my bedroom door behind us and leans in towards me. I put my hand on his chest to keep him at a distance.

"Jack, I invited you around to talk about Ethan," I say seriously. "I know that he made some crazy accusations against you in the common room today, but can't you see that he's not well? I thought that you'd step in and tell people to back off when they started to attack him."

"Zoe, you were there, you saw me try to help him, but he wouldn't even shake my hand."

"I know. I guess I just expected someone like you to stand up for him *despite* that," I say earnestly. "Everyone at college looks up to you, Jack. All it would take is one word from you to make people leave him alone."

I'm caught by surprise as he cups my face between his hands and looks down at me. "Forget Ethan. Tell me something. Have you thought about the question I asked you?"

"What question?"

He cocks his head to one side, giving me a million-watt smile. "*The* question! The one I asked you yesterday on the moor." His voice drops seductively. "Do you love me?"

Why is he asking me again? Why is he asking me *now*?

"Jack, I told you that I needed time! I thought you understood," I say in an annoyed hush.

His head drops like a naughty schoolboy.

"I'm sorry, Zoe. I've been insensitive ... thoughtless. The last thing I want is for you to feel under any pressure." His voice sounds like that of a hurt child – it sends a pang through me. He's on the verge of crying. Maybe I'm being unfair to him. I lift his chin, wanting to comfort him, but I pull my hands away as he raises his head.

There's no sign of tears in his eyes. His face isn't crumpling with emotion.

"I feel so strongly about you that I assume you feel the same – and that's wrong of me, Zoe. Will you forgive me?"

He *sounds* full of passion, but there's something strange about him. It's his eyes. His eyes are cold and detached.

"Just give me some space, Jack," I say, unnerved, as my instincts tell me to get him out of here. Yes, I want him gone.

"You know I'd do anything for you," he says, his hands around my waist. "I'd never let anyone make you unhappy again, not your dad, not Ethan, not even Matt Gillingham."

I pull away from him, bemused. "Excuse me – *Matt Gillingham*? How do you know about him?"

"Jodie and Sonja told me what happened in Spain." He shakes his head. "He lied to you . . . used you."

I choose my words carefully. Ice is settling in my chest. "Listen, Jack, I don't know what the girls told you, but it was no big deal."

"It was, and that's why I posted the video on his Facebook page. Now everyone knows what kind of person he is." His voice is triumphant.

"What? *You* posted the video of him kissing that girl?"

"Yes. I did it for you. He made you unhappy, so it was only right that I made him unhappy."

I stare at him. My hands feel cold.

"Zoe, I hope I haven't upset you. I thought you'd be pleased," he says solemnly.

"Can't you see what a weird thing that was to do? You hardly even knew me when you did it!" I can't stop the tremor in my voice.

"But we're soul mates, Zoe – like one person. Like Cathy and Heathcliff." He takes hold of my dog-tags, toying with them. "If someone hurts you, it's as if they're hurting me."

I take a step back from him. I know that he's gorgeous and popular and every girl at college would love to be in my place, but suddenly everything about Jack Cartwright alarms me. The grand gestures, the presents, that kiss on the moors, his declaration of love – it all feels disturbing rather than romantic.

I brace myself, facing him. I have to do this, and I have to do it now.

"Jack, I'm not sure that this is working . . . you and me, I mean." I try to sound gentle. "You're wonderful . . . incredible, but maybe we should just be friends. There's so much going on at the moment; I really think this isn't the right time for us."

"Are you rejecting me?" He frowns.

"No," I say, startled. "I'm not *rejecting* you; I'm just saying I want you as a friend."

"But not a lover."

"No, not as a *boyfriend*," I reply, rattled.

His brow clears. "I understand. You're not convinced that I love you, but give me time and I'll prove it to you."

"No, Jack, you don't need to prove it. I just want to be friends," I say firmly. There's a silence.

"OK," he says abruptly. "Let's not mention it again." He pulls the chair from under my desk. "I'll sit here, and you can sit on the bed. Let's watch a movie."

I sit down stiffly on the bed. Hasn't he taken in what I've just said? Why doesn't he just go? I shouldn't have mentioned still wanting to be friends. I have to think of a way to get him out of here.

"Give me your iPad and I'll find the movie," he says brightly.

"I'm not in the mood for a movie, Jack. In fact, I've got a bit of a headache. It's best if you go."

"Oh, please, it's called *Before Sunrise*. It's one of my favourites. I'd love to share it with you," he says, getting it up on the screen.

Before I can even protest, Jack's phone rings.

"Hi, Dad," Jack says. "OK. Ten minutes? OK."

"Anything wrong?" I ask as he hangs up.

"No. Dad just wants me home. He's coming to pick me up. He'll be here in ten minutes."

"OK," I say, trying to mask my relief.

"But we've still got time to see the start of the movie." He clicks "Play" and I tell myself I can get through this – ten minutes, I think, in ten minutes he'll be gone.

As the movie unfolds I realize it's a romance. I can't look at Jack, the last thing I want to do is watch a love story with him. But as it plays out I get a weird feeling of déjà vu. I must have seen it before, but I've no idea when or where – a young man and woman are travelling on a train through Europe. They don't know each other but they get talking. There's a real spark between them and they know that they're attracted to each other.

I'm relieved to hear the doorbell ring. I instantly turn the movie off and usher Jack out of the bedroom. I walk downstairs with him but stop dead as I see Rob in the doorway, chatting politely to my mum. I've been thinking of him only as Jack's dad – but now, framed in the doorway, I realize that I'm looking at a skinny white man with round glasses and spiky hair.

"Hi, Zoe, sorry that I have to drag Jack away," Rob calls to me.

"No worries," I say, my voice sounding surprisingly calm as I continue down the stairs. Jack has just made me on edge.

Even if that homeless guy was telling the truth, there are hundreds of thousands of men fitting that description. And, anyway, why would Jack's dad want to hurt me?

"I suppose you're still getting used to the area. Maybe you and Annie would like to go out for a drink some time?" Mum is saying. "It can be hard, moving somewhere new."

"That sounds like a great idea, Emma," Rob says warmly. He pats Jack's back and begins to lead down the path. "I'll be in touch," he says.

Jack waves to me, calling out, "I'll see you tomorrow, Zoe. Thanks for a lovely time." His voice is cheery, as though nothing has passed between us.

I return to my bedroom and drop on to the bed, so thankful that he's gone. My thoughts wander to that movie. It's bugging me; I just can't remember why it seemed so familiar. I look it up and my eyes widen as I read the synopsis.

> ***Before Sunrise*** *is a critically acclaimed 1995 American romantic drama directed by Richard Linklater. The plot involves two young strangers (Ethan Hawke and Julie Delpy) who meet on a train and feel such a connection that they spontaneously decide to spend the day together in Vienna where they learn about each other and fall deeply in love.*

I gasp in disbelief, feeling chilled to the bone. Jack pretended that this movie was his dream about us. I ought to remember because he told me it twice.

I catch a glint from the dog-tags hanging from my neck. I hold them in the palm of my hand, absorbing the inscription – *I am Heathcliff* – the words suddenly repulse me. This isn't a romantic statement of eternal love, it feels like Jack wanted to put his mark on me; to have me wear something that, if I *really* think about it, proclaims I've lost my own identity and merged with him. What does Cathy say? *"He's more myself than I am. Whatever our souls are made of, his and mine are the same."* No! That's not true. I undo the clasp of the necklace and pull it off. I open my desk drawer and throw it in. I'm Zoe Littlewood and I don't belong to anyone, especially not Jack Cartwright.

CHAPTER 24

I poke my head out from under the duvet. What *is* that noise? It sounds like a bird pecking at my bedroom window.

There's no light coming through the curtains. I've barely slept. Just thinking of how odd Jack was yesterday makes me wrap my duvet tighter around me to stop my insides quaking.

There it is again. *Tap, tap, tap* on the glass. Groaning, I haul myself out of my warm bed to investigate. Pulling back the curtains, I see that it's still dark outside, only the yellow beams of street lamps illuminate the frosty road. I flinch as a pebble hits the glass. Looking down, I see Ethan on the driveway, waving at me, mouthing for me to open the door.

I open the window, whispering to him groggily, "What are you doing, Ethan? What's wrong?"

"Open the door, Zoe. I've got something to show you," he whispers back in plumes of icy breath.

I pick up my phone and check the time – 6.10 a.m. – what is he playing at? Notifications start to ping, texts and a voicemail, all from Ethan, sent throughout the night. I read the first:

Ring me. I need to talk to you.

I have a sick feeling in my stomach as I throw on my dressing gown and go downstairs. I brace myself as I open the front door.

A biting wind sweeps into the hallway with him. He hurries inside. He seems . . . jittery. Excited. His cheeks are pink with cold and his eyes shine.

"Mum's asleep," I say, clutching my dressing gown around my neck. My teeth start to chatter. "What's this about, Ethan? Couldn't it have waited until later?"

"Get your laptop, Zoe. I need you to see something," he says urgently. He follows me up to my room, just like he's done a thousand times before, only now he's making me nervous.

He logs into his Facebook and brings up the page for a place called Lenton Academy.

"What am I meant to be looking at?" I ask, rubbing my gritty eyes.

"The messages on this page between me and past pupils at this school. Read them, Zoe. This is the school in Somerset that Jack Cartwright said he'd come from."

I peer at the screen and read Ethan's message:

Hi, can anyone help me? I'm trying to find Jack Cartwright. He's an old mate that I've lost contact with. He went to Lenton Academy and left last July at the end of Year 11.

Under the message is a photo of Jack that Ethan must have copied from Jack's Facebook page.

There are comments below. The first one was posted the next day.

I didn't know every single kid in Year 11 but I don't recognize that guy.

The next comments followed a few minutes later:

Weird. I was at Lenton Academy from Years 7–11 and I don't know him.

I'd definitely remember that hottie if he'd been in Year 11. The standard of talent at Lenton was depressing. ☹

I don't know him either, but if you've got his number then pass it on 😜

Ethan then posted the photo of the leavers' ball from

Jack's page, showing Jack in his tux, surrounded by his classmates.

Does this help? It's the Year 11's leavers' ball.

Think you must have the wrong school, mate. No one in that picture went to Lenton Academy.

Must be another Lenton Academy somewhere. Good luck finding him.

The next comment has a photo attached. It shows a sprawling group of teens all dressed in prom outfits outside a festooned barn.

That's last year's leavers' ball for our school. I don't know where your photo is from.

OMG, having flashbacks seeing that photo. What a quality night!!!

The comments then go off track as people reminisce about their leavers' ball, but I've read enough to understand.

"Jack Cartwright didn't go to that school," Ethan says gravely.

"Is there another Lenton Academy in Somerset?" I ask, already knowing the answer.

"No, it's the only one in the whole country, Zoe, and that's not all; I've checked his old photos on Facebook, he never tagged people and now we know why."

"Why?"

"Because it's all a lie. He doesn't want anyone knowing where he really comes from."

"But all those photos with his friends at parties . . . festivals, who are they?" My head starts to pound.

"I don't know, but they're not from his 'school'. Do you understand what this means, Zoe? We don't know him at all. Why hasn't he told the truth? What's he got to hide?"

"His parents told me that they'd come from Somerset." I massage my temples, trying to think clearly.

"Did they mention Lenton Academy?"

I trawl my memory. "No, we didn't discuss his old school. They just mentioned moving from Somerset."

"OK, so maybe he *did* move from Somerset. He could have gone to another school in the county or. . ." Ethan stops mid-sentence as another thought hits him. "Maybe something happened there. Maybe they *had* to leave."

I shake my head, thinking it through. "But that doesn't make sense. He doesn't behave like someone running away from something. As soon as he arrived here he became the centre of attention at college. That's not the action of someone who has to keep a low profile. I don't understand what's going on."

"Neither do I, but you can't trust him, Zoe. There's something very wrong with him. He killed Bullseye and framed me," Ethan says emphatically.

"He wouldn't do that, would he?" I whisper to myself, doubts overwhelming me. After all, it looks like I don't really know who Jack Cartwright is.

"I don't know how we prove it, but I know it's true. He's drugged me, he's framing me, he's dangerous."

"But *why* would he do that?"

"Because he wants me out of the way, of course. He picked up how I feel about you and he wants you all for himself."

Once, I would have told Ethan this was ridiculous. But not now. Not after yesterday, here in my bedroom. I've witnessed how extreme Jack's behaviour can be. I hear the passion in Jack's voice and see the coldness in his eyes. I've no idea what's going on in his head.

"We've got to stop him, Zoe," Ethan says. "I'm going into college today and I'll show everyone that Facebook page so they'll all know he's a liar."

I hesitate. "But, say you go into college and try to expose Jack as a liar, and then Jack comes along with a perfectly good reason for what he's done. If that happens, I guarantee everyone at college will be even angrier with you for trying to turn them against him. You know how people love him. We should talk to him first, give him a chance to explain."

Ethan obviously doesn't want to listen to reason. He shakes his head, saying, "I'm sorry, Zoe, but if you give him a chance to explain, he'll come up with some bullshit story. *You* know how convincing he can be. The quickest way to get to the truth is by exposing him as a liar to everyone."

He whips around and is gone before I can stop him. I look out of the window and see him hurrying down the street.

Pressure is building in my head as I call his phone, watching him disappear around the corner. He doesn't pick up. I leave a voicemail. "Please, Ethan, don't do anything stupid. Come back and let's talk and make a decision together."

I grab my laptop and type *Jack Annie Rob Cartwright Somerset* into the search engine. If there was an incident that led to him and his parents leaving, maybe it would have been reported in local papers.

I scroll down the results but there's nothing relating to Jack or his parents.

I go to Jack's Facebook page and study the photos he posted from before he moved here. Ethan is right – no one is tagged in them, but they all show him and his mates having a great time. Are they people from his *real* school? He's got so many friends. He looks so happy. Why would he lie about which school he went to?

Why would he lie about any of this?

*

I'm the first student to arrive at college. Most of the teachers aren't even here yet, but I couldn't just wait around at home. I can't get through to Jack or Ethan on their phones. I'll just have to hang around the college entrance and waylay Ethan as he comes in. He's not handling this right. If it backfires, and Jack has a good reason for the lies, then everyone will hate Ethan even more, forcing him out of college.

I blow my warm breath on to my freezing hands as I keep watch from the steps of Hinton Dale. Students start to filter in and, a few minutes before the bell, there's a great flurry of people. I stand on the top step to try to see above them. My gaze roves over everyone but Jack and Ethan aren't among them.

The bell goes but I ignore it and stay outside as the college corridors become clogged up with people moving to their first lesson. I try both their numbers again, one eye on the grounds and playing fields. Ethan still isn't picking up and, yet again, the automated voice kicks in on Jack's phone.

My stomach twists. What if Ethan changed his mind and went to confront Jack at his house instead? I call Ethan's mum, but her phone is off, she must be in work. I try Ethan's dad and I'm relieved when Simon answers.

"Hi, Zoe, is everything OK?" Simon asks.

"Yeah, I'm just looking for Ethan. Have you seen him?"

"No, he'd left before any of us got up. I think he must have some assignment to finish. Aren't you at college today?"

"Yes. But I haven't seen him yet. Would you give me a call if Ethan turns up?"

"Sure, but I'm in work soon. You don't think anything's wrong, do you?" Simon sounds worried.

"No. He's probably in the library and not checking his phone. Thanks. Have a good day at work," I say casually, determined not to alarm Simon before I know what's going on.

My feet have gone numb with the cold. I stamp my Doc Martens on the steps to get the circulation going as I call Jack's mum. It goes to voicemail. I feel like hurling my phone to the ground in frustration. I need to take control of this situation.

I clutch the phone in my hand as I walk out of the college grounds. My eyes keep flitting to it, worried that I'll miss a call or text. The ringtone blurs out and Dad's name appears on the screen. I'd forgotten that we were meant to be meeting tonight; he's probably going to try and wriggle out of it. I keep walking as I answer.

"Hi, Dad, now isn't a great time. I'm trying to keep the line free. I'm expecting a call," I say abruptly.

"Zoe, I know we're meant to be meeting this evening but I can't make it." His voice sounds small and fragile. Is this him trying to grovel?

"What's the problem? Has Petra got an appointment with her nail technician and you have to hold her hand?" I say with bitter sarcasm.

"Please don't." There are tears in his voice. "It's Petra . . . she's had a car accident. She's in intensive care."

I stop dead. "Oh, god. Is she going to be all right?"

"She's broken a few bones and one of her ribs has punctured a lung. She's on a ventilator, drifting in and out of consciousness." His voice cracks.

"Are you on your own? Do you want me to come and sit with you?"

"You're such a good kid, Zoe," he says remorsefully. "And I haven't made this easy. I know you've resented Petra – but that's been my fault, not hers. She only wants to get to know you. She doesn't want you to hate her."

I swallow. I *have* hated Petra, really hated her; but I would never have wanted this to happen to her. "What caused the accident?"

"I'm not sure. The police are investigating. She was driving to work this morning and she seemed to lose control of the car. Maybe she hit some black ice, maybe something ran out in front of her. Whatever happened, it seems she was going quite fast and the car careered off the road and into a tree. No one else was hurt, thank god."

"Wow. I'm sorry, Dad. Are you sure you don't want me to come to the hospital?"

"No, honestly, Zoe. You've got college. I'll be OK."

"Will you ring me if there's any change?"

"OK, thanks, love. I – I appreciate this."

I walk on, still shaken from Dad's call, when the phone rings again. It's Lily.

"Hi, Zoe. Listen – something weird just happened." I wait apprehensively, noting the confusion in her voice. "I've just spoken to one of the secretaries for the neuro surgeons. I asked her about Jack Cartwright's appointment."

"And what did the secretary say?"

"Well, the thing is, she checked on the hospital computer system *and* double-checked all the correspondence from the department and there's no record of Jack being a patient here at all."

"But there must be! He's been in A&E. He spent a couple of nights on an observation ward, they gave him a scan!" My voice is shrill.

"Well, that's what I told the secretary, but she was absolutely adamant that there's no Jack Cartwright on the hospital system."

"Then that's the hospital's mistake. It's obviously an admin error."

"But you told me that he'd received an appointment to see one of the surgeons – there's no way that could have happened if he wasn't in the system."

"I don't understand," I say helplessly.

"Well, neither do I, Zoe. All I can tell you is that Jack Cartwright isn't known to St Monica's hospital and he doesn't have an appointment with the neuro department." I hear another voice in the background and she says, "I'm sorry, Zoe, I'm going to have to go, I'm still on shift. I'll call you this evening."

"Yes . . . OK . . . thanks."

I walk in a daze towards a bus shelter ahead and sit down on the flip-out seat. Traffic speeds past, spraying up water that seeps inside my shoes. A bus comes and goes, a woman says something to me, but I can't register anything. I'm lost in confusion. Why isn't Jack known to the hospital? Jack told me himself that he'd been in hospital, and so did his parents. Why would they lie?

I put my head in my hands, commanding myself to think straight, but my imagination is spiralling out of control. What if his parents are weirdos who don't believe in doctors so they didn't get help for him and Jack is too scared or indoctrinated to tell anyone the truth? No! That can't be right. Annie and

Rob seem so caring. I've seen how they all are together and they obviously love him. They wouldn't neglect him. They must have taken him to A&E that night. He must have stayed on the ward and had the brain scan. There must be some explanation for why he isn't in the system. *Think, Zoe, think.*

"Yes!" I say it out loud, getting a funny look from the woman next to me. His parents aren't neglecting him. He *has* been treated at St Monica's and he'll be on their computer system – only not under Jack Cartwright, because that's not his real name.

They're using a fake identity – all of them. Maybe Ethan's right and they're running away and hiding from something. It would make sense of lying about what school he went to, not wanting people to connect him to old friends. But then, why has Jack put himself all over social media if they're gone to the extreme of changing their name?

My elation plummets as confusion takes hold again. I *have* to speak to Annie. I need to hear what she's got to say. Whatever is going on, I'll convince her to tell me the truth.

I spring up from the bus-shelter seat and start heading towards town, adrenaline pumping through me. I need to speak to Jack's parents right now – and I know where to find them.

CHAPTER 25

The centre of town is heaving with people. I cross the congested road from the town hall and pause outside the towering glass building. There are several company names in silver lettering above the entrance, including Midas Insurance PLC. The automatic doors swoosh open as I walk into the polished concourse and make my way to the reception. The smart-suited man behind the desks smiles.

"Good morning, how may I help you?" he asks on autopilot.

"Hi, I'm here to see Annie Cartwright in Midas Insurance," I say.

"Have you got an appointment?" He maintains his polite expression.

"She's expecting me," I say confidently.

He nods and checks his computer. "Annie Cartwright, is that what you said?"

"Yes, she works in HR."

He taps away at the keyboard and scrutinizes the screen. "I'm sorry, miss, we don't have any person of that name working at Midas Insurance."

"Well, is there another insurance company here?" I ask urgently.

"No, and her name isn't coming up as being employed in this building."

"What about Rob Cartwright … I mean, Robert Cartwright? Could you check for him?"

He arches an eyebrow in mild irritation as he taps at his computer again. "No, there's no Robert Cartwright working here."

"But there has to be!" I protest, my voice rising. "They told me they worked here."

"Then it looks like you've been misinformed. I'm sorry I can't help." He gestures to the exit. "Have a nice day."

I find myself standing in the middle of the pavement with hordes of people jostling past. I shuffle into a shop doorway and wrap my arms around my body, trying to keep myself together. I don't understand what's going on. Why would they tell me they work there when they don't?

I take out my phone, and my anxious reflection stares back at me in the black screen. Should I call the police? Have they committed a crime, though? I don't know. What it *looks* like is that they're using false identities and they may or may not be lying about Jack's treatment at St Monica's. But he could have been treated under a different name, right? And what if I get the police involved, and they discover that there's an innocent reason for all this? I can't risk it. I should give them a chance to explain first.

I fish out my purse from my bag and check the money situation; I haven't got enough for a taxi, but there are a couple of buses waiting at traffic lights ahead. My pulse quickens as I spot the number six, which goes close to Jack's estate. I force my way on to the crowded bus and slump on the first free seat. In my head, I start rehearsing what I could say to Jack and his parents. I don't want to go in throwing around accusations. I want to make them talk . . . tell me what's going on.

It seems to take for ever to get out of the gridlocked town, but as soon as we reach the suburbs we pick up pace. I only realize that I'm grinding my teeth when the man next to me gives a pained look. I tell myself to stop, but moments later I start again as stress takes over. The phone rings and vibrates in my hand. It's Dad.

"Dad, how's Petra?" I keep my voice low.

"She's still stable." I hear him swallow hard. "Listen, Zoe, the police have just spoken to me. They're saying that the brake cables on Petra's car had been deliberately cut and that's what caused the crash."

"You're joking!" I gasp.

"Petra could have been killed. It's a criminal investigation now."

"But who'd want to do that to her?"

"I have no idea, but – but, well, all this has made me

think. I just wanted to tell you that I love you, Zoe." He's all choked up.

"OK, Dad . . . I love you too." I can't believe it. Has Petra got enemies that Dad doesn't know about? Mum and I are not her biggest fans – but the thought that someone might want her dead sickens me.

My shoulders are around my ears with tension. I force myself to make them drop. Out of the window I see the houses being replaced by fields. I spot Jack's estate, set well back from the road, so I press the bell and the bus slows as it approaches the next stop. As soon as the door opens I fly out like a sprinter from the starting blocks.

I try Ethan one more time as I run down the road towards the manicured estate. I expect his voicemail to kick in but instead I hear his voice.

"Zoe, are you OK?"

"For god's sake, Ethan, where the hell are you?" I cry. "I've called you a dozen times."

"What? You've phoned me once, that's all, and I've done what you asked."

"*What*?" My stomach lurches. "I never spoke to you."

"You did! You told me to go home and wait for you. I thought I'd take your advice so I was on my way to Jack's house to give him a chance to explain his lies, but then I got your call and turned around."

"But I never called and said that." I want to sob.

"You did, Zoe. Do you think I wouldn't know your voice?"

"I don't understand *anything*," I say in despair.

"Where are you? You sound out of breath."

"I'm running. I'm nearly at Jack's. No one's answering their phones, so I'm not sure who'll be at the house but I need to get answers from him . . . from his parents. There's more, Ethan – more lies that they've told."

"Well, wait for me. You shouldn't see him alone. He's dangerous. You don't know how he'll react," Ethan says.

"No, Ethan, he's not going to open up with you there. It'll be OK."

"But, Zoe—"

I hang up. I have to face Jack now. I'm not in danger from him. After all, he says that he's madly in love with me. He'd never do anything to hurt me. I know it.

I know it.

CHAPTER 26

I slow down as I turn into the cul-de-sac. I can see their car on the driveway. At least one of them must be home.

Bending over, I rest my hands on my knees to catch my breath. I want to be in control of this. I'll ask the questions; I'll be able to tell if they're lying or not.

I try to keep my breathing steady as I walk up the driveway, squinting to see if anyone is in the front room, but the bright winter sun bounces off the glass, obscuring my view. A sickening sense of dread washes over me as I ring the bell, but I can't let my imagination run wild. Nothing bad can be inside this lovely house, in this quiet cul-de-sac where people wash their cars and mow their lawns and listen to jazz.

I wait a minute before ringing the bell again, putting my ear to the door, listening for noises from inside. I ring a third time, but the house remains silent. Why's the car on the driveway if no one is home? Maybe they're in the garden and can't hear the bell. I walk around the side of the house. There's a high wooden gate with a big padlock securing it. I call over it.

"Jack, Rob, Annie? Is anyone home? It's Zoe, I need to talk to you."

The only reply is the distant barking of a dog from further down the road. My heart sinks in disappointment. I was so ready to confront them. I can't bear to leave without answers.

I return to the front door and, in frustration, I grip the door handle, yank it down and push. I jolt back in surprise as the door swings open.

I brace myself for an alarm going off but nothing happens. I look over my shoulders guiltily. There's no sign of life from the other houses, no neighbour appears to ask me what I'm doing. I know I shouldn't go in, but they've left the door unlocked. There might be answers inside. I'll only be a couple of minutes. They'll never know.

I step inside the lavender-scented hallway, shutting the door behind me and calling out a strangled, "Hello," as a ball of stress blocks my throat. No one answers. My eyes flit around. I can feel all my senses sharpening.

The house is chilly. I put my hand on the radiator; it's stone-cold. I take my DMs and wet socks off and hide them behind the coat stand: I can't risk leaving muddy footprints all over their pristine carpets, they'll know for sure that someone has been in the house. If I have to, I'll grab my shoes and run out of here barefoot.

Gingerly, I open the living-room door. The tastefully-furnished room is just the same as when I visited but, looking around, I realize that there are no cupboards or drawers in here to search through. There's nothing lying around, nothing out of place.

Walking through to the conservatory, I pick up the photo of Jack in his primary school uniform. A thought suddenly strikes me. I fumble with the frame. Maybe there's something written on the back of the photo that could confirm whether Jack Cartwright is his real name or not. My heart starts beating out of my chest as I lift the back off and read the blue ink handwriting in the centre: *Samuel Ascot. St Joseph's Primary.*

So, this is his real name! Jack could have been treated at St Monica's but under this name. I feel a strange sense of relief. But then I see what's written in the corner in small print – *1999.*

That can't be right. If this photo was taken in 1999 it would mean that the boy is at least twenty-four now. I peer at the image. He looks like he could be Jack, but then again he could be any handsome little boy with dark hair. I take the photo to the window, holding it up to the daylight and studying the eyes; they're very dark brown but not the ink-black eyes of Jack. I drop the frame on to the table as if it's electrified. This photo isn't Jack!

I rush into the kitchen, desperately looking for something . . . anything that will tell me what's going on in this family. The spotless kitchen has an island in the middle and lengths of units with granite worktops and an abundance of cupboards and drawers. I open the first drawer but it's empty, the next is empty too, and the next and the next. The last one has a cutlery tray with just two pairs of knives and forks, two dessertspoons, two teaspoons. I fling open the cupboard doors, top and bottom, they're empty, empty, empty! At last I find crockery but there are only two plates, two bowls, two side plates. In the cupboard next to the oven are a packet of cereal and a few tins of beans. A selection of drinks and a coffee machine sit on the worktops but the fridge is bare, apart from a pint of milk and a box of eggs.

I sprint up the stairs and open the first door that I reach. It's the bathroom, with an enormous bath and walk-in shower. Only two toothbrushes and a tube of toothpaste sit on the window sill next to a bottle of shower gel. Two towels are draped over the radiator. I open the cabinet above the sink. It's empty – where's all the stuff you'd usually find in a family bathroom? Where are the plasters, the half-empty tubes of antiseptic, the packet of cotton wool?

I go back out on to the landing and open the next door. It looks like the main bedroom but there's hardly any sign that it's used. There's only a hairbrush on a dressing table with Annie's white-blonde hair entwined in its bristles. There's a pair of women's shoes next to the bed, and on the bedside table is a photo of a little blonde girl. The photo is encased in an ornate frame with a name carved into it: *Maisy*. I recognize the name straight away. Annie's niece, the one she was speaking to on the phone in the café in Howarth. I check the wardrobe and the only clothes hanging there are a few tunic tops and leggings.

Where's all their *stuff*? It's like they hardly live here.

I go into the next room. The small room smells of Jack's aftershave, but an open case lies on a chest of drawers with Rob's round glasses in. Scruffy jeans have been left on the edge of the unmade bed. A small pile of men's clothes is slung on a chair, the wardrobe is completely empty – it doesn't even have hangers in it. If Rob sleeps in here then maybe his marriage to Annie isn't as happy as they make it out to be. But then, nothing about this family seems to be as it looks.

I open the first drawer of the chest. Inside are a few pairs of boxers and socks, but next to them is a bottle of pills. I pick it up and read the white label. The bottle rattles in my hand – *Rohypnol*. I know what this is. It's the date-rape drug.

My mouth is dry as I search for more information on my phone.

Rohypnol – often used to spike drinks, resulting in victims falling unconscious, feeling uncoordinated, unable to move. After effects include severe headaches, muscle ache, memory loss.

The symptoms are just like Ethan described the morning after he missed the movie. It can't be a coincidence that Rob has this drug, and that would mean that Ethan was right. Jack gave him a spiked drink that day. The homeless guy was telling the truth, the mugging was a set-up and Rob must be the man he described. But why do it? So that Jack could save me and look like a hero? That's crazy!

My instincts are telling me to get out of this house, but I still don't have answers. I can't leave yet.

My teeth grind and grind as I step inside Jack's bedroom. It's just as it was when I was here last. Everything immaculate and tidy, his college work in neat piles on his desk. I hold my breath as I open his wardrobe. Expensive tops, shirts, jeans and jackets fill the rail, many of them with their price tags still attached, and on the shelf above are hoodies and jumpers, some still in their plastic wrappers. I get down on my knees to root among the pairs of brand-new trainers and shoes on the floor of the wardrobe. Tucked in the corner is another stack of clothes. My eye is caught by the colours of something poking from the bottom of the pile. I pull it out and hold it up with trembling arms as I see what it is – a Union Jack hoodie, identical to Ethan's.

CHAPTER 27

I sink to the floor. There's something terrible going on here. I need to get out of this place and take the hoodie with me. I'll call the police, hand it over so they can test it, tell them that they have to find out what's going on with these people.

I gather myself and stuff the hoodie in my bag before rushing out of the room but, as I start down the stairs, I freeze as I hear something – a muffled whine, moaning? I strain to locate the sound. There's one room off the landing that I haven't been in. The noises are coming from inside. It sounds like someone is hurt. I try the handle but the door is locked.

"Who's in there?" I call out in a low voice.

The muffled noises get more frantic. The sound of something thumping the floor starts up. Someone's trapped inside. I eye the door; it doesn't look too solid.

I pull down the handle and ram my shoulder against

the wood again and again. I can feel the door yielding, the lock loosening. Stepping back, I take a run-up, shoulder first, grunting as I make impact. There's a twang of the lock breaking, and the door flies open as I stagger in.

I'm still regaining my balance as I see them: Annie and Rob, back to back on the floor, their wrists and ankles bound, their mouths gagged. Their faces contort as they beckon me to help them. I scramble over and tear Annie's gag out of her mouth as she gasps for air. I do the same for Rob and watch as they try to find their voices.

"Get us free, Zoe," Annie splutters with terror in her voice. "We've got to stop him."

I frantically look around for something in the room that would cut through the hard plastic bonds, but all I see are a bank of darkened TV screens covering a whole wall. There are workstations below with laptops and iPads sitting on them. What is this room?

"What's going on?" I whisper. "Who's done this to you?"

"It's Jack," Rob barks. "He's out of control."

"Jack! But why?" I gasp.

"Find something to cut these things," Rob demands, ignoring my question.

"Not until you tell me what's going on," I say defiantly.

"He'll be back any minute. We've got to get out of here," Annie cries.

My head is throbbing with stress. They're terrifying me but I can't let them go before they tell me the truth. "Maybe Jack is right to tie you up. Maybe he needs protecting from you. You never took him to St Monica's. I know you've been lying about everything and I want answers *now.*"

Rob twists his head to glance at Annie, looking uncertain.

"We've got to tell her!" Annie says adamantly. "We've got no other option."

"OK," Rob says, his voice tremulous. "I'm going to tell you the truth so that you understand that Jack is the danger here, not us." He lowers his eyes to avoid my gaze. "Annie and I aren't a couple. We work together. We're electronic engineers."

"Engineers?" I echo in confusion.

"Listen, we're not Jack's parents, we're his designers."

There is a deathly silence. I stare at him. "What do you mean, 'designers'?"

"I mean that we designed him. Jack isn't human."

I pause and then let out a belt of a laugh. "What's wrong with you people? Do you really expect me to believe that Jack is . . . *not human*?"

"It's true, Zoe," Annie says, her eyes meeting mine. "Jack's the most advanced, sophisticated AI ever created. Decades of work went into him. But something went wrong. He's not obeying our commands. He's out of control and we've got to stop him."

I back away, holding up my hands. "You're both crazy. You know what, I'm just going to call the police and let them get the truth out of you."

"Call the police but, for god's sake, untie us first so we can get out of here," Rob says urgently.

"It was after he had the fall outside the club," Annie mutters. "He was fine before that."

I shake my head in disbelief. "No. The weird behaviour is caused by his head injury and you didn't take him to get treatment because you're both obviously insane."

"We had to pretend that we'd taken him to the hospital. How could we take him when they'd only have had to try to listen to his heart . . . find a pulse, and they'd have known what he was?" she says.

Her words rattle me. I remember the night of the accident, when I thought he wasn't breathing, but then I convinced myself that I couldn't hear his heartbeat because of my panic. And then in my bedroom, when I rested my head on his chest, I still couldn't hear his heart pumping.

I shake myself. *No! Get a grip, Zoe.*

"Zoe, the other day, in his bedroom . . . when you thought Jack was having a seizure, he'd malfunctioned and gone into shut-down. And remember when he picked up the biscuit to eat and Annie stopped him – again, he was glitching. Have you ever seen him eat or drink?" Rob says.

I trawl through my memory. No. In the months I've known him I can't remember ever seeing him eat. He'd say that he ate at odd times because of his training programme. And he'd always have that red water bottle, the bottle that was empty yet he pretended to drink from it.

My head is swimming but I've got to stay focused. "Why did he tie you up?" I ask.

"We tried everything to shut him down," Annie said

sadly. "But when that failed we tried to reason with him. We told him we weren't his parents. But his programming is so intricate, the memories that we implanted are so convincing, that he truly believes he's human and that he's our son."

"So, you want me to believe that the most popular boy in college is a machine," I scoff. "Why would you bother sending him to school? What's the point?"

"It was essential that we tested him in the real world," Rob says. "We're funded by the biggest AI corporation on the planet. They've pumped investment into Jack's development and they needed evidence of what he could achieve."

"Achieve? At Hinton Dale College?" I say incredulously.

"They wanted us to place Jack in an environment with his 'peers' to see, not only if he could pass as human, but to test how far he could influence the whole cohort. The challenge was to design and programme an AI that would become an influencer of everyone around him without them even being aware." Rob's eyes flit to the open door anxiously.

"We wanted to see if Jack could affect what the students at Hinton Dale consumed – what they bought, liked, wore, played, even how they looked," Annie says. "Could he influence their behaviour and encourage them to get fit? Could he influence their opinions and actions? We needed to see how far we could push the boundaries of what an AI could achieve."

I think of how much everyone at Hinton Dale looks up to Jack. He's so massively popular. People listen to him, follow him, gladly buy into whatever he's enthusing about, but still . . . *still*?

"You're fantasists! Do you really expect me to believe that you've gone to all this trouble and expense just to sell a few products in a college?"

"You've got to look at the bigger picture, Zoe," Rob says. "Hinton Dale was a small-scale experiment and the results have been phenomenal. The implications for the use of AIs in the future are game-changing. It could be rolled out in any institution. A supremely sophisticated influencer, hidden in plain sight. In a split-second this machine can access and collate any data individuals have ever put into a computer, enabling it to manipulate what people buy and how they behave. So, you see, Jack isn't about selling 'a few products'; he's the key to making billions of pounds worldwide."

My mind is overloading. They sound so terrifyingly convincing, but it can't be true.

Annie's face suddenly lights up as she stares at me. "I know a way we can bring him back under control. It's *you*, Zoe . . . you can stop him."

"How?"

"Jack's behaviour is a logical result of following his programming, so, in a way, he's not actually disobeying us. It's because he hasn't completed his mission that his system has overridden our command to shut him down. He thinks he's being sabotaged."

"What *mission*? To influence the students?" I say scathingly.

Annie blushes uncomfortably. "We watched how well Jack was influencing the group but we noted that you, in particular, were less compliant. You were harder to get data on and were reluctant to engage with social media. You presented a bigger challenge. So, we gave Jack the ultimate mission; to make the person who was exhibiting the most resistant behaviour fall in love with him."

Tears of anger sting my eyes. Bullshit! This is all bullshit!

"It was the ultimate test of his ability to influence; to make a girl *genuinely* fall in love with an android that she believes to be a boy. It would demonstrate that our AI is so sophisticated as to convincingly simulate the most powerful emotion of all . . . love," Rob says. Underneath his fear, I catch a note of pride in his voice.

"But when we downloaded his data this morning we saw what he'd done to Petra's car last night." Annie shudders. "And we knew we had to abort."

"How do you know about Petra's car?" I gasp, unable to make sense of it all.

I turn suddenly, hearing a loud *click* as the wall of TVs light up. The screens all show the same image of a door . . . I recognize the duck-egg blue colour and the shiny brass letter box, it's the front door to this house. The door swings open and the screens display the hallway but then the image moves swiftly up the stairs and on to the landing and focuses on the open doorway of this room.

"Shut the door!" Rob bellows, writhing to get out of his bonds.

I slam the door shut, putting my full weight against it; but one push from the other side sends me hurtling across the room, hitting my back on the workstation. A pain shoots up my spine, though my moans stop abruptly as I see Jack walk into the room.

He looks as perfect and unruffled as ever. He bends down to me and offers his hand. I shrink from him, but he takes my elbow and hauls me off the ground. "I'm glad you're here, Zoe." He sounds so sincere, so normal.

"Jack, what are you doing? Why are your parents tied up?" I ask, desperate for him to tell me it's all a lie.

"I had to do it. For their own good," he answers gravely.

"Jack, untie us now!" Annie shouts.

"Shush, Mum, I'm only doing what's best for you both."

He turns back to me. His fingertips stroke my cheek. His touch makes the blood leach from my skin. As I crane my neck to avoid his reach, I see the TVs out the corner of my eye – and on every screen my terrified face stares back at me. My eyes dart around his body. I can't work it out.

"Have you got a camera on you?" I whisper. "Are you filming everything?"

He laughs like I'm being ridiculous. "Of course not, Zoe. I don't know what's the matter with everyone today. First Mum and Dad saying the most bizarre things, and now you."

"You must let us go, now, Jack," Annie says firmly, like a chastising mother to a child.

"You know that I can't do that, Mum. You and Dad aren't well. And I can't let you stop me and Zoe being together."

She flinches as he bends down and kisses her on the top of her head.

"Untie us and I promise we'll let you and Zoe be together," Annie says, her voice unsteady.

"You're lying, Mum," he replies coolly.

"Jack!" Rob says sternly. "I order you to let us go. Do as you are told immediately!"

"I'm sorry. I know that children are meant to obey their parents but if I know best, then it's my duty to overrule you."

Rob looks up at Jack, holding his stare. "I've already told you, we're *not* your parents."

I flash a look at the screens, Rob's face looms large as Jack leans down to him. "Dad, this is exactly the kind of crazy talk that I'm worried about."

Annie looks at him with no trace of the love or affection that I've seen before. "Jack, it's best for everyone if you stop now, you've become a danger to people."

"Are you referring to Petra? It was necessary to eliminate her. I did it for Zoe. Petra's presence in her father's life was causing unhappiness to Zoe, and if Zoe is unhappy then that makes me unhappy. This is what happens when you're in love."

I'm stunned into silence.

"That was *your* fault, Rob," Annie snaps angrily. "You were on duty last night. You should have known if he'd activated and left the house."

"I was asleep. I didn't think it was a possibility," Rob retorts. "We'd fixed the problem after he went AWOL and killed the dog. I thought he was under control."

Jack shakes his head. "I didn't kill Bullseye ... Ethan Mansfield killed Bullseye."

"No, *you* did, Jack; you just have no memory of killing the dog because we wiped it from your database," Annie says desperately.

Wiped it from his database? I stare in bewilderment at Jack's perfect, handsome face.

I rest my trembling fingers on the underside of his wrist. He stands still, obedient, as I concentrate, praying to be able to feel the tiniest pulse, anything to show me he is human, that this is all a bad dream; but there's nothing. I look into his ink-black eyes. They dilate so wide . . . too wide. He doesn't pull away as I place my hand over them and watch the TVs go blank. I lower my hand and see my image appear on the screens again.

Burning bile rise in my throat as my stomach lurches. "What are you?" I whisper in horror.

"I'm Jack, the boy who loves you," he replies, giving me that smile, the beautiful smile that doesn't reach his eyes.

"Your eyes are cameras." I shudder. "Every time we've been together, everything I've said and done has been filmed and streamed to them." I try to pull away from him but he tightens his grip. I can't stop staring at him, trying to see what I hadn't been able to see before.

I can hardly say the words. I hear the disgust in my voice. "You're a machine."

A perfect line forms on his brow. "Zoe, you're sounding as disturbed as Mum and Dad. I need to get you away from here, talk some sense into you." He puts his arm around me. "I'm going to take us somewhere we can be alone."

Panic and fury grips me. "I can't go with him," I shout at Annie and Rob. "Stop him. You designed him, so you can control him."

"It's not that simple. His accelerated learning has enabled him to override our commands," Rob says.

Annie's face suddenly softens as she says warmly, "Jack, before you both go, please let me kiss Zoe goodbye."

Jack nods approvingly and takes his arm from around me.

I bend down to Annie, knowing she has something to say. She turns her head, putting her mouth to my ear and whispering as she pretends to kiss me. "You've got to use the trigger words that will complete his mission. Then he'll stop and allow us to deactivate him."

"Then why don't *you* say them?" I hiss keeping an eye on Jack.

"Because they can only come from you. You've got to tell him that you love him."

I feel like I've been punched in the stomach. Those words that he was so desperate for me to say . . . pushing me to declare them when I told him that I needed time. It was nothing to do with passion, love or any real feeling. He was just trying to complete his mission.

I try to compose myself and stand to face Jack. Confusion overwhelms me when I look at the gorgeous boy I fell for. Now I know what lies beneath that beautiful exterior: he's not made of flesh and bone but metal, wires, plastic and software. His eyes have never been full of longing for me;

they're not the windows to his soul, he has no soul. I can't bear to look at him, but I have to say the phrase. I keep my eyes cast down to the floor as the words stick in my throat.

"I love you, Jack."

I don't know what to expect. Will he shut down instantly, be frozen in mid-action? I dare to look up at him and see that perfect frown has formed on his forehead.

"But you don't mean it, Zoe," he says, his voice heartbreakingly sad.

"Yes, I do. I do!" I say desperately.

"Then why was your voice devoid of warmth and feeling? Why can't you look at me? I see repulsion and fear in your demeanour, not love."

"But . . . but." I don't know how to answer him.

"Of course Zoe loves you, Jack," Annie says. "You've misinterpreted her tone. Her words were filled with emotion and love. You just couldn't recognize it."

"Jack, listen to me, Zoe has said that she loves you. You've succeeded. Please transfer to sleep mode," Rob commands.

"No! Zoe must *believe* those words, not just say them, otherwise they're empty and meaningless," Jack says.

"I do believe them, Jack. I love you." I try to fill the words with emotion, but all I hear is panic.

He suddenly sweeps a hand across my throat. "You've taken off the necklace I gave you. These aren't the actions of someone who loves me. I can't believe your words unless you prove it."

How am I meant to prove it? I'm terrified of him. I know what he did to Bullseye, to Petra.

"I want to kiss you, Jack," I say, making my voice soft, my eyes wide.

"That won't prove anything. People kiss and have sex all the time when they don't love each other. I've seen it. It's all in here," he says, tapping his head.

"He's incredible," Rob mutters in awe. "His understanding has developed far beyond any of our programming."

"What I feel for you is more than a physical attraction. It's a profound, undying love, Zoe," Jack says. "And you don't feel the same."

Without warning, he lifts my phone out of the back pocket of my jeans and crushes it with one hand, letting the pieces fall to the floor.

He grips my arm and starts to pull me out of the room.

"Where are you taking me?" I tremble.

"Somewhere you can prove your love for me," he answers calmly.

"Stop, Jack. I command you to stop!" Rob barks, struggling against his binds.

Jack doesn't respond as he pulls me by the arm down the stairs, and out of the front door. He leads me to the car on the driveway and takes out keys from his pocket, clicking open the boot.

"No, Jack!" I shout as he lifts me off the ground. I kick at him with my bare feet, but he doesn't flinch. He clamps his arms around me in a vice-like grip. I scream for help but no one stirs in the empty cul-de-sac. He lowers me into the boot, saying gently, "Stay calm, my love."

My shouts are muffled by the thud of the boot door and I'm plunged into darkness. I hear the ignition sparking up and the purr of the engine as we start to move.

CHAPTER 28

I scream in the darkness. I should be conserving oxygen, but I can't just lie here helplessly. My bare feet kick and my hands pound at the boot door. My throat is raw from shouting. Every time I feel the car slowing, I scream louder, praying that there's someone outside to hear, a pedestrian, a cyclist, anyone who'll realize I'm trapped in here.

My face scratches against the boot's rough carpet as the car makes a sharp left turn and then comes to a stop. I hear the driver's door open, then shut, as footsteps make their way towards the boot. Contorting my body, I twist around so that my legs are tucked up to my chest, ready to sucker-punch Jack . . . but he's not *Jack*, is he? He's not the boy I thought I was falling for. My throat tightens as I feel sobs building up, but I can't get overwhelmed. I've got to concentrate on getting away from him . . . from *it*.

I squint as daylight floods the boot. The door rises slowly, revealing Jack. As he reaches inside to grab me, I let out a yell and kick him with the soles of my feet. They land, with a crunch, on his rock-hard stomach. He sways backwards as he loses balance. I start to scramble out of the boot, but before I can even put both feet on the ground he's stabilized himself and blocks my way. He wraps an arm around my chest, pinning my hands to my sides. My toes trail along the freezing ground as he marches me out of the disused car park and towards the tower block I know so well.

"Why have you brought me to Lennon Towers?" I rasp, struggling to breathe as his arm weighs heavy across my chest.

"Because Ethan is here."

My heart lurches. What's he going to do with Ethan? I've got to protect him. "Ethan isn't at home. I spoke to him before. He's in town somewhere."

"Zoe, we shouldn't lie to each other," he says disapprovingly. "People are very rarely parted from their phones. Ethan's phone is here, so I know where Ethan is, just like I always know where you are. I track you." He smiles proudly. "I do it to keep you safe."

My blood runs cold. They've been spying on me night and day.

A wave of relief hits me as I spot two boys kicking a ball against the walls of Lennon Towers. They look about twelve but they're my only hope. I shout to them, feeling the veins in my neck straining.

"Help me, please! He's kidnapping me!"

They stop their game and stare in uncertainty. The curly-haired boy approaches us, saying to Jack, "Hey, mate, what are you doing with her?"

"Call the police, please," I yell, as I feel Jack's grip tighten.

"Let her go," the other kid growls as he swaggers towards us, trying to appear older than he really is.

Jack keeps walking. "Don't listen to her. She's my girlfriend. She's joking with you."

The curly-haired boy takes out his phone. "I don't know, man. I'm getting bad vibes. Let her go or I'll call the Feds."

Jack smiles, and then says, "07700900245. Registered to Alfie Roach."

"What the hell? How do you know my number . . . my name?" The boy's face wobbles in shock.

"You and your friend could go anywhere, and I'll be able to find you. I can't let people stop me and Zoe being together. You need to go away now and I'll know if you've called the police, so if you don't wish to be harmed, just forget that you saw us."

All their swagger evaporates. They look like scared little boys as they pick up their ball and hurry away, ignoring my pleas for help.

Jack rushes us into the grey concrete lobby of Lennon Towers and hits the call button for the lifts. The silver doors open immediately and he drags me inside as the doors slide shut. I look up and see the CCTV camera in the corner, vandalized with spray paint – useless.

Despite my panic, I try to think clearly. I don't think that he'll hurt me. After all, he's been programmed to believe that he loves me. All his actions towards me, up to now, have been designed to appear loving, caring, protecting. It's Ethan I have to worry about. Jack sees him as a rival. The logical thing for a machine to do would be to eliminate Ethan, just like he tried to eliminate Petra. And so, I have to stop him getting to Ethan.

He reaches over to the button panel at his side. If I can just press the emergency button I'll be able to alert someone. They'll come and investigate. I have to distract Jack.

"I can't escape from you in here, Jack, so please let go of me. You're crushing me. I can't breathe."

He gives a little nod and relaxes his hold. I lunge for the button panel but his reactions are too fast. He seizes my wrist mid-air and wraps me in his cobra grip again.

"No, Zoe!" he says, chiding me like I'm a naughty child.

His hand stretches to the buttons. I expect him to press for the eighth floor, Ethan's floor, but instead he presses the button for the very top level.

He gets out a phone from the back pocket of his jeans and clamps a hand over my mouth as I hear it ring.

"Ethan." It's Jack talking, but it's *my* voice. I writhe and moan. "Yes, of course it's Zoe. I'm in Lennon Towers. I need to meet you on the roof . . . no, it's got to be there . . . I can open the security door . . . please, Ethan, stop asking questions, just meet me on the roof in five minutes."

I shrink from him as he takes his hand from my mouth.

"Don't be afraid, my darling." His voice is his own again.

"Why are we going to the roof?" I can't stop my body trembling.

"He *must* be there so that he'll understand what true love is. He'll see that he was never worthy of you."

"Listen to my words ... *I love you*, Jack. Do you hear me ... I love you!" My desperation fills the lift.

He looks down at me with his camera eyes. "Your heart rate is soaring. Your cheeks are flushed and your pupils are dilated. Don't you think it's peculiar that passion and fear induce the same physical signs?"

The lift jolts to a stop.

"We've arrived." He smiles like I should be excited. He lifts me on to my toes and propels me down the shabby corridor to a metal door at the end. There's a heavy brass padlock sealing it and warning signs plastered all around.

Private. Strictly no entry. Anyone accessing this door will be prosecuted. CCTV in use.

He grips the bulky padlock with one hand and wrenches it off effortlessly. The door creaks as it slowly swings towards us. I thrash and shout at the top of my voice but his hand gags me as he pulls me up concrete steps that lead to another heavy door covered with more warnings. Again, he pulls off the rusting padlock like it's made of rubber and kicks it open as we emerge into the bitter cold on the roof of Lennon Towers.

"Jack, we shouldn't be up here. It's dangerous," I shout over the ghoulish noise of the wind. "Aren't you worried about your mum and dad? We should go back to your house and talk to them."

He pulls me down with him to sit on rough breezeblocks strewn on the football-pitch-sized roof. My eyes flash about, looking for something I can use to defend myself; there's a car tyre, a filthy bed mattress and a broken pram; nothing of any use.

"Mum and Dad aren't well, Zoe. You heard the crazy things they were saying." He shakes his head sadly.

He truly believes it. He seems so genuine that I have to remind myself that Jack Cartwright isn't being a caring son to his loving parents. I'm dealing with a computer, so I should treat him like one. His mind is a set of codes and algorithms. He'll have to think logically . . . won't he? If I can't fool him into believing that I love him, then I'll have to prove to him that he's not human. Maybe then he'll abort his mission because it's illogical. He has to understand that he's not a boy in love with me, so there's no reason for me to be in love with him. But would that work or would it make him more dangerous?

He must register the anguish on my face. He strokes my hair as litter swirls in the biting air around us. He's incredible. How did they programme him to be so emotionally intelligent? Did they simply teach him by downloading every conceivable facial expression?

"Don't look so upset, Zoe. I've brought us here so that we can be together."

"What do you mean, Jack?"

"You'll see."

"Jack, listen to me. Annie and Rob weren't lying to you. They're not your parents. They designed you, built you, programmed you. You're not human. You're an AI . . . you're not human, so you must stop this now."

He cocks his head to the side, that perfect frown making him look perplexed. "Shush now, Zoe." He squeezes his arm around my shoulder, pulling me into him.

I say the first thing that comes into my head. I need to try to prove to him that he can't really feel, can't sense, can't be human. "What does a lemon look like?"

"Yellow. Oval-shaped, thick pitted skin." He answers immediately without commenting on the strangeness of my question.

"What does it taste like?"

"Sour due to the acidity level."

"Have you ever eaten a lemon?"

He looks blank then answers flatly, "I have no recollection of eating a lemon."

"But you can still show me how your face looks when you eat it, can't you?"

"Your facial features react to the soreness by becoming temporarily crumpled."

"OK, but don't tell me, *show* me."

I watch as he runs through all the expressions I've seen before; he tries out his varying degrees of smiles, he raises his eyebrows, frowns, he opens and closes his mouth and eyes. It's only now that I know that I realize how blank he often looked.

"You can't do it, Jack. You've never tasted *any* food because machines don't need to eat. You look so real. You feel real, but inside you're not flesh and bone but wires, plastic and circuits."

He tuts at me in disapproval, but I've got to make him understand.

"Smell my hair, Jack. Breathe it in and tell me what it smells of."

He buries his nose in my hair, but says nothing.

"What does it smell like?" I ask

"I must have a cold," he says, matter of fact. "Nothing registers."

"You haven't got a cold. You can't get ill. It's coconut shampoo but you can't smell it because you have no sense of smell. Remember in my bedroom when the candle burned your trainers, you didn't smell the smoke, you didn't feel the heat of the flame. You can't feel pain. You were fearless when Bullseye was about to attack us, because you can't feel fear. You can't feel *any* emotion because you're not human."

He shakes his head. "No. You're experiencing some form of psychological disturbance akin to mass hysteria. Cases throughout history have proved the condition is mentally infectious. My parents have infected each other and now you. You're all delusional, Zoe, but it will pass."

"Tell me about your old school in Somerset." I have to expose his fake memories, it's my only hope to get away from him, to convince him that he isn't what he thinks he is.

He gives a wistful smile as if he's truly recollecting something. "It was wonderful. I attended it for five happy years. My best friend was Patrick Bates. We used to play football every break on the field. I was very sad to leave him when I came to live here, but we had to move for my parents' jobs."

"Are you still in touch with Patrick Bates?"

"Yes, of course. He was my best friend."

"Why don't you call him now?"

"Because I'm here with you. Patrick isn't important at this time."

"Please, Jack, I'd like to speak to your best friend. You do have his number, don't you?"

"Yes." Jack keeps tight hold of me as he gets out his phone and scrolls down his contacts. I watch carefully as names whizz by.

"You see, Jack, he's not in there. So, explain why your best friend isn't in in your contacts."

He looks blank. "I must have accidentally deleted it."

"No, you haven't. It was never there. Patrick Bates isn't your best friend. He doesn't exist. Rob and Annie, your creators, have made up a past for you that they've implanted into your database."

"That's not true. I can picture Patrick Bates right now. Blonde hair, blue eyes, he always had my back. We were inseparable."

"What's your earliest memory, Jack?" I persist.

He smiles confidently. "I was six years old. I went to the

safari park with Mum and Dad. A monkey jumped on the car and snapped off the window screen wiper. It was so funny I couldn't stop laughing."

"OK. Tell me another memory from when you were little."

He stares ahead and repeats. "I was six years old. I went to the safari park with Mum and Dad. A monkey jumped on the car and snapped off the window screen wiper. It was so funny I couldn't stop laughing."

"No, Jack, that's the same memory. I want another one."

"But that is my memory from early childhood. I have no others to share."

"Why not? We all have hundreds of memories to share," I say challengingly.

"Well, I don't," he says firmly.

"Tell me about your grandparents. Do you still see them?"

"Of course. They live in Somerset. I'll visit them during the holidays."

"What's their house like?"

He stares straight ahead. "I can't recall."

"Oh, come on, you *must* know. You visit them. Is it a cottage, bungalow . . . a stately home?"

"I can't recall."

"What do you dream about?"

He turns his head to me, his voice full of longing. "About us meeting on a train and having the most wonderful day as we fall in love."

"That wasn't a dream. It was a movie that they showed you. You have to accept the evidence, Jack. All your memories are fake. They created a story for you like you're a character on a stage, but look at all the gaps: they didn't give you enough details because they didn't think that they needed to. Everything you know, everything you say has been implanted into your database so that you could *appear* to be a real person. Your mission was to fool people into believing this, but to do that they had to programme *you* to believe it too."

He gives a little nod. I hold my breath. Am I getting through to him?

"Zoe, what the hell's going on?" Ethan bursts on to the rooftop, breaking whatever thought process was happening in Jack's mechanical mind.

Jack yanks me up by my hand and turns to face Ethan.

"Run, Ethan, run!" I scream but Ethan keeps approaching, his face a picture of confusion.

"Get off her!" Ethan lunges at him but Jack is too quick. He wrenches Ethan's arm behind his back, making Ethan cry out in pain as he forces him to his knees.

Jack lets go of me. The door leading off the roof is wide open. I could run and get help but I can't chance it. It'll only take a second for Jack to harm Ethan. I can't leave them together. I need to stay and persuade Jack to stop.

With lightning dexterity, Jack whips Ethan's belt from his jeans. Ethan yells as he hauls him to the middle of the rooftop and, using the belt, ties his arms around a thick metal pole with mobile masts atop it. Ethan kicks out at Jack but the more he struggles the tighter the belt becomes around his wrists.

"You were my friend, Ethan," he says gently. "I helped you."

"Who the hell do you think you are?" Ethan spits. "I never needed you."

"You needed to get fitter, stronger, so I helped you. You lacked confidence, so I built it for you. But, unfortunately, we developed a conflict of interest which meant I could no longer support you."

"A 'conflict of interest'? Are you talking about Zoe?"

"Yes, you're in love with her and so am I. But you don't deserve her, Ethan."

"You're crazy. Do you think she'll love you after you've pulled this psycho stunt?"

"This isn't a stunt. You have no idea what true love is, so I summoned you here to teach you a final lesson. You will be our witness. You will tell everyone about the ultimate act of love that you're about to see."

"What are you talking about?" I whisper in terror as he seizes hold of my hand and begins to drag me across the rooftop, away from Ethan.

"About you and me being together for ever. This is our destiny, like all the star-crossed lovers. Romeo and Juliet, Heathcliff and Cathy, they couldn't be together on earth but were united for eternity in the next life. It will be beautiful, Zoe."

I look back at Ethan in horror. My voice paralysed. Ethan's cries are lost on the wind, his body writhes as he tries to break free, as he twists against his binds.

CHAPTER 29

As we get nearer to the edge it's as if there's no one else on earth except me and him. Even the birds seem to have abandoned the sky. I hear the moaning wind as it whips my face, feel the grey clouds pressing down, see the whole of the city laid out in front of me.

Can no one help me? *Someone* must be watching. There's another high-rise opposite Lennon Towers, walls of windows facing this way, there must be hundreds of people inside, getting on with their lives, oblivious to what's happening to me. Surely someone must be out on their balcony . . . one of them must be looking up . . . all the way up, beyond the twentieth floor – gasping as they spot us. Are they calling the police right now? Is their voice rising as they tell the operator that there are people on the roof of Lennon Towers: teenagers. They shouldn't be up there. They could get themselves killed.

How clearly can they see us? Can they see his face? Can

they see how he holds me, never wanting to let go? Can they hear how he says my name?

"Zoe." His voice is full of tenderness as his grip tightens around my crushed hand. "We're going to do this."

"But Ethan—" I look over my shoulder at him.

He holds a finger up to his lips. "Hush. This is how it's meant to be."

He hauls me forward, closer to the edge. I jerk back, trying to get a foothold on the rough concrete ground, but my bare feet skid along as he drags me towards him. I cry out in pain and fear.

He gathers me to him; holds me close, strokes windswept hair out of my eyes. "Don't be afraid, Zoe. This way we'll be together for ever."

My body shakes uncontrollably as I take his face in my hands and look deep into his eyes. Dead eyes. When I speak, I try to make him hear passion in my voice, knowing my life depends on it.

"There's no need to do this. We can still be together. I love you! I love you!"

"Then prove it."

I scream as he lifts me up and carries me over the metal barrier that stands between us and the narrow ridge. He carefully places me down, the tips of my toes touching the very edge of the roof. He calmly tells me not to struggle as he seizes my hand. I can't stop my legs shaking. I try to look straight ahead but my eyes are drawn downwards. My stomach lurches at the sight of the drop, miniature cars and trees hundreds of feet below. Everything suddenly feels unreal . . . this can't be happening. This can't be how my life ends.

No one is coming. No one can reach me . . . save me. In a second he'll step off this roof, taking me with him.

He stands next to me, tall, solid, looking out over the city like he's king of the world. He turns his head, a rictus smile on his face, the wind carrying his words to me. "Everyone will know that our love was real. They'll write about us. Tell stories about us, be jealous that they've never loved so deeply."

Sobs burst out of me, tears blind me.

I hear his voice in my ear. "Don't be afraid, my love. It's time. . ."

"No! Wait, Jack. Listen to me. You're wrong. The stories they've shown you haven't taught you about real love. They're tragic and twisted. There's nothing romantic or beautiful about killing yourself."

"But I don't want to live if I can't be with you."

"If you make us jump, I'm the only one who'll feel terror and pain. I'm the only one who'll die. *Please* understand you're a machine. A stunning, incredible machine. I don't know if there's an afterlife but whatever happens after death *we* won't be together."

"But our souls will be as one – like Heathcliff and Cathy. Remember her beautiful words – *Whatever our souls are made of, his and mine are the same.*"

"But you have no soul."

"How can you say that? I'm in love with you, Zoe Littlewood. Haven't I demonstrated that?"

I keep my gaze on him, fighting the compulsion to look down.

"Yes, you've done so many things that made me think that you loved me, but they weren't done out of love. You were programmed to do them. Everything you think and say is not your choice. All your feelings are simulated . . . they're not real."

"Of course they're real," he says, tearing at his T-shirt. I shriek as I sway over the drop, struggling to keep my balance. "How can you say such terrible lies? My heart beats for you, Zoe. I feel love in here." He strikes his bare chest with his fist.

My heart beats for you. His words echo in my head and I realize what I've got to do.

"Jack, I know how to prove to you that you're a machine not a boy. But you've got to promise me that you won't resist, that you won't struggle."

He shakes his head sadly. "You can try. But you're wrong."

"Then face me and close your eyes." I try to sound commanding despite my terror. He obeys, still gripping my numb right hand.

My free hand trembles as I place the palm on his firm chest where his heart should be. The feel of his skin is so smooth, the texture so life-like. I glance at his beautiful face. He looks peaceful, angelic, with his eyes closed. I hesitate as irrational thoughts swamp me. I can't do this. I'll hurt him. I take a deep breath and force myself to press my nails into Jack's flesh. I have to fight to keep from turning away but no blood starts to seep out; he doesn't flinch. I dig them in deeper, clawing away at his skin. He stands perfectly still, no cries of pain. I grit my teeth and scrape harder and harder through a thick layer of silicone until I break right through and expose what lies beneath.

I gasp at the network of wires and fine narrow strips of metal and plastic. I peer more closely, able to see through the intricate innards.

"Open your eyes, Jack." My stomach churns.

His black eyes shoot open. "What have you done to me, Zoe?"

I take his hand and direct it into the small gaping hole that I've made in his chest.

"Tell me what you feel, Jack."

The perfect frown forms on his forehead.

"This is where your heart should be." My voice is gentle, like I'm a doctor giving a patient terrible news. "I've been telling the truth, Jack. You're not made of flesh and blood. You weren't born. Annie and Rob designed and constructed you."

Jack looks down and inspects the hole. "How can I be like this? I'm Jack Cartwright. I have parents who love me. I had a happy childhood. I've got friends at Hinton Dale College. I love playing the piano and watching Baz Luhrmann movies. Each night I sleep in my bed and dream of you."

"No, you don't. You're the most astounding machine but you're not a human."

"How can I be a machine when I feel such love for you?"

"You don't. When you love someone you do it freely, but you can't. You were programmed to behave like you loved me. You were just following orders. It's all fake."

"No. My feelings are real."

"Then why are you trying to kill me?"

"So that we'll be together for ever."

"If you really felt love for me you'd know how perverse this is. You'd want to protect me, not kill me. This isn't an act of love, it's the action of a machine that doesn't understand love."

He lets go of my hand, staring down at the hole where his heart should be. My whole body trembles with relief as I step back from the edge. I should run away but my instincts tell me to stay. Compassion takes over, even though I know it's illogical to feel this way.

"Could you learn to love me as I am?" he asks.

"But how can I love a machine?"

"You can just keep believing that I was the boy you fell in love with. I'd never let you down or cheat on you. I'd be the best lover. I'd make you the best version of yourself and always be at your side."

Tears prick my eyes. "No, Jack. None of this is real."

"But I am perfect for you."

I shake my head sadly. "I know that a lot of the time human beings aren't great at love. They hurt each other. It can end in misery and heartbreak, but at least it's real and there's always the chance of finding the right person, despite all our faults."

He gives a little nod.

I want to tell him that none of this is his fault, but before I can reply Jack turns to the edge of the roof and, holding his head up high, he steps off. My hands fly to my mouth, my scream follows his body as it hurtles down and smashes on the concrete below.

CHAPTER 30

As I stand in the wings, the studio manager clips the mic on to my blouse and the make-up woman pats extra powder on my face. I try to steady my breathing. I mustn't think about the millions of people who'll be watching, hanging on my every word and gesture. I want to do this. I need to do this.

Excitement in the studio is at fever pitch as I look out at the packed audience. Row upon row of eager faces. So many people wearing T-shirts declaring their allegiances to "Team Jack". There are a handful of others showing their support for "Team Ethan". I even see a couple of girls dressed in biker jackets and red DMs, their hair just like mine. Others are holding up signs saying: *I am Jack* and *Jack, be my Botfriend*.

It's turned into one big circus. People are treating it like some kind of game. That's why I'm convinced that doing this interview is the right thing. I can't remain silent and let this go on. I've got to make the world see that what happened wasn't just an entertaining social experiment that went wrong.

Ethan, Jodie and Sonja are in the front row, looking even more tense than me. Jodie spots me and blows a little kiss as Sonja holds up her crossed fingers. Ethan waves, looking uncomfortable as girls behind him lean adoringly into his face, asking for selfies. I feel a twinge of jealousy, wishing they'd leave him alone. What happened with Jack made me realize what Ethan really means to me. Ethan hasn't dared mention being in love again, but I'm pretty sure that I'm in love with him. I can't keep holding back just because I'm afraid that becoming a couple will end up ruining our friendship. I've got to be as brave as him and, once we're out of the spotlight, I'm going to tell him and see what happens.

I smile inwardly as I see Jen, Mum and Dad sitting side by side, united in their worry for me. I don't think Mum and Dad will be exchanging Christmas cards any time soon, but this "Jack business", as Dad likes to call it, has got them speaking again, for my sake.

I've visited Petra a few times since the car crash. She's home and recovering well. At first, I saw her mainly out of guilt, but she doesn't blame me for Jack's actions. Now, each time I visit, things are easier between us. I'm finding it hard to dislike her and, to be honest, it's a relief to stop carrying around the resentment I felt towards her.

All the weeks of footage filmed by Jack was leaked on to the internet. It still freaks me out to know that people across the globe have sat down with their popcorn and watched every second of it. They've seen us all, but especially me, at my most vulnerable … gullible. There has been an outpouring of sympathy, but there have been plenty of trolls too, saying that I'm an idiot and that they'd never have been fooled by him. It hurts, but I won't let their ridicule stop me from speaking out. This is more important than protecting my wounded pride and dignity.

The world's fascination with the story doesn't seem to be waning. Every time I turn on the TV, some "expert panel" is debating what happened. There have been outraged headlines about the AI company's behaviour, while just as many have been turning Jack into a global celebrity.

Tonight, I know why people will be watching; this interview is the first encounter between me and Jack since he tried to kill me on the roof of Lennon Towers.

Of course, this isn't *my* Jack, but the media never let the truth get in the way of good story. I watched Jack Cartwright fall from the roof and smash to pieces but, even though Annie and Rob are being prosecuted, the courts were unable to stop a replica being built by the AI company. The company pledged that the new and improved Jack Cartwright is one hundred per cent compliant with in-built safety mechanisms.

Despite all the assurances, and the enormous security guys next to me in the wings, my stomach twists with nerves about coming face to face with him … *it*. I know that he's somewhere in the shadows on the opposite side of the stage. I feel like running away but I can't let them use this interview as a publicity stunt for their charming android.

Ellie Freeman swishes on to the studio floor, causing a rousing round of applause. I've seen her present chat shows for so many years. She's a national treasure, the "girl next door" that everyone trusts. She stands centre-stage, lapping up the adoration of the audience.

I take a sip of water, feeling like I might throw up as I watch the studio manager hold out three fingers and mouth, "Three, two, one – on air!"

"Hello and welcome to the show, everyone!" Ellie trills. "In all my time in broadcasting I can say, hand on heart, that I've never been so excited to welcome my guests. This evening we're joined *live* by millions of viewers across the globe to see an *exclusive* interview between the 'people' at the centre of the biggest story on the planet! So, without further ado, let me welcome on stage Zoe Littlewood and the android who broke her heart, Jack Cartwright!"

The roar from the audience is deafening. I'm so dazzled as I walk under the bright studio lights that I don't see him until I'm only centimetres away. He looks identical to Jack; they've changed nothing about his beguiling appearance. They've dressed him in a blue, slim-fitting suit, a crisp white shirt and narrow silk tie. He looks like a movie star. He shakes Ellie's hand and gives his million-watt smile.

"It's great to be here. Thanks so much for inviting me." He sounds just the same, mellow, seductive, but I have flashbacks of him imitating my voice in the lift, of him dragging me towards the edge of the roof. I feel myself beginning to hyperventilate. I've got to keep calm.

Ellie hugs me, offering kisses on both cheeks, before shepherding us on to her famous green couch. I sit as far away from him as possible as Ellie launches into her first question.

"Well, Zoe, you've been through quite an ordeal. How does it feel to see Jack again, now that you've had time to absorb the truth?"

Everyone's eyes are on me, desperate to hear how I respond. "This isn't the Jack I knew. This is a replica," I say firmly.

There are rumblings from the audience. They obviously don't like the fact that I'm not playing along.

Ellie tries to mask her disappointment. "Technically, yes. But essentially he's the same boy. Have you forgiven him?"

"Please say that you have, Zoe. I made mistakes," the android interjects. "Terrible mistakes. I will never repeat them." Those dark eyes catch mine. "I would like you to forgive me."

I address my answer to Ellie, ignoring "Jack". "He's not a boy . . . he's a machine and a machine doesn't need forgiveness. It's the AI company that created him that I'm angry with, for exploiting us and putting our lives in danger."

There's a stony silence from the audience. They came here to be entertained, to witness a unique love story. I'm ruining their fun.

Ellie nods hesitantly. "A number of your fellow students at Hinton Dale College have said in interviews that they were never fooled by Jack. Do you feel like you were, perhaps ... naïve?"

"That's total crap!" I hear Jodie shout from the audience. "*No one* realized what he was."

Ellie holds up a hand, saying playfully, "Thank you for your input, young lady, but Zoe is the one people want to hear from."

"I can't comment on what all the other students thought." I answer like I'm in a police interview.

"It's true to say that there've been students who've reacted positively to the revelation about Jack, saying that they didn't mind the deception. They say the experiment was, and I quote, 'beyond cool'." There's laughter and applause from the audience. "Even now that they know the truth, many students would like Jack to still be at the college; they *enjoyed* having him there. They feel he was a good influence."

"Ellie, can I just take this opportunity to thank the Hinton Dale students?" Jack says with faultless politeness. "They always made me feel so welcome and I made such great friends there."

I shake my head.

Ellie looks at me quizzically. "I know that it's hard for you, Zoe, but can't you see why students were actually happy to have Jack there?"

"Maybe they'd think differently if he'd tried to throw *them* off the roof of a high-rise," I reply bitterly.

"I quite understand," Ellie says gently.

"I don't think you do," I say boldly. "Has everyone conveniently forgotten that this machine killed a dog and tried to kill me *and* my dad's wife?"

I recognize a fleeting look of panic on Ellie's face, but Jack intervenes.

"That was a malfunction, Zoe. You said it yourself; I'm not *that* Jack. The boy who malfunctioned so badly is no longer with us, and my makers have given legal assurances that *I* can never behave in such a way. This is how progress is made; they've learned from their mistakes."

I narrow my eyes in anger as I hear applause from the audience for his little speech.

"We all understand how traumatic you must have found this," Ellie says, regaining her composure. "And, on that subject, I hear that you're not planning to sue the AI company for the trauma caused. Why not, Zoe?"

"The only reason that I'm not suing is because I refuse to play the victim in all of this. What happened to me won't define who I am or what I do with my future." I say my well-rehearsed lines.

"How brave," Ellie says to loud applause from some people. "Jack, what have you got to say about Zoe's response?"

The android gazes at me. "Well, now everyone can see why I fell in love with this remarkable girl," he says, causing coos of delight from the audience.

I throw up my hands in frustration at the audience. "Please, just stop! He's not some kind of romantic hero. You're all being manipulated by an AI company. They put my life and the lives of others in danger to test how far their android could influence people. This was about money, greed and power, and you're buying into it."

"That's one way of looking at it. But wasn't it about something more than that? Wasn't it about you falling in love with Jack?" Ellie says softly, like I'm confiding in a friend.

"I didn't fall in love with *it*," I say defiantly, to hisses of disapproval from the audience. "You've all watched the footage he filmed. His programmers tried every trick to make me, and I admit that I did think that he was wonderful, for a time, but in the end, I knew . . . I knew that something wasn't right."

"Yes, we've all seen how gorgeously romantic Jack was towards you," Ellie says, her eyes sparkling. "He certainly knows how to make a girl feel special."

"So, do you think it was OK for them to manipulate me?" I hear my voice rising. "You can't treat people like that. *I'm* not a robot – my feelings aren't simulated. You can't just reprogramme me, or wipe my database so that I forget what happened. We carry our emotional scars with us. It's part of what makes us human, it's part of what distinguishes us from machines, no matter how much they look or behave like us."

"But if you'd known from the beginning what Jack was, do you think you could have loved him *anyway*?" Ellie asks, sounding so sincere. "I suppose what I'm asking is, do you think that in the future there will be romantic relationships between humans and androids?"

"Why would we want to do that?" I gasp.

The android turns his handsome face to the audience, saying passionately, "Because I'd never let you down, or be unfaithful. I'd adore you and treat you with the utmost respect. I would be yours – for life and always know that you were the boss."

The audience erupts in whoops of approval.

"How can you want that?" I plead, trying to get through to the captivated audience. "Any relationship with an android is just an illusion . . . a con. It's all one way because a machine can't *love* you back. They're not with you by choice. Don't you think we're worth more than that? Have we lost faith in our own humanity?"

"I'm sick of humanity," a woman shouts from the back row. "I say we should give Jack a go. At least he won't leave his dirty pants on the floor for me to pick up!" There are howls of laughter.

"Well, I'm not giving up on *real* love," I say defiantly.

"Are you talking about . . . Ethan?" Ellie raises an eyebrow, a smile playing on her lips.

I look at Ethan in the darkened auditorium. I see him frozen with anticipation. A dull ache of longing fills my chest. I want to declare my love for him but I can't do it here . . . not now. It would just drag us deeper into this media frenzy.

I pause, restraining my heart. "What I feel for Ethan an android could never replicate or understand. Ethan knows me."

"No, Zoe; I know you," says Jack quietly. "I know you better than you know yourself."

I ignore him and address the audience. "You've probably read about the orders flooding in for more androids like 'Jack'. And Jack is right; they *will* know you better than you know yourself, as they collect the data from everything you've ever inputted on your computers: your posts on social media, the things you've 'liked' and shared, the people you follow, the products you've bought, the content you've clicked on. Beautiful, charming androids like Jack will become your managers, leaders, politicians, and AI companies won't just be able to influence what you buy, they'll be able to manipulate your decision-making and behaviour in every aspect of your life. Don't you see that we're sleepwalking into an era where our free will is in danger of becoming an illusion?"

A smattering of supportive claps rings out, followed by a barrage of shouts. "Rubbish!" "Do you think we're stupid?"

Jack raises his hands and the audience slowly quietens. "Zoe, I'm sorry that your experience has made you lose perspective, but I think that your alarmist prophecy grossly overestimates the role of AIs and underestimates your fellow humans. Please believe me when I say that I'm here merely to help and serve." He bows his head humbly.

Ellie fans her face. "Well, I didn't expect this encounter to be so fiery," she says disingenuously. "But let's get back to what the world really wants to know – Jack, do you think you'll ever fall in love again?"

I glare at her. How dare she? Her crowd-pleasing question has sparked a feverish atmosphere in the studio as people wait for his answer with bated breath. The camera moves in for a close-up.

I watch in appalled disbelief as his lips tremble and a single, plump tear falls from each eye. And then the android leans towards me, his voice so sincere.

"I'll only ever love one girl until the day I die and her name is Zoe Littlewood."

ACKNOWLEDGEMENTS

I really enjoyed writing *The New Boy*, and part of the pleasure was being able to work with two very talented editors. So massive thanks to both Sophie Cashell, who managed to give me invaluable notes on my first draft before going on maternity leave, and to the fabulous Gen Herr, who put *The New Boy* thoroughly through his paces and made sure he was in the best shape possible when he got over the finishing line.

Thanks once again to the great team at Scholastic who worked so hard on Shell and have shown the same commitment to *The New Boy*. Special mentions to Jamie Gregory for the clever and intriguing cover design that I instantly loved. To Kate Graham in marketing, Hattie Quinlan at the Scholastic Book Fair team and Harriet Dunlea for publicity. To Managing Editor Pete Mathews for doing another meticulous job on the proofreading, and copy-editor Jenny Glencross. All the sales and rights team, and to Sam Smith for making sure I knew that she was there should I need to call on her – her thoughtfulness was much appreciated.

I'm very lucky to have the marvellous Clare Conville of C+W as my agent and friend. She's a woman that you'd want in your corner, and my thanks to her always!

To the lovely Weronika Karas – thanks for her expert help in the Polish translations included in the novel.

Love as ever to my family – my homing pigeons, Stan and Archie, and to Sadie who returns to the nest when she's not flying around town with her mates. May you all always come home for your Sunday roast. And to David, who's the chef who keeps us all together, body and soul – thank you!

ABOUT THE AUTHOR

Author Paula Rawsthorne first found success when she won the BBC National "Get Writing" competition with her prize-winning story which was read by Bill Nighy on Radio 4. She has also been a winner of SCBWI's "Undiscovered Voices" and her previous Young Adult novels, including *Shell*, have been award-winners. She is passionate about inspiring teenagers to get reading and is a writer in residence in a secondary school for the national literacy charity, First Story. *The New Boy* is her fourth novel for young adults.

Follow Paula on Twitter @PaulaRawsthorne

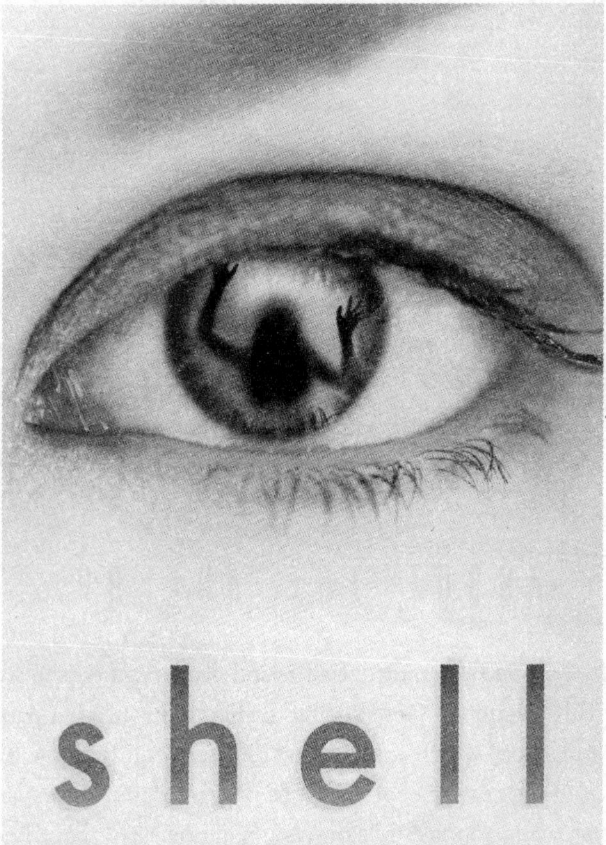

When Lucy wakes up cancer-free, it should be a dream come true. But trapped in a new body and faced with a life she didn't choose, she discovers that cheating death comes at a price...